Unusually Hot

John McGinn

BEDROOM
BOOKS

Winchester, UK
Washington, USA

First published by Bedroom Books, 2014
Bedroom Books is an imprint of John Hunt Publishing Ltd., Laurel House, Station Approach,
Alresford, Hants, SO24 9JH, UK
office1@jhpbooks.net
www.johnhuntpublishing.com
www.bedroom-books.com

For distributor details and how to order please visit the 'Ordering' section on our website.

Text copyright: John McGinn 2013

ISBN: 978 1 78279 010 5

A CIP catalogue record for this book is available from the British Library.

Design: Stuart Davies

Printed and bound in the USA by Edwards Brothers Malloy

We operate a distinctive and ethical publishing philosophy in all
areas of our business, from our global network of authors to
production and worldwide distribution.

Unusually Hot

Unusually Hot

igged back the last mouthful of his pint of Foster's. It
othing like the real thing, merely a faded, British version
at Australian beer. His taste buds desperately tried to
emories of Sydney sun and Bondi surf from the gassy
t failed miserably.

rned to the television mounted on the wall of the small
eone had changed the channel from the rugby and
d just appeared on a weather map. The young lady
apologised for the recent bad behaviour of the climate
recast that the temperature would soon change for the
act become unusually hot, for this time of year.

ll overcast sky outside really didn't want to agree.

only one more day in this dump,' he whispered to
he looked around at the equally bored looking, lunch
mers in the tavern.

d some loud voices from outside and turned around to
gh the open window.

shouted and ducked, as something hard bounced off
d.

ace appeared in the window. 'Sorry luv, I didn't mean
lly hit you.'

bed the side of his head, 'No harm done.'

ent, he's Australian. I told you so. Push me in, girls,'
brunette to her companions.

tched as his self-confessed assailant struggled
window.

stuck. Hold my bag, luv, please,' she said to Greg at
point.

ou should go around to the front door?' he
he took the white leather item.

this girl always finishes what she starts,' she

CONTENTS

Foreword

Or really four sentences why you should[...]
of short stories...

You don't have the time or inclinati[...]
novel.

1. Your Internet and TV are broken[...]
2. The girlfriend is acting a little w[...]
   she may be a werewolf but neec[...]
3. You're a lady who likes an e[...]
   dumped by an inconsiderate, p[...]
   head and you want revenge.
4. You're blonde. So what? Well[...]
   you've still got his credit card[...]

Greg sw[...]
tasted n[...]
of a gre[...]
extract [...]
nectar bu[...]
He tu[...]
pub. Sor[...]
Wales ha[...]
presenter[...]
and she f[...]
better, in[...]
The du[...]
'Huh,[...]
himself, a[...]
time custo[...]
He hea[...]
look throu[...]
'Jeez,' h[...]
his forehea[...]
A girl's[...]
for it to rea[...]
Greg ru[...]
'That ac[...]
shouted the[...]
Greg w[...]
through the[...]
'My ass i[...]
the half way[...]
'Maybe[...]
suggested, a[...]
'No way,[...]

laughed.

The lady turned to her friends outside, 'Shove harder but don't snag my tights. Jason here can catch me,' and held her arms open towards him.

'Jason?' he asked, getting the hint and standing up from his seat.

'Donovan, don't you know him? You look like him,' she said, giving a flash of purple knickers as both legs finally clambered through the small wooden frame.

Greg helped her down and ended up with his hands on her waist whilst her arms were around his neck.

'This is cosy,' she purred, 'And we haven't been introduced. I'm Welsh. What's your name, Jason?'

Before he could answer, a woman's voice started shouting.

'Wynne Evans. I saw you climbing in the window. I will have you barred again, young lady. You broke three glasses last time!'

Greg turned around to see that the woman from behind the bar had come over to have a few words.

'Wynne?' he repeated, beginning to doubt his eyes and wriggling from her grasp.

'S'alright luv, I'm not a bloke. It's short for Wynnefred, see,' she explained. 'But don't call me Fred either or I'll lamp you one.'

'Bonzer, g'day to you and pleased to make your acquaintance,' replied Greg and he bowed in a theatrical manner.

'An Australian gentleman, eh? Well, OMG to that. Just call me Welsh,' and she pointed at her tight red T-shirt.

Greg read the slogan on the front, 'Welsh and Proud.'

His eyes surveyed the two raised mounds, trying to poke through the 'e' and 'u'.

'Yes, erm… very proud,' he answered, 'No, I mean good…'

'Shit, he's looking at my nipples,' shouted Welsh and instinctively covered them with both hands.

'Told you to wear a bra,' said a girl's voice.

'You're a right tart sometimes,' said another.

Greg turned away from the pointy bits, to see that two other young women were standing behind the smiling bar lady.

'As funny as this may seem, girls, you have been warned before that you live in a chapel going community. Silly goings-on, like this, will not occur in my tavern. You three are all barred for two weeks again. Wynne, you'll end up with a bad back, if you don't look after your boobs properly. Now be gone with you, I have decent folk to serve,' chided the woman before walking back to the bar.

Greg watched one of the new girls make a chatterbox sign with her hand, behind the bar lady's back whilst the other turned to Welsh and asked, 'You bringing the boyfriend, then?'

He started to speak, 'I'm not her...'

Welsh cut him off. 'Come on Croc, let's have some fun.'

'That's Crocodile Dundee, I guess. Well ok then. I do have a real name; it's Greg,' he replied.

'Love that name. Did you see where my weapon went? It hit you on the head, remember?' asked Welsh.

'It flew under the next table. Did you say weapon... could I have been hurt?' Greg asked.

Welsh disappeared in a flurry of legs, tights and purple knickers, under the table, before jumping up and shouting, '*En Garde*, you harlots.'

Her two companions panicked and delved into their handbags, as she advanced towards them.

Greg watched as they suddenly engaged in a mock sword-fight, which ended in one girl falling to the floor, clutching her boob and shouting, 'It is the end, I am leeked.'

'Get out now before I call Sergeant Williams,' shouted the bar lady.

Welsh and the other girl yanked up their mortally wounded mate and ran for the door.

'Sorry, Blodwen, see you in chapel,' shouted Welsh, as they left.

Greg remained standing by his table, wondering what to do. He could see now that they had been fighting with leeks, the green and white vegetable symbol of the Welsh nation. There were a few battered leaves on the floor and a slight oniony smell in the air.

'Well go on then, boyo. They've invited you; I heard them. Just make sure they don't get you into any trouble,' advised the oracle from behind the bar.

'I could do with a bit of a laugh after the last few weeks. Are they safe to be around with?' asked Greg.

'This time of year, the girls like to let off a bit of steam. Still full of summer fire, even though it's autumn, they are. Go along with them. You only live once, mun,' replied Blodwen.

Greg grabbed his coat and bag before waving to the woman and heading for the door.

He looked up and down the street when he reached the pavement but couldn't see anyone around.

After tutting to himself about a missed opportunity, he started walking back to his digs. Greg had rented a small house, several streets away.

'At least it's not raining,' he muttered. The weather had been pretty awful recently and it still looked a complete contrast to the earlier forecast of the leggy weathergirl. 'Hot, for this time of year...' Hot for whom, he wondered?

Greg had almost turned the corner by the post office, when something whistled past his ear and bounced off a nearby telegraph pole. He looked around, heard giggles and half guessed an attack seemed imminent, so he ducked. Two more green and white objects flew over his head and he shouted out, 'Missed me, girls.'

'Didn't we just, Jason,' said Welsh, stepping out from the butcher's doorway.

'He's a quick mover,' shouted one of her mates.

'Lovely ass, be nice fried with a few leeks. I could eat him all up,' shouted the other.

'Hands off ladies, I found Mr Foster.' Welsh walked closer to him, smiling broadly.

'Who are your friends?' asked Greg.

'These two hot ladies are Tanya and Rebecca but you can call them Tan and Bex,' replied Welsh.

'Doesn't anybody around here use their normal names?' he inquired.

'Who said we're normal?' replied one of the young women.

The two girls assumed model poses, before wrapping their arms around each other and smooching.

'Are they erm…?' asked Greg, turning to Welsh.

'Never turn your back…' warned Welsh.

He felt both of his buttocks being grabbed.

'Not lezzies, just animals,' explained Bex.

'Evil ones,' added Tan, giving a cackle. 'My name means fire in Welsh.'

'Does it really? Well back home, there's a saying 'Take a Bex and have a lie down'…he countered.

The girls all laughed.

'Did your boyfriend just try it on with me, Welsh?' asked Bex. 'I think he wants all three of us,' she said, tossing her long blonde hair over her shoulder.

The three girls surrounded him.

'Well, I'd love to party with all of you but I've only got a day left in Wales and I still have to write up a report. I can't really get too drunk with you lot,' said Greg.

'And there's nowhere to go in this village anyway. We've been banned from the pub,' replied Tan.

'Let's go back to your place,' suggested Welsh.

'Yes, pleeeease…' added Bex. 'We'll be very good and Welsh won't mind if you read her T-shirt again. You can do mine as well, it's in brail…'

'Oh really?' asked Greg, with a smile, as he led the trio of girls along the narrow lane back to his cottage.

* * *

A month ago Greg had been sitting in a meeting, at the offices of *Stalking the Myth*, an Aussie magazine with the aim of investigating anything unusual ranging from legends to the paranormal.

'We're going to have a series of de-bunking stories from abroad,' said the blonde editor, looking over the top of her spectacles at the assembled staff members.

'Abroad as in Africa and America, Sheila; not just Tasmania...' replied the suspicious man, sitting next to him.

'Quite. We've written about loads of Aboriginal stuff, early convict-settler ghosts in attics, etc. in the two year history of the magazine and have a good customer base of readers wanting home grown stories, but the demographic could surely be improved with some tasty items from other places. Don't forget that this nation is made up of immigrants. They would love a few so-called 'old country' memories,' said Sheila.

'Maybe not if we disproved a legend. How about the Red Indians discovering Britain for instance?' Greg asked.

'If you could quote reasonable evidence, I'll take it and give you a knighthood,' laughed Sheila.

'Or make him Big Chief Overseas Tales?' suggested a business suited lady, opposite.

'More likely Running Dog, after that Thai takeaway curry we ordered last night...' added the suspicious man.

After the laughter had subsided, the editor continued.

'I have permission from the directors to fund a trip to somewhere in Europe for starters. Which one of the four roving reporters fancies a bash at it, this month?' asked Sheila.

'My daughter's expecting and it's due anytime,' replied the suited lady. 'Count me out. What about you, Gus?' she asked the suspicious man.

'I had the last trip to NZ; Canterbury Tsunami still affecting goldfish, remember?' he laughed. 'Anyway, I have booked a week off.'

'So it's Greg or Suzanne,' said Sheila, first looking at him and then the brunette next to Gus.

'How about we arm wrestle?' suggested the athletically built lady, sitting up straighter.

Greg recognised a six-foot tall gym bunny when he saw one and she knew that he'd hurt his right wrist after falling off his cycle on the commute to work. He didn't feel too happy with the challenge but felt it unmanly to disagree.

Gus came to the rescue.

'Let's toss, alien heads or forked tails?' he asked and produced a coin from his pocket.

'Pardon?' asked Greg, looking at the metal disc placed on the table.

'Oh, this? I picked it up at that Star Trek convention last year, for my article, 'Do Vulcans Really Exist?' in the September issue,' explained Gus.

'Remind me how it ended?' asked Suzanne. 'Before I joined, you see...'

'Only one Mr Spock didn't wear plastic ear extensions. We're still waiting for the sample of his green blood that he promised...' replied Gus, sniggering.

Sheila picked up the coin.

'Your choice, guys?' she asked.

'I'll be an alien, if that's alright Gus?' asked Suzanne.

'No worries, you need more of a blue face though,' replied Greg. 'I'll be happy with the forked end.'

Sheila tossed the coin with a flick of her thumb and all the onlookers craned their necks to see the result, as the coin clattered onto the wooden table.

'You have your wish, Greg,' said Sheila with a grin. 'You're off to check out the tales in Wales.'

'Wales? You said Italy or Spain or...' spluttered Greg.

'I said Europe, actually. The Principality of Wales is a hotbed of myths and legends. If you spend a few days researching the Internet for ideas, we'll organise a flight to Cardiport and you can chase the yellow dahlia,' replied Sheila.

'That'll be Cardiff and daffodils, then...' answered Greg.

'Easy, you see,' said Sheila. 'Talking like a local already; I hear the girls all wear tall black hats, chequered skirts and eat seaweed...'

'And it rains and rains,' added Suzanne, laughing. 'You'll need a good fire to dry you out.'

* * *

'What are you girls having for dinner? I had planned to eat some of the steak pie at the pub again but your sword-fighting antics put paid to that,' asked Greg.

Welsh gently replaced the ornament onto the shelf that she had been examining. The cottage rooms were full of interesting nick-nacks and Greg had taken a few pictures to aid his research.

'Sorry we messed that up for you. We were going to have a snack there as well,' she said, pulling a sad face.

'We could always eat Jason,' suggested Tan.

'Stop it, Tan. He's a visitor to our little village,' said Bex, sinking into a soft armchair. 'Cosy place you have here. How'd you find it?'

'Well that's just it. I didn't...' he replied.

'The village found him. It's a funny little place, isn't it, Greg? What are you doing here?' Welsh asked.

'Research for an Australian magazine; I'm writing an article on myths of Wales and trying to find out if any of them are true.' he replied.

'Mermaids, hobgoblins and headless sheep...Whoo,' said Bex,

in a ghostly voice.

Greg laughed. 'Stuff like that. I may as well have copied it from the Internet. This place seemed odd though. I found the name of the village in an old book at Carmarthen library. There seemed to be several spellings but when I looked it up, it didn't appear on any map. I drove along a misty valley early one morning on the way to check out a castle, when I saw the sign to Llandraig. I turned off the main road and saw this cottage to let, straight away.'

'And I bet the owner stood in the front garden and tended the flowers...' Tan said.

'That's right. He told me that he'd bought the place not long ago and to leave the money when I left. I haven't seen him since. Very trusting, if you ask me, I think he might have been French,' said Greg.

'That'll be Maurice. We've met him. A lovely little man,' said Bex.

'We had a barbecue with him once,' added Tan, grinning.

'I burped onions all night, those French men...' laughed Bex.

'Have you got plenty of food, Greg?' asked Welsh. 'You could cook for us. Aussies are supposed to be great at that type of thing.'

'There's an old grill around the back and plenty of charcoal in the shed, but the weather's not good,' answered Greg.

'Look outside, the sun's come out. It can change very quickly in this valley. I think they call it a local weather system,' explained Welsh.

Greg walked to the door and went into the back garden. Sure enough, in the few minutes since they had started chatting, the sky had cleared and a bright yellow September sun beamed down on him.

'I can't believe it. Looks like either the village or you girls control the weather. Maybe my mobile will work, now that it's cleared up?' he asked, taking it out of his pocket.

'Doubt it,' replied Welsh. 'No visitor has received or sent a message out of Llandraig yet. The mountains either side of the valley, stop all the phone signals,' she explained.

'You're right,' said Greg, staring at the blank screen. 'I guess that's why there's no television or radio in the cottage. How does the pub have a signal? Satellite TV maybe? Even that's a bit odd because my satnav won't work. This village seems to have no coordinates and is not on a map...'

'There's loads of food in the fridge,' shouted Bex from the kitchen. 'Sausages, bacon and salad stuff.'

'Are you going through my property, whilst Welsh attempts to distract me?' he laughed.

'He's got some cool shirts and leopard skin underpants,' added Tan's voice from another direction.

'No, Tan. Come out of the bedroom, if you don't mind,' shouted an embarrassed Greg.

'Please wear them for the barbecue, Greg,' pleaded Welsh.

'It'll be fun. If you get cold, we have ways of warming you up. Your girlfriend might get really hot with you,' teased Tan.

'We like handling fresh meat at a barbecue...' whispered Bex in his ear. Her hot breath made him shudder.

'Hope you don't mind if I go for a smoke?' asked Tan. 'Nasty habit, I know.'

Greg looked at her. He could see sweat on her brow.

'Are you ok, Tan? You're looking a little red,' asked Greg.

'It's the national colour and she's probably looking forward to seeing you cooking,' suggested Bex. 'We're all pretty hungry.'

'You sort out the sausages and stuff, Bex. I'll help Greg get dressed and prepare the salad,' instructed Welsh. 'Hope you don't want a smoke as well, girl, or I'll end up doing the cooking myself.'

Greg watched Tan put a cigarette to her lips and start puffing. He watched the end glow red, as she inhaled deeply, before walking to the side of the house. Smoke hung in the air where she had stood and tickled his nostrils.

'Phew, what's she smoking?' asked Greg, as he followed Welsh back into the house. 'Something smells wacky and sulphurous.'

'A special Welsh shag. Fancy some?' she answered and kissed him on the lips.

'Thanks for that,' he smiled. 'Did you know you're really hot? Your lips, I mean. They almost burn. They feel really nice. You haven't got a fever, have you?'

'If I have, it's to see you in leopard skin underpants…' she answered. 'Get 'em off,' and she started clawing at his buttons.

A minute later, Greg stood there naked, with his hands over his private parts.

'Listen Welsh; is this really a good idea? I hardly know you girls. I have work to do and a plane to catch, later tomorrow,' he said.

'*Bydd ddistaw* Greg,' replied Welsh, holding up a finger to her lips. She then lifted up the lower front edge of her T-shirt over her tummy and continued to raise it over her head.

Greg's idea of writing a myth report instantly disappeared, as Welsh's secret points were revealed.

'We'd like you to stay here with us,' said Welsh, dropping her top to the floor and putting her hands behind her head to maximise her feminine appearance.

'We can show you genuine Celtic magic, in exchange for a touch of your body,' said Bex's voice, behind him and to his left.

He hadn't heard her come back into the lounge and when he turned left, to see her grinning face, he quickly started to move one hand from his bits to cover his ass.

Before it reached its destination, he felt a firm squeeze of his right buttock.

His head immediately turned to the right to see Tan looking at his back and licking her lips. That odd smell of Welsh shag tickled his nose again.

'Nice buns, Greg,' said the fire-girl. Her hand moved from his derriere to stroke his back. 'I'm sure that if we're really nice to you, we could change your mind about leaving so soon. There are lots of local tales that we can tell you and special things to see. I need another cigarette, I'm feeling hot...'

Greg looked around at the three smiling girls; the topless Welsh with her outstanding unharnessed assets, Bex with her amazing warm breath trying to nuzzle his left ear and Tan tapping a cigarette out of a packet and placing it between her full ruby red Celtic lips.

He watched as Tan inhaled and the cigarette tip burned red. She deliberately blew the smoke gently in his direction and the unusual vapour climbed up his nostrils to stroke his olfactory nerves.

The smell relaxed him for a few seconds until a thought occurred to him.

'You didn't light that cigarette, Tan...' he said.

'A hidden talent,' Tan replied. 'Tales to tell, secrets to be learned...'

'So there is something going on here in the village. This'll make a scoop for me and *Stalking the Myth*. I bet that French guy who rented me the cottage has a story or two. You said that he stayed,' said Greg, inhaling more of Tan's smoke.

'Oh, yes. After we showed him a few interesting things and ate, he just couldn't leave the place,' said Bex.

'That might explain a few things. Over the years, there have been a few stories of missing persons in the county. I always check police records as well as local libraries. In Australia, for instance, dingoes can pick off people lost in the outback and there's also tales of backpackers falling in love with the jungle, going native and living off the land.' Greg explained. 'It's rather tempting to disappear with you three beauties...'

'Tidy,' the three girls said in unison.

Greg laughed. 'That is so Welsh.'

Before he could say anything else, Tan and Bex grabbed each

of his arms and held them behind his back.

'Go Welsh,' encouraged Tan.

Greg watched the voluptuous Celt kneel down and place a hand each side of her boobs.

He couldn't wriggle away as his member lay enveloped by her flesh. She started moving her breasts slowly and deliberately up and down his shaft.

Her assets were soft but not like he expected. This act usually required some lubrication, in his experience, but they seemed to have a natural slippery feel, almost like touching a snake. He watched the tip of his growing phallus, disappear in those beautiful Welsh hillocks and reappear a second later in the valley, a little more engorged, a little more excited, over and over…

Greg started thrusting, he couldn't help it. Bex and Tan joined in with their free hands on his buttocks, squeezing and pushing him harder into Welsh's cleavage.

'This is amazing,' he groaned. 'And to think I didn't want to go to Wales…'

'Our legends will pop your cork,' replied Welsh, panting a little with the exertion of the tit-massage. She sped up her efforts and leant her head forward, in order to touch his tip with her tongue, on his upward stroke.

'Jeez,' shouted Greg, as the Celtic taste buds sent tales of castles, princesses and romance through his shaft, then along the nerves to his visual cortex. His next thrust generated visions of mermaids, shipwrecks and coracles. His mind swam like a Welsh salmon, fighting to reach an upriver place to spawn. His seed burned inside him, eager to invade the flesh of the buxom Welsh beauty.

'Welcome to the village,' whispered Welsh. 'Abandon your resistance.'

Greg could hold back no longer and his sperm forced a fiery path through his pulsing member and doused Welsh's breasts in an Aussie sea of hot desire.

He finally watched, breathless, as Bex and Tan each took a fingerful from her chest and tasted his brew.

'Better than Foster's,' said Bex.

'Could do with a dash of chilli,' suggested Tan.

Greg looked at Welsh as she lifted up a boob in turn and licked the pink flesh all the way to the tips. He could feel himself falling in love with the Celtic princess. She seemed to have fire in her eyes as she smiled back at him.

'I am just so hot for you, *Cariad*,' she said, and suddenly leant forward to take his phallus in her mouth.

'Yeowch,' exclaimed Greg, as he felt like he'd dipped his wick in a red hot volcano.

She pulled away, just as quickly and her retreating lips felt like the burning tyres of a dragster as they caught the rim of his helmet.

He looked down in panic to check for rubber skid marks, but his manhood stood intact, pointing at the smiling face of his most favourite woman ever…

'Oi, emu-face,' said a voice, pulling him out of the love trance.

Tan held out a pair of animal-skin briefs towards him.

'Put these on, you're cooking,' she instructed and lit another cigarette.

'You've got a lighter somewhere, Tan. I just can't see it…' he said, as he balanced on one leg trying to drag on the skimpy attire.

'I'll do the salad,' said Bex, stroking his back again. 'Greg can load up the charcoal from the shed onto the grill. Tan and Welsh can get the stuff from the fridge. I'm really hungry now.'

'Sure thing,' said Greg, looking at Bex's boobs. 'Do I get to read brail stories later or stick to learning Welsh?'

'You're a naughty boy,' said Tan, delivering a stinging slap to his ass. 'And maybe you'd like me to teach you how to smoke, behind the bike shed?' she added, raising an eyebrow.

'Cool,' answered Greg, running barefoot to the old wooden

building. He just wanted to get the meal out of the way so he could explore his new friends...

A few minutes later, they were all in the back yard around the small wooden table that Bex had carried out from the kitchen. An array of chopped tomatoes, lettuce, cucumber, plates and cutlery lay before them.

Greg had loaded up the cast metal base of the outdoor cooker with fuel and placed the metal grill on top. Bex had placed a second small side table from the lounge near to it and the other girls had arranged opened packets of sausages and bacon on top, next to some metal tongs.

'Think we have everything,' said Greg, standing next to the stack of food, with his arms crossed facing the girls, manly biceps bulging in the autumn sun and his tanned surfer pecs teasing the three women. He felt every inch the king of Llandraig with his trio of worshipping Celtic ladies eyeing up his body.

'And how are you going to light it?' asked Bex.

'Kookaburra shit,' exclaimed Greg. 'No matches.'

'Allow me,' said Tan. 'Move back Greg.'

Greg joined the other two girls, to watch Tan bend over in front of the grill. He couldn't see her face but her hands were on her hips and she seemed to be looking down examining the top of the barbecue.

He admired the curve of her ass in the tight denim jeans, when he heard a crackle and saw smoke beginning to rise from the grill. Tan turned around smiling and winked at him.

'How the heck did you do that? I'm sure I could see your hands. You must have held the lighter in your mouth. I sprayed lighting fluid on the coals. You could've lost your eyebrows...' he warned.

'She's pretty thick skinned when you get to know her,' giggled Welsh.

Greg walked over to the grill.

'It's burning definitely. I don't think I should put the sausages on yet. I could spray a bit more fluid on it to perk up the flames or maybe Tan wants to give it a blow?' he teased as he turned to the girls.

'You asking for another blow job, Greg?' inquired Bex, laughing.

'Light me up, girls,' invited Greg, looking at the hot Celtic ladies eying up his almost naked body.

The girls looked at one another and laughed. They linked arms and pursed their lips at him.

'Burn baby burn,' replied Welsh, as she dropped her mystical mask, to reveal her true scaly form.

Greg could only watch in astonishment as Tan and Bex did likewise and their beautiful purplish-red reptilian bodies sparkled in the late afternoon sun.

He found his voice, 'you - you're evil things with pointy tails...'

'Correction, we're hot chicks with pointy tails,' replied Welsh, flexing her leathery wings.

'And it's barbecue time,' added Tan, tasting his fear by flicking out her forked tongue.

Greg's manly torso turned to toast, in the flaming crossfire from the mouths of the lady dragons. His final charred thought being, 'Wales is unusually hot, this time of year'...

13/13/13

Victor drummed his fingers on the table, in front of the laptop that he and his female colleague were staring at. He frowned as he watched the blue revolving band, hovering over the words, 'TRANSACTION IN PROGRESS'.

'There's less than a minute left, Samantha. We're in deep shit,' he said, fingering his collar and loosening his tie. 'What's wrong with the damn thing?'

'The fact that the whole world has switched off all non-essential communication, maybe, or that we're on the seventh leg of our plan, where an ancient Romanian server is trying to link up with a Mexican satellite,' she answered calmly.

'Seventh leg… we're using a crippled octopus? Maybe the computer has frozen? Is there time to press the refresh button? Has the deal gone through and we don't know?' he shouted and used his shirt sleeve to wipe the sweat from his brow.

'Quiet. It's like the scary moment in sci-fi films; I'm the sexy, redheaded computer geek, you're the clever knob-head, now just shut up and watch…' she scolded.

Victor turned to look up towards the electric clock on the wall. It still showed midnight, as it had done for several minutes. He next looked down at the LED display of the black metal cased device, plugged into one of the laptop communication ports.

Seventeen, sixteen, fifteen; it relentlessly counted down…

* * *

Almost six months previously, to the day, Victor Mason had been summoned to a meeting with the directors of the small research firm that he worked for, Maple and Phillips, a partnership set up during the second world war, to fund clandestine operations against the Axis powers. With the founders now long gone, the small business made its money from the occasional government contract, which usually involved discovering ways to run, make or buy things cheaper, so long as it made those in political power look better than the opposition.

'Just once I wish we were asked to fix something, by throwing money at it,' said the redhead to Victor's left. She wore a crisply laundered white laboratory coat with her hair tied back in a pony-tail.

Victor looked down at her pale, nylon clad, crossed legs, his eyes taking in the outline of her thigh as it bulged against the chair base. He mentally pulled the tights down to the top of her patent black shoes and wondered whether to remove the footwear first, or just pull the lot off in one go…

He jumped as she elbowed him.

'Are you listening? I hope you don't mess up this presentation, Victor. This is the chance for the pay day of a lifetime and it'll be a damn sight more interesting than sourcing the cheapest bed pans in the world for the NHS,' she reminded him.

'Sorry Samantha.' He turned to see her looking at him severely, over the top of her dark rimmed glasses. Victor had tried, but just couldn't work out how every pose that she assumed looked sexy. 'I'll do my best,' he answered, meekly.

'Good. Anyone know who's attending from the heavens with the manna?' Samantha Boyd asked the others waiting patiently at the table.

'Word is, from Director Jones, that we have the top civil servant at the treasury and someone high up in the home office. This theory of yours, Vic, had caused a bit of a flap,' answered a balding man in his sixties.

'It's not a theory, Ed. The maths show it's a fact so that makes Victor's work a discovery. This thing could go worldwide and give those of us involved a fat bonus,' she pointed out.

Ed replied, 'The last bonus ended up at two hundred pounds, for re-sharpening used blunt syringe needles and sending them to China. Last week, my doc had to jab me three times to take blood. I bet the crafty chinks sold them back to the NHS.'

'Well this discovery of Victor's is no little prick like you Ed,' laughed another man, dressed in a blue business suit. He pushed his gelled hair back to accentuate the side parting. 'From an accountant's point of view, it's a winner. A solid twelve inch cock of certainty,' and he winked at Samantha.

'You wish, Nigel... It's Victor here who's done the hard work,' she said, gently squeezing his shoulder.

'Quiet, you lot. I can hear Jones' voice down the corridor. The party's about to begin...' hushed Ed.

* * *

'Fucking wankers,' cursed Samantha loudly, after Victor closed the door of their laboratory.

Victor just stood inside the entrance biting his lip. The creases in his best un-ironed shirt looked even more slept in than normal.

'How dare they just take it from us? Six months of theorising, cross checking, late nights and shit coffee/cocoa from that tit of a machine,' she bawled.

He finally spoke, 'the story of my life, Samantha...'

'Life; did you really say life? I've given up offers of dates at fancy restaurants with a doctor and a top lawyer just to see this project through. I've abandoned the gym to live on junk food and late night takeaways, when we needed to see results by the next day. I've spent so much time with you that my sex life has shrivelled smaller than a nun's vibrator,' she replied.

'Well, I thought you liked working...' he started to say.

Samantha cut him off. 'Sorry Victor, I didn't mean it like that. You've worked hard; we both have and deserve a reward better than having our project... our baby, taken away from us at birth.'

'There's nothing we can do,' he replied. 'Anyhow, you don't look too bad on all those burgers. I note you always had the low fat option.'

'Thanks Victor.' She looked him in the eye and gave a curious smile.

'I've been around a bit, you know. There is something we can do. May I kiss you and explain?' she asked.

Before Victor could answer, she had her tongue in his mouth. He could hardly respond. A few minutes ago he felt like throwing himself off a cliff and now the younger woman that he'd been almost too shy to look in the eye for the last six months explored his tonsils…

* * *

About nine months before that negative meeting, Victor had been talking to the lady who'd become his assistant and had worked by his side now, for many weeks. The department of education had asked Maple and Phillips to investigate the possibility of changing the terms of the school year. A variation already existed across the UK, but the secretary of state wanted to see what could be gained from a radical alteration. Their suggestion had been a four-day school week, with terms extending into the summer. It seemed obvious that the teachers, with vested interests in the long holiday, would object, as would some parents about childcare. The accompanying letter said that every great scheme had a starting point and the firm could check through as many permutations of school attendance as it thought necessary. The bottom line of the brief had been to save money, lots of it.

After obtaining costs from the education department for daily use of fuel during winter heating of schools, and combining them with a future cost escalator, they carried out a similar study on teachers' salaries. They reasoned that the cost of books and materials would be almost the same, whatever the term length. It quickly became clear that an eight-week long winter holiday and summer school would be a great cost saver. The problem often quoted of young children being put at danger, due to British summer/winter time, would be greatly helped plus the lowered number of vehicles travelling at twilight would help traffic congestion and safety at peak times.

Victor had been in charge of the logistics and initially delegated various tasks to those helpers that had time to spare from other duties at the firm or were actually assigned to him. Once these were in place, he busied himself with the number of days available in the year. He soon took this a few stages further into hours and minutes; until, being a perfectionist, a study of calendars came about.

'So what's this odd thing that you've discovered, then, Victor, more computer number crunching for me?' asked Samantha, after the project had been running a few weeks.

'Afraid so,' he replied. 'I've been going through the dates on the calendar and it's quite interesting.'

'Three hundred and sixty five days and an extra one in leap years...' she laughed.

'Indeed, Samantha and obviously the extra day every four years is added, because the three six five number is not accurate enough to mark the time that the Earth takes to travel around the sun,' he explained to her slightly bored face.

'Ok,' she nodded.

'Well, most adults and children know the abbreviations B.C. and A.D. but not many know just how and when they came about. We all know that it's linked to the Bible, but it seems pretty obvious to me that everyone didn't change the way they counted the weeks and seasons just because a rather talented baby had been born out of wedlock and shared digs with a few animals. Someone devised a system a few years later, once Christianity had become established,' Victor explained.

'So who decided the start date?' asked Samantha.

'Dennis the Short,' he said and grinned.

Samantha laughed, 'Yeah right…'

'No joke. That's the translation of *Dionysius Exiguus*. Presumably named after his stature, this clever little monk from the sixth century took the Julian calendar imposed by the Romans on Celtic Britain, plus its own empire, and introduced a start date, approximately linked to the birth of Jesus,' he explained.

'Alright, so where do I come into this?' She looked at him with her head to one side, gently biting her lower lip. He mentally changed her lipstick colour from red to dark pink and accentuated the Cupid's bow…

'Victor, you ok?' she asked.

'Oh sorry, Samantha, just painting… I mean thinking about what you could do for me…' he replied.

'And…' she said.

'Well Dennis did a great job and so did Pope Gregory the Thirteenth, when it became clear that the calendar seemed too short. The latter managed to convince most of the Catholic world to drop ten days in the year 1582. Put simply, the eleventh of March became the twenty first. Not every country followed straight away. Russia and Greece only changed in the nineteenth century. Because the discrepancy is about three days, every four hundred years, the last two takers had to lose more than ten days. The current difference is usually quoted at thirteen days, between the old Julian calendar and today's Gregorian,' he replied.

'Interesting stuff but how does this help the school term project?' asked Samantha.

'Only indirectly; I'm pretty certain that the old fashioned maths is a little out and there's another thirteen minutes that should be lost,' he replied.

'Hmm; lots of 'thirteens'… you have the pope, the calendar difference and your theory. You're not superstitious, I hope?' she remarked.

'It's thirteen minutes, thirteen seconds actually...' he added, thinking about her observation.

'How will this save or even make anyone any money?' she asked.

'A mercenary question,' he answered and laughed. 'So many modern things depend on exact time; nuclear power plants, scientific missions to Mars, Microsoft's next software, etc. Believe it or not, they all need constant monitoring and tweaking. I reckon that my formula should eliminate all that; we can literally forget about fixing time.'

'I'm guessing that you think Maple and Phillips will be able to sell this to the UK government?' she inquired, raising a perfectly manicured eyebrow.

'Of course; the military and research boys will want it. The Yanks will be all over it, not to mention the growing BRIC economies.' He smiled and continued, 'It says in my employment contract that I will participate to the tune of five per cent of any profits, if M&P's turnover doubles in one year, after a successful project.'

'I forgot about that clause; put in no doubt, because no one thought it could ever happen. Ok then, show me your findings. I'll have to set up a program to go through all the calculations. This could take weeks. I guess that we keep it secret at the moment and then you have more claim to the prize?' inquired Samantha.

'That's a good suggestion. We can delegate some work to the others, if the task fits in with the school study. Who knows? We might be famous one day and get a piece in Wikipedia,' he said and laughed.

Samantha joined in. He noted that her earlier look of disinterest had been replaced with one of hungry attention. She turned before walking slowly away to fetch her notebook and he watched the back of her crisp, tight lab-coat hug her hips, the alternating creases in the fabric looking like imaginary hands, squeezing her peach-like ass…

* * *

Several weeks after first engaging Samantha on his clandestine project, Victor drew her to one side for a progress report.

'It's getting harder and harder to hide this from the others,' he said to her, after looking down the corridor and closing the door of a little used back room. 'I overheard Ed say that he thought we were either getting lazy, or one of us has become a mole sent to spy on them.'

Samantha laughed, 'you were earwigging, though…'

'Has anyone said anything to you?' he asked.

She took off her glasses and sucked the end of one of the arms. 'Well, now you mention it, Shelley's inquired about a part of the analysis program that I asked her to help me with. She wondered why it went back to several thousand years B.C., instead of forward five years, as specified in the government contract, to twenty eighteen.'

'And how did you answer?' asked Victor, mesmerised by the red lips of his sultry assistant.

'I waffled and said that I thought there might be another area where M&P could use the work, and that it made sense to complete it now,' she answered.

'More or less true, then,' he nodded.

'Apart from the little white lie about it being sanctioned by the M&P directors… I forgot that Shelley had an affair with one of them a year ago. I hope she doesn't mention it to him,' she said, putting her spectacles on again.

'Hmm… how's the analysis going anyway? We haven't compared notes for a while,' he asked.

'I don't think there's a lot more that can be done. The research part of the program has pulled up lots of references to the various types of calendars with their pluses and minuses. It's all been correlated with the theories of the old monks and the Bible etc. and it would seem that you're completely right, Victor. The present calendar's all wrong. When you add it up since the year one, Anno Domini, it's been losing a few more seconds every year than the other experts predicted,' she answered.

'Time is getting out of hand...' he replied.

'You're not a Time Lord by any chance? I saw you drinking lots of cocktails at the last Christmas do. Doctor Woo Woo, maybe?' she suggested.

'Ha-ha, not a chance, unless my work helps with some further understanding of quantum physics,' he answered. 'Thinking about it, I wouldn't mind going back thirty odd years and telling my history teacher, Mr Foulkes, that he'd been completely wrong about Britain having a manned base on Mars by the year two thousand.'

Samantha laughed. 'You're quite funny for a man of your age, Victor. I like that. Everyone person I date thinks they're either Peter Pan or Peter Stringfellow. You must be the only chap here who hasn't made a pass at me. It's been a pleasure working with you. Just remember me in your will...'

'Always the gold-digger, Samantha... Don't worry; I won't forget you, when they pay up. If I'd been younger and bolder, I'd have swept you off your pretty heels. With any luck I will be able to take early retirement. I fancy starting a collection of gold coins and maybe dealing in them. I've got a couple of sovereigns already,' he replied.

'We have something in common; I love gold too, since a job that I worked on a couple of years ago. Ever seen inside a gold vault? It totally changes your perspective on life,' asked Samantha.

'I think if I ever did that I wouldn't want to come out,' he laughed. 'I think I understand why the deceased Pharaohs wanted to be locked away with their hoard. Who needs food and water, when you own the ultimate precious metal?'

'Maybe you'll get the chance, if this works out,' she replied. 'I think it's time we came clean with the team or at least our main helpers.'

'You're correct. I'll try and get them together tomorrow, at dinner time. Will you back me up? It'll be a good trial run for the interview with the directors, one day soon,' he asked.

'Of course,' she winked, 'we're partners in crime...'

'Erm... we haven't actually done anything dishonest yet, have we, Samantha?' he asked, as once again he watched the desirable lady walk out the door.

* * *

'I knew you two were up to something,' said Ed. 'I even thought sometimes that you were having an affair.'

Victor tried not to look at Samantha. 'Of course not, we're colleagues.'

She had sat next to him and leaned over pretending to kiss his ear.

'Give over,' he laughed, trying to be serious. 'Ok chaps and chap-esses, you've been given a basic report of our progress a day ago and should have had time to read it. Do you have any questions or violent disagreements? I'll deal with the former; Samantha the Rottweiler will look after the rest...'

'I thought she looked like an old dog,' muttered Ed to his neighbour.

'With more tricks than you'll ever know,' she laughed. 'Victor's really come up trumps in my opinion and the calculations stack up.'

'Surely people have looked at this time thing, over the centuries?' asked Ed's neighbour.

Victor looked at the technician sternly, as Samantha had instructed him to do.

'Of course Rodney; from initially crossing off days, by carving

27

on cave walls, to today's twenty first century recording and measuring instruments, combined with giant computers. It gets more and more accurate over the centuries and my formula finally cracks it. All the others were like junior school sums, with answers and little remainders, mine divides exactly,' answered Victor.

'But it only works if the world stops for thirteen minutes and erm...' Rodney referred to his copy of the report, 'And thirteen seconds.'

'Well, not actually stop. We can all breathe but communication and non-essential use of electricity must stop for that period. The world will continue to orbit around the sun but that short period of electromagnetic silence or as near to it as humanly possible will allow the man-made magnet that has been superimposed on the planet to collapse and the Earth will return to its correct spin and orbit. An almost infinitesimally small change but just enough,' explained Samantha.

'You're saying that the discovery and use of electricity over the last hundred or so years is affecting the Earth's speed of rotation? Even if your collapse to normal EM theory is correct, surely when everything is turned back on, it will go wrong again?' asked Ed.

'Correct, Ed. That's why a managed plan of switching everything back on, at more or less opposite sides of the Earth, at the same time, will keep the balance. Even when running at full tilt, the power usage in the west will be reasonably close to that of the developing east. It's not likely that everyone from China will move to London in the near future, to unbalance it again,' replied Victor.

'There are enough takeaways in the West End anyway,' said Samantha.

'Ok, so say if the directors go with this idea; I think the fact that the calendar is a bit off has been known for decades. There have been several attempts to add varying amounts of time. I seem to recall reading that, a few hundred years ago, the dates were moved forward a couple of weeks overnight so the peasants protested about their stolen wages and missing parts of their lives,' replied a stern faced man sitting opposite her. 'What's to stop all the 'End of The World' nutters and religious freaks having a party? What about terrorists and freedom fighters in the Middle East and South America? They're not going to listen to any orders and turn off their bomb timers,' asked Rodney.

'Statistically speaking, there are not enough of them for their power usage to make any difference. Anyway, they don't control the generators, governments do,' answered Samantha. 'The fact is that this is going to save the military powers chunks of money in testing and regulating timing devices, in medical and hospital situations, and simplify computer chip research. No one sensible will say no. Once the big powers go for it, we're away...' said Samantha. 'Is everyone in?'

A general nodding of heads, from the six people present in the room, passed the vote.

'No need for Plan B then, Victor,' noted Rodney.

'Erm...' Victor turned to Samantha and shook his head.

'You said Sam would pole dance to get the male vote,' laughed Ed.

'I'll pole dance on your head if you want.' offered Samantha, glowering.

'Right then, the meeting's over everyone, and thanks for attending. I'll be pushing on with a presentation to the board ASAP and I'll let you know if we need more help. For the time being, I'd be grateful if you'd just finish your allotted tasks,' said Victor.

After the others had departed, Samantha closed the door.

'I'll swing for that dick Ed one day. He's such a caveman. He really thinks women belong in the kitchen,' complained Samantha. 'I hate being called Sam and he knows it. It's a man's name. Do I look like a bloke?' she asked and stuck her bosom out.

'Not at all, you're very pretty,' replied Victor, admiring the bumps under her jumper, visible through her unbuttoned lab-coat. 'You're all woman,' he added.

'Thanks, Victor. You're a gentleman,' she smiled. 'I'll get in touch with the secretary to the board, explain the position and arrange an appointment for the presentation. I guess two weeks should allow us to tidy up any loose ends?'

'Fine, Samantha, I'll be in my office,' he replied.

Ten minutes later she knocked on his door. It had been fully open but she still tapped with her knuckles out of courtesy.

'Hi Victor, I've got the date. You're not going to believe me,' she said.

'Try me,' he answered, looking mystified.

'One o'clock in the board room, two weeks today,' she said.

'And...' he replied.

'It's the thirteenth of the month at thirteen hundred hours...' she said, smiling.

* * *

'So you see, Victor, we've spent too much time and invested too much effort to let those government tossers take total control of our project,' said Samantha, after letting him breathe again.

He inhaled deeply and licked his lips, which were still fresh with the taste of her sweet saliva. The unexpected snog had caught him totally unawares and his mind spun with questions about her intentions. Her perfume ran around his nasal sinuses, before sneaking up to his brain, to give the sensible cortex a good kicking.

'Well what do you propose, Samantha? Feel free to kiss me again while you're thinking,' he said, hopefully.

'Ha-ha. I'm just expressing my thanks for trusting me to work with you. It would have been easy to ask for another temp to check over your ideas and she'd never have guessed the reason.

You could have kept all the glory and bonus for yourself,' she replied.

'Huh, in case you misheard, there is no bonus,' he said, seeing the chance of another sultry lip collision receding.

'Ah, I'll let you into a secret. You asked me because you could see that I seem a foxy lady,' said Samantha.

'Ok, so you're a redhead…' he replied.

'Foxy doesn't always have to be red,' she explained. 'Try a fuck-able, intelligent lady with a large cunning gene.'

'I reckon that I'm looking at one…' he said, carefully.

'And imagine mixing her with a clever boy, who's had his toy taken away, by a big bully,' she said. 'Well the ruffian needs to be taught a lesson.'

'Compensation would be better than fisticuffs,' he replied.

'Gold bullion suit you sir?' she answered and smiled broadly.

Victor looked at her lips. 'Say that first word again.'

Samantha spelt it out, 'G. O. L. D.'

'You're going to turn this fiasco into gold? I don't think so,' he said.

'I'm going to powder my nose, lock the door and give you a special presentation. Trust me, it's foxy…' said Samantha, before she walked into the corridor, on her way to the ladies' locker room.

Victor twiddled his thumbs for a couple of minutes, wondering about what could happen next. Maybe Samantha had plans of defecting to China with the secrets or had totally flipped with the pressure, he mused.

She came back just as he considered putting the kettle on. He watched her lock the door and deliberately leave the key in the lock before walking over to him, where he sat at a workbench. The redhead carried a clipboard and a cream coloured cardboard folder.

'I've had several jobs, you know,' she said, as she came closer.

'I guessed that. Model maybe or geisha girl?' he asked,

cheekily.

'A good foxy guess but much more mundane; I graduated with a masters in computing, I then followed that with some teaching and a stint at a bank,' she explained.

'That explains your programing ability. Did you get a good mortgage deal at the bank?' he asked.

'Not just any institution; the Bank of England, actually,' she replied.

'I smell something dodgy here. I'm not sure I want to be involved...' said Victor, who now had a worried look on his face. 'I'm no criminal.'

'Maybe I can show you something to change your mind.' She passed over the clipboard.

Victor took it from her. He saw a blank front page, so flipped it over. On the next sheet, written in large red capitals were the words 'THIRTEEN MILLION POUNDS STERLING'.

'Split fifty/fifty but this is all yours,' she said.

He looked over to see that Samantha had started to unbutton her lab-coat.

'That's a large...' His mouth stopped in mid-sentence as she dropped the garment to the floor.

'A genuine redhead just for you, Victor; want to catch this fox?' she asked, in a totally naked, apart from black nylons, way.

He looked down at the fiery red triangle between her legs. Samantha raised her left foot onto the chair next to him, to reinforce the message.

'Do you want in or out?' she asked and took off her glasses, to suck the arm in her usual fashion. 'Or maybe both, Victor?' she added.

Samantha reached over to his collar and pulled to encourage him closer. He got up from his chair and she met him with her lips, in a smouldering kiss.

Victor couldn't resist stroking the soft white flesh of her hip, around the black suspender belt. A little twang with his thumb helped to convince him of its reality. He looked down at her white boobs with their delicate pink nipples and noticed how the number of freckles rapidly increased towards her neck and shoulders.

She laughed and asked, 'Counting them? Don't bother, it'll take too long. Anyway, I have an easier task for your clever mind...'

Samantha took his right hand and separated the first two fingers from the others before guiding them between her open legs. The coarse orange forest easily parted, as his fingers landed on her target. He felt a little used, as she tightly gripped his right hand and pressed it backwards and forwards. Her clitoris hardened under his fingertips and she closed her eyes, moaning softly at his enforced touch.

'Thirteen million pounds,' she said and thrust his two fingers, into her impatient fox's mouth. 'Half of it and me...'

She released her grip on Victor's hand and opened her eyes to look at him. The pupils inside Samantha's green irises narrowed, to focus and scan his face for signs of agreement. He felt the zip of his trousers being forcefully tugged down.

'Let's rob a bank,' she said, as his trousers fell to the floor. Samantha continued to undo his shirt buttons and pull it partly off, until it remained hanging from his right wrist.

Victor continued his partly clothed fingering of her innermost parts, as she locked herself onto his mouth again. Samantha's soft but firm lips bullied his own into submission and he could feel his stubble grazing her pretty face. His hand became moist with her juices, as he alternately pushed second knuckle deep into her, before returning to finger-tip massage the crinkled skin, covering her fun button.

She finally rewarded his digital effort, by a strong muscular contraction holding his fingers captive for a few seconds, before expelling him with a series of short aftershocks.

'Wow; pretty amazing, you clever boy,' Samantha said,

smiling broadly and removing the dangling shirt, from his now free, right arm. She lifted her leg down from the chair. 'I do so love a man in socks,' she laughed. 'Leave them on and fuck me,'

Victor watched her lean over the bench to present her trim posterior towards him. Her untrimmed orange bush, beckoned him in and without further invitation, he slipped his manhood inside her and went fox hunting...

'I guess this means we're partners,' the vixen asked the perspiring scientist, a couple of minutes later.

Victor continued his attempts to squash her pale body into the wooden surface of the worktop. 'Yes, yes, yes,' he exclaimed as he finally shot into the cornered animal, and added, 'in crime...'

* * *

Once fully clothed and tidied up, the pair sat together in the café opposite the Maple and Philips building, discussing business over a couple of frothy cappuccinos.

'Let me get this right, Samantha. When you worked on a recent contract at the Bank of England, you were in charge of a major part of a new computer installation. It kept track of international loans involving hundreds of millions of sterling. Obviously before being put into proper use, it had to be tested with fake transactions. Only you knew all the codes or passwords to do this, because of your position,' said Victor, before taking a bite of the biscuit that came with his coffee.

Samantha didn't answer at first. She simply smiled and dipped her teaspoon into the cappuccino bubbles, before emptying it, upside down on the tip of her tongue. Victor once again watched in admiration, at how almost every action of the redhead turned him on, as she retrieved a missed bit at the corner of her upper lip, with a sexy lick.

'That's right,' she finally answered, 'and I accidentally forgot to cancel them after installation at the bank so they're still active.'

'Ok, why share this with me? Haven't you wanted to dip into the cash machine before?' he inquired.

'Many a time, but the problem is it would register in nanoseconds as an illegal transaction, triggering an immediate internet search for the computer or access device used, not to mention alerting New Scotland Yard, MI5 and MI6. I'd be arrested before I made it to the end of the street,' she answered, pulling a sad face.

'So how has the position changed?' he asked.

'It's your theory about the calendar, Victor. In order to correct that electromagnetic problem building up, you recommend closing down all communication etc., effectively meaning that all major computers are oblivious to time for thirteen minutes and thirteen seconds. Rather than being pissed off that the government has stolen our scheme, we should actually be encouraging them to push it through with the other international powers,' she replied.

'Ah-ha, and maybe you can do something sneaky in that catch up period?' he said, and raised an eyebrow.

'Thirteen million worth of sneakiness actually and I suggest we push for the end of year twenty thirteen,' she suggested.

'Why exactly?' he asked.

'The bank's program is set up to not only recognise twelve months of the year. We used a false thirteenth month for the trial transactions. I can get the system to think that the short closedown is an extra but normal day, dated 13.13.13,' she answered. The alarm systems won't be triggered and new Porsche, here we come.'

'And you need my thirteen minutes and thirteen seconds miniature day...' he mused. 'Do I get to fuck you again?' he inquired.

'The den's all yours, Victor and I'll be ordering my car while you're counting your money,' Samantha answered. She reached out to feel the bulge in the front of his trousers. 'That monk Dennis the Short unwittingly set this up for us, so I think I'll change your name to Den the Impaler...'

* * *

Fifteen, fourteen, thirteen...

Suddenly the laptop screen went blank.

'Shit,' shouted Victor.

'Connection must be interrupted,' said Samantha calmly and he watched her fingers dance across the keyboard.

The screen lit up, 'TRANSACTION COMPLETE<£13MILL FROM BOE TO FOX>ON 13.13.13'.

'Well fuck me, you did it,' said Victor after reading the screen, several times.

'I'll fuck you later; pass me the small screwdriver set first, Victor. We have to destroy the evidence,' said Samantha, with no hint of emotion.

He brought over a box of tools and watched as she quickly stripped the hard drive out of the small computer and dismembered the special modem connection device that she had constructed. Various parts were subjected to a severe hammer beating on the kitchen floor, before being wrapped up in several used shopping bags. She scraped identification stickers off the laptop base and several other parts before packing those as well.

'Alright Victor, let's go to that New Year Party as our cover, and welcome in twenty fourteen, the Year of the Porsche,' she laughed.

Victor couldn't resist slapping her tight millionaire ass, as she bent over to put on her heels. He did up his top button and straightened his tie. He looked forward to their forthcoming holiday in Switzerland in a week's time and helped her carry the bags of smashed-up electronics. After locking up the front door to his flat, he walked into town with Samantha, depositing parts in random refuse bins along the way. The New Year fireworks, crackling overhead on the cloudless night, combined with the red fox on his arm, made him feel so good that he could hardly believe it.

'I'm the luckiest man, alive,' he said to Samantha.

'Lucky thirteen, I told you so,' she replied.

'And when we get to Switzerland, the plan is to take me to a bank with a private storage vault, that you've organised just for us, where the money will be present as gold bars?' he asked, as a group of drunken revellers shouted new year greetings to them, from across the street.

'You'll be able to touch and count all of them. They weigh a kilogram each. There'll be over three hundred and forty, depending on the exchange rate. The spot price of gold's around thirty five thousand pounds a kilo at present,' replied Samantha.

'Wow. Obviously we'd attract attention if we bought a huge mansion straight away,' he noted.

'Exactly, I'm taking three bars and picking up a right hand drive Porsche to drive back across Europe on my own. You'd better think of some way to convert your share into cash,' she advised.

'I'd like to think that the ideas will reveal themselves when I touch the precious metal,' he answered.

'That's fine. You'll have plenty of time in the vault,' she said.

A week later, they were ushered into the rear room of a private depository in Berne and the manager explained to them how to use the facility.

'Our customers require strict anonymity, of course, so there are no logs of visitors signing in and out. If myself or the deputy manager is not available, you may still gain twenty-four hour access by using the exterior keypad and similarly the control to your personal vault. I will be finishing my shift in five minutes. When you leave; simply key in your code to your inner door, the exterior door will lock itself. If you're wondering what the other vaults contain, you will have to use your imagination because we never ask and we never enter them. Every night the air is purged and replaced with pure nitrogen for an hour, to cleanse and help preserve any stored rare artefacts. If you have no questions then you may proceed with your business,' said the pin-stripe suited man, in a strong French accent.

After he had left them to return to the front desk, Victor giggled like an excited schoolboy. 'We're nearly here. Show me the money, honey,' he said to Samantha.

'Journey's end,' she replied, smiling and turned to tap some numbers into a complicated looking keyboard.

He heard a loud click as a latch disengaged and the door slid open in front of them. Samantha took his hand and tugged him inside.

Victor looked at the pile of sparkling gold bars stacked on the stainless steel floor. His eyes almost rolled like the spinning reels of a gambling machine, about to hit the jackpot. In his mind he could see his new favourite numbers lining up one by one; thirteen, thirteen, thirteen…

A few minutes later, Samantha stood just outside the door, having just carried out a Porsche 911's worth taster, in a reinforced sack.

'See you in thirteen weeks, Victor, as agreed,' she shouted.

Victor didn't hear. He had considering taking thirteen bars of gold and his mind busily worked out how much money he could spend per minute, over the next thirteen weeks. Neither did he hear the click as the vault-door closed behind him, after Samantha dialled in code 13.13.13.

Knot

Dave looked out of the rear bedroom window at his beloved vegetable patch and shrub collection. He'd been carefully tending the many plants for years; watering, pruning, digging, composting and anything else that he could do to improve his garden.

He shook his head in sorrow at the scene that now greeted his eyes. In the last two months, his life's work had been overrun by a pernicious plant, which grew so fast and tall that it crowded out all the other competition.

The prize-winning marrows of last year and the delicious King Edward potatoes had been replaced by the six-foot tall bamboo-like stems of the green-leafed monster. He could hardly see the greenhouse now and had simply given up trying to keep the rapidly spreading armada of invading plants under control.

'You can untie me now, master,' said a voice behind him.

'Oh sorry, Opia.' He turned around to face the young oriental girl, who had just spoken. 'Miles away, I'm afraid; just thinking about my veg. I still can't believe what weird force of nature or bad luck has dumped that forest of that evil weed on my back garden.'

'Please show me the bonds again in the mirror, before you start, *Nawashi*,' asked Opia.

Dave picked up the large mirror that he'd taken from the landing wall earlier and also adjusted the full-length floor standing one, so that the girl on the bed could see her reflection.

'A little more to the left, please,' she asked before commenting, 'you have learnt so much from me. Your knots are beautiful and feel so sexy. Please pull my ankles once more...'

Dave obliged and smiled as his large hands wrapped around the delicate ankles of the willing prisoner. He rocked her legs back and forth. This had the effect of tightening the single jute rope that bound her hands and feet behind her back, to the intricate design encircling her hips.

Opia pressed her face into the pillow and gently moaned as the motion allowed a single carefully placed knot to rub her fun button. He continued his actions for a couple of minutes until her slim body tightened and shook.

Dave couldn't resist kissing the tiny, size three feet that he held, which seemed smaller than his own hands.

Opia giggled and wriggled at his unexpected touch.

From his standing up position, Dave could still see out of the window. It almost looked as if the foliage had grown another couple of inches, in response to his half hour of fun with this oriental girl only half his age.

He looked down at her jute entwined, naked buttocks and for some reason felt that his lost garden might be Opia's fault, so he gave her left bum cheek a firm slap, to match the existing red handprint on the right side.

'Ow… thank you master. Remove the binding now. We have to do some maths before your wife gets home…' said Opia, grinning.

* * *

Three months previously, Dave sat in his Vauxhall Astra twiddling his thumbs. As usual, he had parked by the side of the road, a few hundred yards along from the local college and awaited his wife. As a secretary to the deputy principal, she always finished early on a Wednesday. He'd taken an early retirement/redundancy package at fifty years old, from his job with a multinational chemical group, when the credit crunch had forced it to downsize. He'd worked for the same firm under different trade names, via several takeovers and mergers, for almost thirty years and been faced with relocating to a nonde-script city in the north of England or to 'take the money and run'.

Dave took the latter option, with both him and his wife hoping that some other position would appear locally, and allow them to stay in their North Devon home.

Six months later, apart from a three-week stint as a stand-in school lollipop man, the local employment centre had been completely unable to find a job for a highly skilled industrial biochemist. His main function now had become house husband and taxi driver for his wife. Previously a two car family, they had sold one to conserve funds.

He leaned his elbow on the steering wheel with chin in hand and peered through the rear view mirror at the college entrance, for any sign of his wife.

Several students walked out of the gateway. Dave kept his flagging spirits up by looking out for the pretty girls and trying to make sense of modern undergraduate fashion. The latest idea seemed to be a combination of tights with very short trousers to show off the legs. He hoped that a model or two would walk along in his direction but they all either crossed the road to wait at the bus stop or headed towards the town centre behind him.

'Shit,' Dave uttered, as he jumped to an unexpected loud tap at the driver's window. He half turned around expecting to see a traffic warden or police officer, about to harangue him for waiting partly across someone's front drive and surprisingly saw a vision of loveliness in a black beret, smiling back at him.

The front passenger door opened and his wife climbed into the front seat.

'Let her in then, Dave. She's going to look at the bedroom,' she ordered.

'Oh, erm… ok then, Janet,' he answered, understanding now. They had discussed renting out their spare room to make some extra money. His wife had found out that it would be tax-free and had placed a note on the accommodation notice board at the college.

He opened the driver's door after looking in the mirror and

said, 'Hi, I'm Dave,' before tipping the driver's seat forward, to allow their prospective tenant to climb into the back seat.

The girl looked oriental in appearance, slimly built and barely five foot tall. She slipped into the narrow gap to the rear seat, with ease. Dave received his earlier wish to get a close up of the latest tights/cut-off jeans look, as her cute rump disappeared into the back of his vehicle. As he retook his position in the front seat and started the car, he had already decided to vote for her, if the wife asked...

'This is Opia,' explained Janet, as he pressed the indicator stalk and pulled away. 'She's Japanese and speaks amazing English. She's enrolled on a botany degree.'

'Ah, you want to be a plant doctor... I love gardening. I've been growing various plants for ages. The back garden started off as bare earth, when we bought the house new. I'm very proud of it now,' remarked Dave.

Opia's head popped into the gap between the front seats. He instantly smelt a lovely flowery perfume.

'That's great. I love to get out into gardens and mingle with the plants. You'll have to let me help you with the weeding, Dave. I'm so excited about this. Will I be able to plant some seeds? I'll probably have to, as part of the course homework,' she replied.

He looked at her almond shaped dark eyes, topped with the rakish black beret, in the rear view mirror and couldn't have wished for more, a smart young girl assistant in his very own garden...

* * *

Three days later, Dave helped Opia move her things into his house. Janet had asked him to take the car around to the temporary lodgings that the college had arranged for her, when she'd arrived from Japan barely a week ago.

'I'm so glad to have my own room. I didn't like living out of cases and sharing at the last place. Your house is very nice. I feel like I could take root and stay here a long time. You are so kind, helping me move my things, Dave. If there's anything that I can do in return, please ask. I insist on helping you in the garden tomorrow after college. The weather forecast is good,' said Opia.

'No problem,' said Dave, a little red-faced after carrying a large heavy suitcase upstairs. She either owns a lot of shoes or is planning on having her own greenhouse upstairs and he'd just carried up the soil, he thought.

'Shall I make you a cup of tea?' she offered. 'You look like a poor plant wilting in the sun.'

'That'll be lovely,' he answered, warming to the smiling Japanese girl by the second. He became convinced that to have someone else in the house, other than his wife, would make being unemployed much more palatable. Their own children had left the nest years ago and he only saw them a few times a year because of their work commitments and distance apart.

Dave bent down to pick up a label that had fallen off one of the cases. 'OPIA FALL,' it said, followed by some oriental style writing and then 'FROM JAPAN.' He handed it to her. 'Better keep this, in case you forget your name. Is it the same in Japanese? I know some countries and religions seem to swop things about.'

'Maybe; I guess the letters in English for my name and pronunciation are European or Latin in origin. It's just a couple of symbols, if you write it in my home language. I do feel a little homesick when I see Japanese writing like this.' She pointed at the label. 'There are so many traditions and ideas that are different from your western thinking. I hope that I get to show you some,' she answered with a smile that made him wish he could turn the clock back.

Dave watched her lithe little body walk into the kitchen. Parts of him that hadn't twitched with desire for a long time were stirring, as his eyes followed the tight red T-shirt. He sat down at the wooden table watching her, as she filled the kettle and chatted away to him. He hardly had chance to say a word as she described the differences between Japanese kitchens and their food.

'Aren't you going to ask how old I am?' she asked all of a sudden. 'Foreign men usually do...'

'Well it had occurred to me but it seemed rude. Eighteen, I guess? I know that Japanese women seem to age well, compared to Europeans,' he replied, really hoping that she wasn't going to say just turned sixteen. He had no idea how advanced the Japanese education system could be, and whether their students went to university much earlier than this country.

'Why thank you, Dave. I'm twenty-five actually. Twenty-six next month,' she grinned. 'I was married for two years. Does that change anything?'

'Absolutely nothing,' he lied, feeling so much happier that he hadn't been starting to lust after a schoolgirl.

'You are correct about Japanese ladies. We can be hard to age and often more experienced at things than we look...' she said, as she placed a mug of tea in front of him, on the table.

Dave watched her closely as she carried on speaking, looking for clues from that typical inscrutable oriental visage. He wondered if she teased him or could there be more to this...

'A lady like me taken out of my native habitat has to be adaptable to survive. I could be lucky and fall on fertile ground. If I want to thrive, I may have to fight my corner against animals, poison and sharpened weapons but I'm here to stay. I'm sure that I'll leave an indelible mark on this place, Dave. I may be a long way from home but I know there'll be things that we can teach one another. We all have souls...' said Opia.

Dave sipped his tea. 'You're a little weird in a cute way. I think that you're more grown up than you look. I'm a biochemist and have a nose for a new discovery. You've got me curious, Opia Fall...'

'Cool,' she grinned. 'You won't regret it, well some of it, anyway.' She winked at him. 'I'd like to rest now. May I join you in the garden tomorrow morning, around nine o'clock? My lectures start later at eleven.'

'Sure,' he said. 'Hope you can handle onions. I've got to tie off the heads to get them ready to lift.'

'Tying and knotting? Right up my street,' she laughed. 'See you tomorrow. I've got food in my room.'

* * *

'So you see, Dave. Opia's having some trouble with the maths, especially the statistics. Apparently it's still at a basic level but she didn't study them in Japan and she's finding it hard. I told her that you used to have to do a lot of calculations and formulae in your old job and you'd probably be able to help her. Hope you don't mind Dave,' said Janet.

'Oh, I suppose I might be able to,' answered Dave, trying not to sound excited.

'Well she has been busy in the garden tidying up. She spent an hour out there the other night. I'm sure that she spoke to some of the bushes at one point. Must be a real botanist if she speaks the plant language,' laughed Janet. 'She's really nice but do you think she's a bit odd?'

'Aren't all boffins that way inclined? I'll have a word and see what I can do. She usually gets home around five and it's ten past now,' replied Dave.

'The front door just clicked. That'll be her now,' said Janet. 'I'll get the tea on. Hello Opia, had a good day?'

'Oh, hello to you both, lots of lectures today and some lab results to go through. I don't suppose that I can have a word later, Dave?' replied Opia.

'Jan's already said about the maths. That's no problem,' said Dave.

Opia smiled, 'Thanks, that's great. If I help you in the garden tomorrow could we look over those results afterwards?'

'No problem. Do you want to join us for dinner?' asked Dave.

'Don't worry about me. I have to use the internet now. I'll use the kitchen later if that's ok. Leave the washing up to me if you want.' Opia gave a cheery wave and went upstairs.

'She'll make someone a nice wife, you know Dave,' said Janet, after she heard the bedroom door close upstairs. 'I'll have to keep an eye on you two, in case you think of trading me in for a younger model.'

'You're all I need, Jan,' Dave fibbed, thinking of those denim shorts…

* * *

The next morning, Dave opened the back door to survey his domain. He took a bite of his piece of toast and after swallowing said, 'Huh.' The night-time breeze had started to shift the broad leaves of the neighbour's sycamore tree onto his lawn. He put his plate back on the kitchen top, pushed his feet into his pre-laced well-worn garden shoes and padded out on to the dew-covered grass.

The smell of an early autumn tingled in the air, even though the weather had remained warm for the time of year. He could just detect another smell, something fresh, like the smell of newly erupting seedlings in his greenhouse but with a hint of decay and cat pee. He didn't like the fragrance.

Dave bent down and picked up the dozen or so examples of the trifoliate foliage. As he did so, he noticed a few weeds shooting up amongst the recently mown grassy green tips. The newcomers were pink and slightly frilly, where immature leaves were starting to form. The edges had started to turn green where the light had stimulated chlorophyll production.

Opia's voice stopped his investigation.

'Morning Dave, what can I do? Would you like me to tidy up inside the greenhouse? The tomatoes are nearly over.'

'Yes please, Opia. Pull them up and strip off any fruit be it red or green. Janet will make chutney with any that do not ripen. I'm thinking of mowing the lawn. There are some odd weeds sprouting up that I don't recognise. If I trim the tops off that'll kill them,' he answered.

'We're all God's creatures, Dave. Some may just be a little more annoying than the others. I would say that one person's weed is just someone else's lost flower...' said Opia.

Dave looked at her smiling face and for some reason, felt that he had been cruel by thinking of clipping the lawn.

'Well, it can't do any harm to leave it a few days,' he said to appease the weed-lady champion.

'What did you think about my onion stem tying, the other day?' she asked.

'Quite amazing what you did with that ball of string. I never learned that in the scouts,' he answered and followed her over to the veg patch.

The previously eighteen-inch or so tall allium stems had been folded over and bound in an intricate fashion. Dave knelt down to look at the attractive little knots and string lattice work, which kept the onion leaves imprisoned.

'I can do a reef knot but these are something else, a Japanese tradition or art form, I guess?' he queried.

'Indeed; most of the skill is genetically in some of us, I think. The ability to trap and hold something, but avoid damage to the parts that you need, has been around for generations,' she answered. He watched as she picked up the ball of string from on top of an upturned bucket, where it had been left a few days ago. Opia pulled out a yard long piece and snipped it off with a pair of rusty scissors.

'Hold out your hand,' she said, so Dave put his upturned palm towards her, mystified.

Opia's hands became a blur as she skilfully bound his fingers and thumbs in an intricate web of triangles, diamonds and loopy knots with the soft string.

'Wow,' he said, as he held up his hand to the sun and looked through his fingers at the sparkly pattern. 'It looks alive and, well... maybe just a little bit kinky.'

Opia gave a little knowing laugh, 'Oh really? Takes one to know one maybe?'

Dave watched her denim shorts as she slinked over to the greenhouse. Red tights were the order of the day, with a short faded denim jacket and black shoes. Opia walked so lightly that she didn't leave footprints in the soil. He tried to do likewise by firstly tip toeing and then gently flat footing across the ground to the shed but failed miserably. She seemed to be at one with the soft fertile surface.

As he watched her bending over, through the algae stained glass, yanking up the tomato plants, his eyes spotted something familiar in the soil just in front of him.

'Damn,' he uttered and bent down to pull up a red tipped weed. The top snapped off in his hands and as he surveyed the surrounding soil, he could see several more of the invaders pushing their leading edge through the crust, to peep for the sunlight.

'Oh no,' he said, 'flipping birds.' He guessed that some of his not so favourite feathered friends had been dropping seeds with the help of the wind. This had been one of the problems in trying to keep a perfect looking garden, all evil horticultural devils gang up to fight you; weeds, slugs, snails, weevils, they all knew where to get a free lunch and a new home.

Dave attempted to remove another rebel with a sharp tug and again ended up holding a crushed pink leaf. He decided that he would have to fetch out the garden fork and lift out the surrounding soil, in order to get at the roots of whatever the plant may be.

'Can you get me a bowl?' shouted Opia from the greenhouse door.

'Ok, I'll pop into the house. I've found some more of those pink blighters growing over here, by the way,' he answered.

'Oh never mind, Dave, we can see to them another day. Chutney comes first...' she laughed.

'Don't even like chutney,' he muttered under his breath as he walked back to the kitchen.

He came back with a metal bowl and held it out as Opia scooped up a selection of red and green tomatoes from a pile on the floor. She repeated the process twice more, which nearly filled the container.

'That should keep Janet happy. You can make me happy next, by showing me how to do the botany calculations and then I'll have to do something special for you. You're looking a little glum. I bet it's the little plants. Don't worry, I know something to take your mind off them,' she said.

They put the tomato plant remains onto the compost heap and went back into the house to clean up. He almost cut off his hand binding with a pair of scissors, prior to washing his hands, but Opia stopped him. She pointed out a just visible loose end. 'Pull this,' she advised.

Dave did as instructed and to his amazement the latticework began to unravel. She pulled off the remains and shook it to produce the original, knot-free, one-yard length of white string.

'Bravo,' he said, flexing his fingers. 'I can't see any marks or damage. Imprisoned but preserved as you said earlier.'

She smiled sweetly at him, 'I will teach you some later. It's called *kinbaku*.'

'Kin-ba-ku,' repeated Dave. 'Ok, it will be nice to learn something new. I'm up for it.'

'You'll just love it,' she replied. 'Can we do the maths in my bedroom? It will save me bringing all the notes downstairs.'

'Ok,' answered Dave. He'd avoided going into her room for

fear of meeting assorted knickers, bras and other feminine attire. He hoped that all underwear etc. would be packed safely into drawers.

He followed her up the stairs after they'd washed their hands. They'd both left their shoes by the door and he couldn't help looking at her slim legs and tiny feet as she stepped up in front of him. He could see the muscles working in her trim calves before telling himself to behave.

Opia pointed to the padded typist's chair in front of the large wooden dressing table that she had transformed into a makeshift desk. Dave sat down, trying not to look around. She took a file out of her rucksack and opened it in front of him.

'This is the homework,' she said. 'We've been growing some pre-weighed geraniums inside clear plastic bags and removed them from the soil. The pots and compost were all weighed and we have to work out just how much oxygen and hydrogen have been taken up to make the new plant structure, from the result tables. We all live and breathe, whether plants or animals, but rarely think about these things, quite interesting really.'

'No problem, Opia. I used to do this kind of thing regularly years ago, when we were developing fertilisers at the factory. We did a bit with rabbits as well, until the anti-vivisectionists found out. I guess we were lucky with the plants that we weren't attacked by Triffid-like monsters demanding equal rights,' he laughed.

'So you've read John Wyndham, the story about a world overtaken by giant plants? Who knows, Dave? It's said that anything's possible.' She laughed.

He drew a few columns on a piece of blank paper and showed her where to put the relevant numbers. Opia asked a few questions and she knelt beside him. He could feel the warmth of her little hand as she took the pen a few times from his grasp, to add up a few numbers.

'It's not so bad,' she said putting her left hand softly on his right shoulder. Her warm voice seemed to massage his brain through his ears and he so wanted to touch her. The room smelt of her unusual Japanese perfume and this only added to the strange situation.

'You're good with figures, Dave. What do you think?' She drew two lines at the bottom and started to write in an answer.

Dave leaned over to read the small handwriting.

'Me.'

Opia turned his swivel chair in her direction.

'What do you think of my figure?' she asked and did a little twirl.

'Erm... very nice of course, you're a pretty young thing, Opia,' he said, a little surprised at the unexpected question.

'I guessed you fancied me. People don't always want Opia Fall around, you know. It's how I present myself, you see...' she said, slightly mysteriously.

'Fancied, well, I erm...'

Dave shut up as she turned away from him and watched her lift up the back of her T-shirt, to reveal a plant tattoo. A bamboo-like stem ran along her spine, with large strong green leaves sprouting out at each alternate nodal joint. He could make out the lower parts of some colourful figures, on either side.

'I know you'll like this because you're a gardener, Dave,' she said, looking over her shoulder.

'I do like tattoos. I'd never have one myself, too squeamish. That's very nice artwork, not at all the 'Do it while he's drunk' stuff that I've seen on some of my mates' arms. It's very arty, is it Japanese?' he asked.

Opia responded by pulling the T-shirt over her head to reveal the full ink illustration on her back.

'Whoa there Opia,' said Dave, turning his head to one side. 'If Jan caught me like this, she'd string me up.'

'What a lovely English phrase... I'd like to teach you to string me up, Dave,' she replied. 'Janet won't be home for hours and I won't tell. Have a proper look,' and she knelt down in front of him with her arms folded to show the full image on her back.

Dave slowly moved his hand away from the side of his head and when certain sure that Opia seemed mostly decent, he started to observe the full design.

The centre backbone plant extended to just shoulder height, the final unfurled leaf tip keen to open onto her soft brown neck. He realised why he hadn't seen any clues that she had tattoos earlier; they were all hidden under her clothes. Small leaves just above her belt gave way to larger ones, which arched across to her shoulders and several spikes of pale yellow flowers crowned the feature. To the left curled a colourful, ferocious looking, wide mouthed, oriental style dragon. Two red lipped, blue finned, coy carp swam in a pebbly pool on her right hip and a branch of flowering blossom dropped pink petals into the waters of her gorgeously narrow waist.

'Wow,' said Dave. He struggled to think of anything else to say about the delicate artwork on the bare skin of the young Japanese girl.

'You like?' she asked.

'I certainly do. It's just incredible,' he replied.

'There's more,' she said and started to stand up. 'I'll show you my roots.'

'Ah,' he said, expecting to see a list of ancestors discretely written on her leg.

With a quick side-to-side movement she bent over and wiggled out of her red tights and denim shorts. The flexible girl then leant so far forward that her palms touched the floor.

'Oh fuck,' whispered Dave as his eyes clocked the ink rocky ground level, just below her belt line and the root architecture running down the crease of her derriere, ending at the top of her inner thighs. Her olive cheeks made the most wonderful plant-pot imaginable.

'Fuck,' he repeated, wondering how the tattoo artist had

managed to keep a steady hand, in such an erotic situation.

'Fukushima, maybe, my home city?' she asked.

'Sorry, Opia; I didn't mean to swear. It's just your tattoo and your body; I'm lost for words.'

Opia returned to a kneeling position.

'It's traditional upon receiving a gift of a plant to show appreciation by caressing it,' advised Opia. 'And I think you want to turn Japanese...'

Dave trembled as he stood up and gently placed his hands on her horizontal soft shoulders to stroke the blossom. He bent his head towards her neck and hovered for a second, as Janet's face came into his mind...

'Not sure? True appreciation is a kiss,' suggested Opia.

Janet's face disappeared under a wide spray of tattoo ink. He completed his movement and felt her warm skin touch his lips and her shoulder press back against his face.

'Now the shoot and down the stem,' she instructed.

Dave didn't think to resist and carried on gently lip-worshipping the Opia plant along her back, as she silently bent over, to place her hands on the floor again.

After kneeling down to kiss her to the end of her tail bone, he leant back a little, to admire the view of her pert behind. Dave hadn't noticed before that the dark wrinkled skin of her outer labial lips made her womanly bits look like the brown stone, at the centre of her peach shaped behind.

Dave so liked peaches.

'And now the roots,' her soft voice encouraged...

* * *

'Don't know what's happened to you this week, Dave. This is the second time that you've not bothered to shave in the morning. You were in your twenties, the last time you behaved like that. The lawn's growing and there's funny weeds popping up all over the back garden. Aren't you well, love?' asked Janet, feeling his forehead, as he sat staring at his full coffee cup on the kitchen table.

Dave shook his head. 'I might have a little virus or something. Don't worry; I guess it'll pass soon.'

'Hello both,' said Opia as she ran into the room. 'I've got to dash, early lecture. I'll just grab a biscuit bar and be off. Are you ok for some more maths at two o'clock, Dave? You've been very helpful.'

She didn't wait for a reply and ran off down the garden path after slamming the front door.

'She's a lovely girl and such a hard worker. I'm glad that you're able to aid her but please trim your grey whiskers before she gets back,' said Janet. 'Is there any chance you can start to build a pile of metal rubbish on the drive, by the side of the house? A scrap man called yesterday and left his mobile number. You've still got that rusty old wheelbarrow. The old freezer and boiler are in the big shed. There's a broken barbecue and the left over copper pipe from the replacement gas installation. I bet you can probably find more stuff if you look and he says he'll buy it. Gerry next door used him and said he paid cash. It all helps, anyway. I'm going to pop into the supermarket for some tea and biscuits for the staff room; otherwise I'd have given Opia a lift. See you at six, love.' She gave him a peck on the stubble.

Dave waited for the noise of her car to drive away. He picked up his coffee cup and walked out of the back door onto the damp lawn, in his slippers and dressing gown. He surveyed the once proud garden area. It still looked a very well-kept plot but on closer inspection, dozens of pink tipped, green leaved weeds were shooting up in every available place. A voice inside him said dig them up but Opia had suggested leaving them, until they were identifiable and maybe they'd be easier to remove later, like some other plants are.

He shook his head and went up to the bathroom to have a

shower. How little his wife knew about Opia, how much he'd learnt about Japanese bedroom etiquette this week and those knots, those beautiful knots…

'Damn weeds,' he uttered, as he caught a glimpse, whilst opening the window before jumping into the hot steaming shower.

* * *

'Opia Fall, it's been ten weeks now since I first met you. You've tied my life in knots, literally. I would never believe that the suitcase I carried inside for you, had been full of Japanese bondage books and ropes, and that my life and imagination could be so enriched by your lovely presence.'

She didn't reply and just grinned around the large rope knot holding her tongue tightly in place.

He looked down at the hogtied and gagged olive skinned girl as she attempted to roll onto her knees and failing twice. She made it the third time and steadied herself by opening her knees as wide as her tethered ankles would allow. This had the effect of placing her posterior into the long promised ultimate female position.

Opia had said that her teaching had nearly ended. He had become a fully-fledged *Nawashi* or rope master. His reward would be her innermost parts. Dave had kissed her, stroked her, roped her and obeyed her but never made love. She said that he must agree to one more Japanese bondage ritual afterwards. He did so without asking the task, such had become his desire for the sensual young lady.

Dave climbed onto the bed with no further delay and positioned himself behind her derriere. He stroked the latticework of rope that outlined her slender form. All his own work; he felt quite proud of himself, looking down on the dragon and coy carp, peeping through the diamond shaped pattern.

He urgently fingered the two crotch ropes apart in order to enter her dark crinkled lips. The plant stared back at him, as he thrust deep into the little lady. The sensual jute rope softly rubbed the base of his phallus and balls as she pressed back to meet him.

Opia's perfume and young, soft, painted skin seemed to invade the whole of his mind, in the same way that the weeds were trying to conquer his garden. The green foliage on her back started to multiply in front of his eyes and her dark pubic hair turned into fast growing stems, which pushed their way through the cytoplasm of his cortex. Lurid green chlorophyll pulsed through his veins as the ropes on Opia's back turned into snaking vines, which wrapped around him and dragged his body closer to the Japanese weed-queen with every movement.

'Opia,' he uttered as the speed of his stroke increased.

'Opia Fall, Opia Fall, Fall Opia, Fallopia...' The words merged into his weed infested brain as he gave the final push.

Dave flopped onto Opia's pretty back a few seconds later in a jungle dream. She had to get his attention by wriggling about underneath him.

He finally pulled away.

'I'm so sorry Opia. I had a weird vision... The sex is amazing but so strange. I thought that I had changed into a plant...' he mumbled, rubbing his eyes. 'Let me untie you.'

'Thank you, Dave. I think you know me now. Don't forget your final challenge...' she answered, as she unwound the jute coils from her torso.

'Oh yes, of course, after a cup of coffee, maybe? I feel drained,' he asked, looking at his complexion in her dressing table mirror and checking that he hadn't changed from white to green...

* * *

An hour later, they were standing outside in the garden, looking at the old chest freezer in the shed.

'Are you sure about this,' Opia? Dave asked.

'To complete the journey of a *Nawashi*, you have to prove that you can escape from a life threatening situation. I will bind you in the rope of death and seal the escape end loop with a padlock. You have to remain there until the winter ice melts and summer arrives, whereupon you may remove the lock and restraints to emerge like a butterfly from your prison,' she explained.

'I'm not staying in that freezer for six months,' he laughed. 'Who'll look after the garden?'

'No worries. That is the legend. In practice, we fill the key opening of a padlock with a sugar or salt solution and then freeze it. The device can be clipped on but not opened until the ice melts, a speeded up variation of winter and summer...' she explained. 'The key is left in the prison of course but is useless until the journey's complete.'

'Ok, I'm up for it. Jan said that the scrap man's collecting all the metal junk around five o'clock so how about we drag the chest out of the shed along to the side of the house and do the challenge there?' he suggested.

'Great idea, Dave, Janet did say something about that. There's a galvanised watering can with a hole in the base, by the green-house. May as well chuck that as well, it leaks on my foot,' she replied.

Dave looked over to the small jungle threatening to engulf the old tomato building. 'Only if you can find it now; I tell you, those flipping weeds are heading for a fall, Opia, when I find my scythe.'

'Sorry Dave, I chucked it on the scrap pile, a couple of days ago because it looked so rusty. I know that I've taken your mind off the garden but haven't you enjoyed yourself being close to me? You wouldn't want to cut me down now, would you?

His mind mentally undressed and tied her up again. 'Erm... no, of course, they're alive, sorry guys,' and he waved to the weeds. Dave watched as they seemed to bow back or did the wind make them move?

'The lock's been in the freezer since yesterday, in the ice box. I'll get the rope and we can get down to business. You can get undressed behind the house. Nobody will see us there. I'll do the arms and chest binding while you're standing, you can then run over, jump in the freezer and I can lean over and hogtie your legs.' she said.

'Ok then,' he said, looking around and taking off his shirt, as Opia ran into the house. He had actually begun to like this crazy bondage stuff. 'Hope it's warm in the freezer,' he laughed to himself.

Three minutes later, Dave was face down on a cushion that Opia had tossed into the floor area of the chest freezer. 'Thanks,' he mumbled, through the knotty mouth gag at the kind thought.

She skilfully and quickly knotted up his bare feet before jamming the padlock into a double loop of rope and clicking it shut, close to his mouth. 'Remember, when it's time, you can pick up the key with your lips and turn it with your teeth.'

Dave grunted and nodded.

'Good luck on your Japanese journey, Dave,' before waving to his grinning face and closing the lid on to the latch.

An old Ford Transit tipper truck pulling up opposite the drive took her attention. 'Is that pile for us, darling? Are you Janet? We did phone to say that we'd be earlier than originally planned,' shouted the driver.

Opia waved them in and the vehicle reversed up the drive. 'Just on time,' she shouted.

The passenger got out and started throwing the rusty metal in the rear, starting with the battered wheelbarrow. She walked over to the older man driving the vehicle who had just climbed out of the cab. He lit a cigarette.

'Sorry darling. Bad habit, I know. Just can't stop the old weed,' he said. 'Quite a pile here, we're going to have to rope this on,

Bert,' he shouted to his mate.

'Ropes and weed, if you had more than two brain cells I could fancy you,' she said quietly to herself.

'Didn't catch that darling, can't turn the diesel off because we've got a knackered battery. Is the freezer to go?' shouted the boss.

Opia nodded and watched as Bert jammed an old nail in the latch before bending it back over.

'Don't want the frozen meat and two veg escaping,' he joked.

'Definitely not,' replied the smiling young lady.

Opia watched as the two large men tipped the freezer onto its side, in order to lift it.

'Some bloody weight here,' swore one of them, as they crashed it up into the back of the truck. 'Don't make them like they used to.'

The boss reached up to the exposed compressor pipework and snipped the copper pipe to allow the coolant to hiss out.

'Fuck the environment. Degassing costs money, we can just crush this now, Bert,' said the boss.

Bert laughed at Opia's frown before the boss offered her a twenty pound note.

'Spend this quick before the old man gets back,' he advised.

She tossed a metal key into the wagon. 'You may as well have this. I'm sad to say he just disappeared one day,' she replied. 'I'm helping his widow sort out the insurance. I have big plans.'

The scrap man pointed at the huge plants in the rear garden as he started to drive away.

'You want to do something about that stuff, love. It'll take over the world, you know. It's Japanese Knotweed, the experts call it Fallopia Japonica...'

Mumbo Jumbo

Adam looked disbelievingly at the row of arms, sticking out of the ready mixed concrete. The driver of the mixer-truck gave a cheery wave to the man standing next to him, before driving away. He left a grey blobby trail from his chute on the dusty African track.

Some of the fingers on the hands were moving. One assumed a V for Victory salute and another seemed to wave at him. There were also two raised fists and a gun impression.

Another man walked up behind them and started taking photographs with a digital camera.

'For Christ's sake, can't you see this is madness? They're all going to die!' shouted Adam.

'It is Benoza's wish that they go to the hidden place,' replied the first man. 'You are not going any closer.'

'But Mesote's in there. She's not part of this. We came to help the village,' said Adam, desperately.

'They know that they will be rewarded for their belief,' replied the second man. 'I have their souls safe, here in the camera. I will take them to Benoza.' He bowed to them and walked away, in the direction of the village.

'How long does the concrete take to set? It still looks wet on top. There's still time...' asked Adam, trying to push past the man at the gate.

'It is always quick setting in this heat. Minutes, usually... They have their breathing tubes, which I won't remove, until their breath no longer lifts a feather.'

'Look, er... is that your name, Mahele?' asked Adam, pointing to the writing on a label above the shirt pocket.

The man nodded.

'Listen, Mahele. I have money. Lots of money... dollars, euros... It's yours. Just let me through to save her.'

Mahele took the brown leather wallet that Adam waved in front of his face and opened it. He fingered the notes and looked back up. His face looked sad.

'The *Dark Spirit* will come after me, if I help you,' he said.

'Damn the spirits. Just take it. I can get you more. You could leave the village,' said Adam. 'You can have the Toyota as well,' and Adam held out the keys.

Mahele smiled a gap toothed grin and took the offering before stepping to one side.

Adam ran through the gate, towards the ghastly scene and shouted back to Mahele, 'Which one is she?'

'I do not know,' the reply came back.

'Bastard!' spat out Adam.

Close enough now, he could see the arms in detail; they were mainly dark skinned and one looked like a tanned Caucasian, making a fist that he instantly discounted.

A vision of the girl flashed into his head. Lovely, pretty, dark skinned Mesote. He tried to remember just what her hands looked like. Her hands, he must have looked at them... They'd been seeing one another for weeks. He couldn't believe his inability to recognise those beautiful hands that had massaged scented oils onto his body only a few days ago.

He could see that several of the hands had stopped moving and the pale skin on the palms had turned a bluish hue.

Feverishly looking from one hand to another, he mentally crossed off the larger hands as male and settled on two adjacent smaller palms.

'Which one?' he asked under his breath. Then he remembered that she'd broken a nail whilst opening a coke can last week. 'Yes,' he said, as he spotted the fractured end, amongst the ten contender fingers and thumbs.

Wondering if he would sink in himself and become stuck, Adam stepped onto the wet cement. The surface appeared very liquid and his feet sank in a few inches before finding a firm base. As he lifted each foot to step closer, the concrete made an awful slurping sound, as if to warn him not to attempt to release any of its captives.

Adam took hold of the hand and felt warmth. In fact, it responded by moving slightly. Could she still be alive or had it been a dying twitch, he asked himself?

He grabbed the grey palm tightly with his own right hand and scooped away at the wet concrete with his left, his idea being to expose her elbow, which lay just below the surface of the material. He grabbed the upper arm and started to pull, gently at first.

Nothing happened initially but, as he increased the pressure, a bulge started to appear in the more solid looking concrete, just under the wet surface film.

He noticed that Mahele had walked over to watch.

'Help me, Mahele, for God's sake,' he pleaded.

Mahele answered, 'I am lost. The *Dark Spirit* within me sees all. I shouldn't have let you interfere. Benoza will have me killed.'

'Look Mahele. I can help you escape afterwards. You'll be fine. Just help me pull Mesote out. I can't do it on my own. I think there's too much weight of concrete on her body or maybe it's the suction?' replied Adam.

Mahele ignored him and simply bent down towards the clear Perspex pipe sticking out of the cement, a few inches away from the arm. He reached into the top left front pocket of his camouflaged shirt and produced a small white feather. This, he carefully balanced on top of the two centimetre wide opening.

Adam had stopped tugging and watched silently as Mahele closed his eyes. 'Benoza has spared her,' Mahele said and opened them again. The feather fluttered off onto the floor.

'She's still breathing!' shouted Adam.

Mahele snapped out of his gloom. 'I help,' he replied, before turning and walking a few yards. He lifted up a piece of canvas and produced a long wooden handled shovel that Adam hadn't noticed before. He then stepped back carefully, next to the buried body and started to drag back dollops of concrete with the edge of the blade.

'Your name? What is your name?' asked Mahele, looking up at Adam, as he carefully dug.

'It's Adam. Adam McKenzie. Shall I pull yet?' answered a very worried Adam.

'A few more seconds, Mr McKenzie. As you said earlier, the suction from the wet cement will hold her like the grasp of a devil,' replied Mahele.

Adam waited what seemed like an eternity. He wondered whether to place the feather back on top of the tube but feared a negative result.

Mahele finally said, 'Now pull with the strength of all your ancestors.'

Adam, tired after the initial exertion in the baking African sun, obeyed and as he thought about the strange comment, seemed to regain his muscle power. In fact, he felt even stronger than before.

The lump in the concrete started to grow. Mahele stopped shovelling when the tip exposed some plastic material, near Mesote's tummy area.

'What's that?' asked Adam. 'Is it her clothes?'

'No,' answered a sweating Mahele, moving to another digging spot and this time using his foot on the shovel, to force it in deeper. 'Keep pulling or the concrete will swallow her again.'

Adam worried that he'd pull her arm off or otherwise injure Mesote but he kept up the pressure. He'd rather have a Mesote with a dislocated shoulder than no Mesote at all...

'The chest areas are always bubble wrapped. If the concrete hardens too fast, the condemned may still move their chests to breath. The face is covered by a mask with an air pipe attached. Sometimes, they stay alive for many hours,' explained Mahele.

'This is barbaric,' said Adam. 'Why are you digging there and not helping me pull?' he then asked.

'Better leverage,' answered Mahele, now pulling back hard on the handle of the buried shovel.

Adam felt a sudden movement and the ground spoke with a loud 'Schloop...'

A large shape, much bigger than Mesote's slender body, started to emerge from the stony prison. Lumpy pieces of part-set aggregate dripped and splatted to the sides as a monstrous grey shape emerged from the depths.

Mahele grunted with the effort and suddenly fell back into the cement as his wooden handle splintered in two.

'Shit!' shouted Adam, as their prize started to disappear and began pulling him under as well.

The concrete had risen up to his shins but he kept his grip and felt sure that the partly rescued hand tried to squeeze his own.

Mahele quickly got back up and dug at the slowly sinking mass with his bare hands to extricate another upper limb.

Adam could work out now what the large shape could be. 'They're lying on sunbeds, aren't they?' he asked.

'It is so one may go to the 'Hidden Place' in comfort and we can prop the arms up, as they leave us,' explained Mahele.

As they both pulled, it became obvious that under the grey lumpy matter, lay a strangely wrapped human body.

Adam could see her feet now, as he struggled to get his own out of the grabbing morass.

'Pull her over to the pipe,' ordered Mahele.

Adam looked around and could see the hosepipe that the mixer truck driver had been using to finally clean out his truck.

With his feet finally out of the concrete and onto solid ground, the task of dragging the prostrate body became easier.

When they reached the pipe, Mahele let go and walked over to a small generator. Adam started frantically clawing at the body's face. A thought occurred to him. Maybe it wasn't Mesote? Maybe someone else had a broken nail? He tried to bury the thought under concrete, in his own mind.

Adam heard the generator start up and felt water spray on to his leg, from the hose nozzle. He grabbed it quickly and redirected it onto the grey figure. The heat from the sun had already started to dry out the freshly exposed cement.

As he pointed it at the face, he didn't see Mesote but instead, a garishly painted mask started to appear. It had features of a sort but looked completely weird to him and he could now see the attached breathing pipe, as Mahele had described.

Adam tried to pick at the edge of the mask in order to remove it, but couldn't, and settled on playing the hose on the rest of the body, to remove the hardening substance. He could clearly see the bubble wrap around the torso and judged that to be protected, so continued with washing down the limbs.

Slim dark female legs appeared from the grey stone. He rubbed at them with his hands to help clean them up. They were warm, very warm. He hoped the warmth indicated life and not just heat from the cement. He knew that concrete gave off latent energy, as part of its setting reaction.

Adam turned his spray to the arms and shoulders. As he knelt down to do this, he looked back at the pretty but seemingly lifeless legs. He felt certain that he recognised them, as the ones that had many times wrapped themselves in ecstasy around his waist over the last few weeks.

'Do not worry. Benoza has said she may live,' said Mahele, who had come to stand by their side. He reached down to feel her foot for a pulse.

Adam turned off the plastic tap near the end of the hose. 'How the hell do you know, Mahele? She's been buried for at least five minutes. What's holding the mask on? I can't get it loose,' he asked.

'Benoza has spoken to me,' answered Mahele. 'When he decides that he wants your soul, he fills you with the *Dark Spirit* and can then talk to you wherever you go.'

'Mumbo Jumbo,' said Adam. 'Can you get the mask and air pipe off?'

He watched Mahele gently lift the head forwards and fiddle directly behind. Adam could then see the grey stained retaining straps, as he slowly pulled the mask to one side.

A damp, mascara stained face appeared, with eyes tightly closed.

'Mesote,' screamed Adam.

He leaned over and put his ear to her mouth. 'I'm not sure...'

'Do not kiss her,' ordered Mahele, adding 'Benoza will know.'

Adam thought about commencing CPR but for some reason disobeyed the instruction and kissed her instead.

He pressed his face to the dry pink unmoving lips that used to moistly kiss him, all over his body and drive him wild.

A split second later, Adam jumped, as her eyelids popped open.

He moved back and she straightened up, coughed and started moving her arms.

'Adam,' she said, weakly. 'What have you done?'

Mesote closed her eyes again but Adam could see that she was breathing. The bubble wrap on her chest moved slowly up and down.

Adam turned to Mahele. 'Have you got any clothes or a blanket?'

Mahele said, 'I have done enough. I must try to escape in your Toyota. This is the key to my old truck. There may be something in there.' He placed a tatty key-ring on the floor next to Adam.

'Why don't you wait for us?' asked Adam. 'I could get you out of the country.'

'That may be so, but you cannot remove the *Dark Spirit*. My only chance is to try to outrun it,' replied Mahele.

Adam could see the frightened look on the man's face.

Mesote opened her eyes and turned to look at him. 'Go, while you have a chance...'

'He is looking at me through your eyes, Mesote. I should never have helped raise you from the dead. Goodbye. Adam the unbeliever, I warn you to be careful...' said Mahele.

The man turned and ran towards Adam's Toyota.

'Please leave my bags!' shouted Adam.

Adam helped Mesote up to a sitting position and steadied her, as they watched Mahele start up the diesel-engined pickup. He first threw two canvas bags out of the window and then waved as he left. The truck bounced the short distance along the track, to meet the main road. As he turned on, Mahele never saw the tanker as it ploughed into the driver's side of his vehicle, pushing it fifty yards sideways along the tarmac, before exploding.

'Christ,' exclaimed Adam. 'We could have been in that.'

'He was dead, before he left us. I knew it,' said Mesote.

'What are you on about? You must be dazed. And why the hell did you climb into a pit and let a bloke cover you in concrete? Have you been drugged, Mesote?' he asked and then hugged her still damp body.

'My skin is burning,' said Mesote, rubbing the sides of her arms. 'It's worse inside this plastic wrapping, Adam.'

'It must be the alkali in the cement. I'm afraid that I'll have to hose you down again. Take off the bubble wrap, Mesote,' he instructed.

'Some man might see me,' she said looking around but obeying him. The plastic had been simply wrapped around her middle a couple of times and quickly fell to the floor. Grey streaks of semi dried cement laced her torso. She held her hands over her small breasts. 'Wet me quickly, Adam. It hurts.'

Adam turned the hose on her and she jumped.

'Cold!' she shouted, cringing in the jet for a few seconds. She then straightened up and began rubbing at the burning stains with her hands.

Adam turned around when he heard sirens behind him. The emergency services were attending Mahele's car crash. Flames were visible in the distance.

'Maybe I should let them know that we have water?' suggested Adam.

'No. You are like a fireman putting out the flames on Mesote. Mahele deserves to burn in hell, for defying the wish of Benoza. Wet me more!' replied Mesote.

'You've gone a bit loopy, Mesote,' said Adam. He enjoyed watching her wash the last traces of cement, from her slim, lithe brown body. She had knickers on, which had now turned red, instead of battleship grey. She looked so much like the girl from his bed now, rather than the grey corpse that he'd pulled from the concrete grave.

Her hands took one last rub up and down her legs before returning to her boobs. She reached out to him and knocked the hose from his hands. It snaked to the floor, spraying water in all directions.

'Make love to me while you still can, Adam.' She started playing with the nipples on her large dark areolae, which had hardened in the cold water spray.

'Not now, silly girl. You're a bit confused. Come over to the old truck. Let's get you covered up,' he replied.

'Adam, you must listen. The *Dark Spirit* is in me. I cannot fight it. Please love me one more time,' she pleaded.

'Listen Mesote; we'll find a real doctor in the next town. You need some rest. The only *Dark Spirit* that I need at the moment is a bottle of navy rum,' he replied

She grabbed his hand and thrust it down the front of her wet knickers. 'You must have me because soon I will be Benoza's.'

He became surprised at her sudden recovery and how forcefully she grabbed his shoulders to bring him down to her height. She followed it with a long, smouldering kiss. 'Get in the back of the car,' she ordered.

The flashing lights and sirens at the nearby accident faded into the background as the dark haired lady almost tore the trousers and shirt off her unwanted rescuer. Adam had never seen her acting so passionately before or so full of lust.

Almost as soon as they'd climaxed, she huddled up naked in a corner of the back seat and started to doze.

'Poor kid,' said Adam as he pulled up his trousers. He draped an old jacket over her sexy little body and watched her quietly snore.

Adam had only met her a few weeks ago. He'd been sent to the area by an oil firm, to get an idea of how the staff could integrate with the local community. Times were different from the old days, when the big oil barons would just ship out the villagers and rape the land. There were drilling prospects here, but the big firms were worried about their image and the likelihood of being sued.

Mesote had grown up a local girl, who had been sent a hundred miles away to the city college with a bursary, in order to study. She had learnt excellent English and returned to work in the local school for a few years, as a sign of respect for her home village. She became the natural first contact for the oil firm, due to her position and knowledge rather than the untrustworthy police and elders.

They had bonded well with one another and within days, were in bed together. He'd already asked her to return to England with him. What he couldn't understand, were the events of the last forty eight hours. He'd kissed her as she left as usual on her way to school, and later he'd driven off with the prospectors, to scour the area for suitable drilling sites. On his return, he had discovered that she'd argued with a powerful local man called Benoza, whom several people claimed had the powers of a witch doctor.

'Mumbo Jumbo more like,' he mumbled to himself. Tricking gullible people and burying the evidence is much more likely, he thought. He'd already decided to put the oil firm's lawyers on the case and have the man arrested.

Adam stroked Mesote's forehead and climbed out of their makeshift bed into the driver's seat. The old truck started up at the first turn of the key. He smiled, thinking that things were beginning to go in his way again, at last.

The battered truck rattled along the track to the tarmac. As he drove along the main road, he watched the continuing clear up of Mahele's crash. There were two medics chatting and smoking next to a body under a sheet. He could see Mahele's camouflaged trousers sticking out at one end. A recovery vehicle dragged the mangled, burnt remains of the Toyota to the side of the road. There existed a chance that it would remain there for months, slowly being stripped of anything useful. He'd decided to report it as stolen, to avoid any questions from the police or insurers.

Adam had mixed feelings about Mahele. On the one hand, he seemed to be in charge of burying his beloved Mesote, yet he eventually helped to pull her out. The dead man seemed to be both employed by and in desperate fear of Benoza. Both he and Mesote had said some weird things about Benoza's all-seeing abilities and sinister powers. The locals obviously thought of him as a modern day evil magician.

The thoughts in Adam's mind then wandered to the other buried hands. Who were those people? Like Mesote, they seemed to go willingly to their death, as though duty bound. Or could it be that if they stayed alive, they were terrified of an even worse existence? The area appeared to be a building site. Another layer of concrete laid down, after removal of the arms, would hide all trace. Then he remembered the second man with the camera, who spoke something about taking away their souls... with a photograph... A shudder went over his whole body. He could see the hairs on the back of his arms, standing on end for a few seconds and he held the steering wheel a little tighter.

At the next stop junction, he turned around to peer at Mesote, lying on the bench seat. 'Hey, beautiful?' he called, but she didn't respond. He drove for over an hour to the next town, constantly checking the cracked rear view mirror, in case they had been followed or for any signs of Mesote waking.

He left her locked in the truck, when he reached the small hotel complex that he'd used before. He felt that he knew and trusted the staff. After questioning the two desk girls if they knew of Benoza, and being satisfied with their laughter at the witch-doctor idea, he carried Mesote inside to their apartment.

It consisted of a bathroom, kitchenette and a bedroom. He didn't want to leave Mesote alone until she had recovered, so gave a desk girl some dollars to go food shopping and find some clothes for his girlfriend.

The receptionist dutifully re-appeared an hour later, with a couple of bags containing fruit, veg and a fresh lump of meat, apparently beef. She also passed Adam an orange dress that she had carried back over her shoulder and a pair of pants from her handbag.

Adam thanked the girl and the noise from the door slamming seemed to wake Mesote, who weakly called out 'Adam, are you there?'

He ran into the bedroom, where he had laid Mesote, an hour earlier. 'I'm here. I have some clothes for you; not much but we can buy some more tomorrow. Whatever you want...'

She pulled herself partly up onto one elbow. 'You shouldn't have interfered, Adam. I spoke against Benoza when you were away. Because of this, he said that he would take my soul, in exchange for the safety of my schoolchildren. He condemned me and filled me with the *Dark Spirit*. He can see what I see. He will kill you for saving me.'

'Listen to me, Mesote. He's a con-man. Maybe he hypnotised you? I don't really know but there's no way he can touch me here. I'm going to make something for dinner. You put on these clothes and have another rest. It'll be about an hour. Just put this *Dark*

Spirit Mumbo Jumbo, out of your head,' replied Adam.

A few minutes later Adam started hacking up pieces of the so called beef, onions and sweet potato with a meat cleaver before dropping it all into a large saucepan, followed by some garlic and chillies. 'Smells good,' he said, a few minutes later, after lifting the lid.

He then went back out to the car and brought in his two canvas bags. A quick rummage in one produced a clean shirt and he placed his notebook, pens and camera from the other, onto the table. 'Phew, what a day,' he said, before sitting at the table and falling asleep, with his head in a bowl of bananas.

Benoza sat at his ex-colonial mahogany desk listening to a police sergeant describing Mahele's accident and the escape of Mesote from her concrete tomb. He beckoned to the man with the digital camera, standing at the doorway.

The man ran over to him and pressed a few buttons on the silver machine before showing the screen to Benoza. He stared at it for a minute until the picture self-cancelled.

'Mumbo Jumbo,' he uttered. 'Huh, fetch me a melon and a large knife.'

The man with the camera went out of the room and returned a minute later, to place the melon and knife on the desk in front of his boss.

'Mumbo Jumbo,' said Benoza, a second time and sliced the melon in two.

When he woke up, Adam ran to the cooker to check the stew. As he did so, he heard movement behind him. He asked, 'Are you feeling a bit better now, Mesote?' and carried on stirring his meal. 'Dinner won't be long. I didn't mean to upset you earlier.'

'You have done so much for me, Adam. I know the right path to take, now,' he heard her say softly.

Adam felt her hand squeeze his behind and turned around, to wait for the kiss…

The next thing that smiling Adam saw was his own reflection, in the shiny surface of the meat cleaver, as it neatly sectioned his skull in two.

Mesote picked up Adam's work camera and took one final picture of his escaping soul...

Five

'Kiss my back,' said Sharon, looking at him over her shoulder, before lifting up the rear of her T-shirt.

Joshua had been taken aback at the request but the ensuing sight, appearing above her low slung trouser waistline, spoke volumes. He quickly obeyed and got down on one knee, with his head just a foot away from her pale flesh.

She smelt of lavender scented deodorant. He inhaled deeply whilst staring at her trim exposed waist.

'Kiss it then,' she reminded him.

Joshua pursed his lips and gently pressed them against her right hip.

'Naughty solicitor,' chided Sharon. 'Maybe you should tell your secretary to go for an early dinner and we can talk business?'

'Erm, y-yes, of course,' stammered Joshua as he stood up and then pressed the talk button on the desk intercom.

'Miss Hendrick, you can go for lunch now. I'll be another twenty minutes with Ms Ryding here,' he said, looking at the speaker and hoping for the right answer.

'Ok Mr Parnell. I'll lock the door behind me. Your next client is tomorrow at 9.30 and Mrs South has dropped off the transfer forms that you asked her to sign.' The voice on the crackly speaker continued, 'It's Sarah's birthday from Alshott and Edwards. We'll be having a drink in the Trumpeter's Arms, if you want to join us. Bye.'

'Ah yes, Sarah. I'd forgotten. Tell you what, take the afternoon off and enjoy yourself. Pick up fifty quid from the petty cash and buy everyone a drink,' said Joshua looking up from the speaker.

'So it's Sharon versus Sarah then? No contest really. Can she do this?' asked Sharon, as she slowly wiggled her hips from side to side and pulled her T-shirt ever higher.

'Why thank you. You're like a different man this week, Mr Parnell. I hope you can come to the pub later,' crackled Miss Hendrick.

'Erm, I think you're very nice but is this wise?' whispered Joshua, taking in Sharon's gyrations with an ever increasing smile.

'Tell me in half an hour. Kiss the other side now.' She stopped moving and poked her left hip at him. He watched as she pulled the left side of her trousers down a little lower.

'You seem to have a magnetic body that I find hard to resist,' answered the solicitor, moving closer.

'Don't I just and you're a helpless piece of metal being pulled towards me...' she replied.

Joshua resumed his previous position but this time gently kissed the top of her left hip.

'Very good, Josh. It's ok if I call you Josh?' she said, fiddling with the button on her trouser waist.

Before he could answer, Sharon lowered her jeans to her knees. Joshua tried to talk but his voice seemed to have dropped to the floor along with her trousers. His mouth could only make a few gasps like a fish out of water.

Sharon stepped out of the jeans and deftly kicked them to one side.

'I bought these knickers last week, after our first appointment. I could tell that you like the colour red. It's a naughty colour and I just know that you're a man who likes to take risks,' she said, pushing her derriere towards him.

Joshua looked at the shapely, loosely wrapped parcel of temptation in front of him. She wore skimpy red silk pants with bows at each side. There didn't seem to be any elastic in the waistline so he guessed that the shiny material itself had actually been tied, to hold them up.

'I know my bum doesn't look big in this,' she giggled and he watched as she grasped both of her buttocks. 'They're very soft,' she said and quickly added, 'and they really like to be kissed.'

'Listen Sharon, I think maybe we should… ' he had found his voice.

'Shush. Give me your hands,' she ordered.

Joshua pressed his palms against hers, which she had held back towards him. She still faced away towards the door and hadn't looked at him for a couple of minutes.

'Push them up under the material,' she said, as she guided the tips of his fingers under the lower edge of her knickers.

Joshua found himself with a hand on each one of her buttocks. The smell of the deodorant on her body, combined with the hot flesh warming his hands felt unlike anything he'd seen or touched before.

'You're worried aren't you, Josh? I can feel your hands trembling,' she asked.

'Well, I… I don't usually do this… I mean I have a wife but she wouldn't be, well… ' he tried to explain.

'She's just not sexy. I guessed that already. That's why I'm going to help you. We both have something that will benefit the other so I'm just completing my side of the deal,' said Sharon.

Joshua Parnell, senior partner in Isaacs, Parnell and Payne, took a deep breath, closed his eyes and tried to forget the lectures in his training, years ago, which forbade personal involvement with clients.

'You're a bad boy, Josh. Now finger me…' said the bartering angel.

* * *

A week ago, Joshua sat twiddling his fingers, in his third floor office. He had been waiting ten minutes for a new client and apart from getting irritated, he had plenty of other work to do.

He glanced over at the files to his left, on top of one of the three tables in his room. He just knew that if he started work on a will or conveyance that the damned woman would turn up.

Miss Hendrick, his secretary/receptionist, also knew just how to deal with late-comers. She would say: 'I'm so sorry. He did wait but may have nipped out the back door by now, to go and visit the library over the road. He had to meet a colleague, you see. I'll buzz him on the intercom to check if he's still there.' Joshua would hear her call and look at the old black and white security monitor behind him that received a signal from the tiny camera on top of a filing cabinet, in the reception room.

He exhaled a bored lungful of air and stood up, wondering whether he had the will to tackle a will. The sun had come out now. This missing client seemed to be the last one of the morning. He could pack up and have a round of golf before going home to see the wife. A vision of her appeared in his mind wearing curlers and shouting at him.

'Mr Parnell. Are you still there? Your next client has arrived.' The crackly voice thankfully shattered the daydream and he turned around to look at the monitor whilst quietly saying, 'I must get a new intercom,' for the hundredth time.

The client had her back to the camera. Joshua could see it looked like a younger lady by her dress sense and hair. He almost dismissed her from his thoughts in order to replace her with the 19th hole, when suddenly she swivelled around to face the camera.

'I feel I'm being watched,' said a soft crackly voice, staring deep into the small eyeball perched on the cabinet. 'Try him again,' ordered the voice. Joshua became mesmerised by the dark lips in sync with the fractured conversation.

'Mr Parnell?' Miss Hendrick waited for a few seconds. 'I don't think he's in. We can rearrange... '

Joshua dived for the talk button when he saw the corners of those beautiful dark lips turn down in disappointment. 'Erm, I'm back. Sorry. Send the young lady straight up.'

He knew it took about 30 seconds for Miss Hendrick to

explain the directions to his room and a little longer to traverse the flights of stairs to the third floor. He nipped over to one of the cabinets and took out a comb to drag through his thinning locks and almost choked on a squirt of mint breath freshener.

The wife reappeared in his head, about to tip a cold dinner over him, this time. The vision disappeared when he heard a soft knocking at the Victorian wood panelled door.

'Oh, erm… come in. It's open,' he shouted, a little too loudly.

A woman confidently strolled in.

'Hi. I'm Sharon Ryding. You must be Mr Parnell. I'm so happy to meet you,' said the brunette with a devilish smile. 'I thought downstairs that you were hiding from me.'

'Oh, no hiding from Ms Ryding… ah, that rhymes. No, no, pleased to meet you too. Take a seat.' He gestured to an ancient dining chair that had the padding sticking out at one front corner and creaked precariously, as the lady gently lowered herself onto it.

Joshua couldn't help noticing how pretty this woman looked. She seemed to be in her early thirties, but her skin looked flawless. He ran a finger around his collar to adjust his shirt. 'It seems to be getting a little hot in here. I'll open the window before we start. Would you like me to order a cold drink for you or a cup of tea?'

As he struggled with the old sash window, he felt her next to him.

'Let me help. You lift that handle while I take this other one. Pull after I count three. One, two, three. Whee. There she goes,' laughed the brunette, as the window opened.

Joshua savoured the cooler air on his face and neck. Sharon had seemed like a hot radiator when she had brushed against him earlier, and he turned around to thank her for helping.

Before he could speak, those dark lips on the monitor which were now ruby red said, 'I'm good at opening things that get stuck. Windows, doors, zips, you name it,' and she winked at him before returning to her seat.

Joshua sat down. His mind raced. Had this young lady just made a pass at him? Surely not, He thought. He looked at her and asked, 'What may I do for you, Ms Ryding?'

She licked around her lips twice before answering. Joshua felt himself going a little cross-eyed as he followed the tongue tip journey.

'Call me Sharon, please. I need your help, Mr Parnell. I have been searching for five men as part of a deal that I entered into. I have one left to find and I think that you may be able to sort out my problem. I do need to be very careful with this matter, though.'

'Well, if it's finding someone regarding an inheritance, for example, we know of tracing agencies and publications where you may advertise. Another option would be to see a private detective' he answered.

'If I fill you in a little, it will become clearer. The first four gentlemen were solicitors. They are no longer, due to meeting me. Don't panic, they're all still alive,' she laughed.

'Well, I should hope so. You don't look like a mass-murderess,' he answered.

'We all have to do things to get what we want... to satisfy our needs, as it were. Sometimes those things seem unobtainable and suddenly, out of the blue or should I say black and white,' she nodded at the monitor behind him, 'Bob's your uncle or should it be Sharon's your new girlfriend?'

Joshua coughed and then remembered to start breathing again. He watched the tongue leave a moist trail as it outlined her beautifully formed scarlet lips again. He could feel his heart pounding.

'Are you suggesting anything that's slightly rude? I'm a happily married man,' he replied wearing his sensible hat.

He watched as Sharon reached over to him, took it off and started licking it before tearing it apart with red lipstick stained teeth and grinning...

Joshua closed his eyes and shook his head.

'Happy?' asked a soft voice. 'I think that you may be missing out on some things. In fact I'm certain that I can help.'

The daydream lips came closer to his face and puckered up. Joshua opened his eyes at the last second before contact, to see that they were actually still over the other side of his desk and talking to him.

'Happy?' the brunette repeated the question. 'I know that I have something that you want and in return you can give me something; information...'

'Well, I really can't tell you anything about my clients, confidentiality and all that. Are you trying to barter with me? I don't quite get it, Ms... er, Sharon.'

She got up from her chair and walked around to his side of the desk. 'I know what you were thinking when you last had your eyes closed. In the same way that I'm good at opening things, I can see through these barriers, such as blanked out windows, doors, even eyelids. Zips are one of my favourite. They hide all sorts of desires. There's a little chap down there quite happy to let me look through your files or your thoughts, after I pay the required penalty.'

The real lips came closer. Joshua froze and then closed his eyes. It is one thing to lust after young ladies and go back home to a shouty wife. It is an altogether scarier thing, to be inches away from your object of desire. He wished in his head that he wasn't there...

'Don't wish like that,' said the soft voice, a second before their lips met.

Joshua popped his eyelids open at the sentence, to meet her deep steely-blues looking into his soul. She took away his breath with the firmness of her kiss. Sharon's lips were soft but muscular. Her tongue-tip forced its way past his lips and made tingly contact. His mouth seemed to run away down his throat to hide in his stomach, which in turn started to shrink. He momentarily visualised himself kissing her naked bottom before his embarrassed mind also legged it. His arms, legs and almost all of his body decided to join them there. All that remained seemed to be his soul with a penis and a tiny bulging tummy.

'I'll take this for safe keeping, Joshua.'

Joshua peeped out of the tiny stomach sphincter and watched as one of Sharon's hands grabbed his soul, before pulling it out of sight. He suddenly felt a sense of relief, as if a burden had been lifted from his shoulders. Not that he seemed to have shoulders anymore. He watched as her other hand reached out and took hold of his penis.

'Oh dear, Joshua; there's no feeling with no body. I'm spanking the monkey but the organ grinder's hiding. Naughty boy; you will be punished.'

Joshua quivered inside the tiny tummy as her face approached. It appeared so large that he felt he may be swallowed whole. Her lips opened and he could see into her mouth; and all the way down her throat into a flaming bowel of fiery, acidic, hellishly steaming acid.

He felt a blast of burning breath which blew his tummy inside out, scattering body parts in all directions. He became a pair of eyeballs spinning around in different directions and felt sick when one eye spun around to look directly into the other one...

'It's ok, I've got you.' A soft voice shouted above the butchered bodily parts. He tried to open his eyes but then remembered that his eyelids were long gone.

'Just do it. Your share of the deal is complete. It's time to collect,' said a soft voice.

Joshua felt someone squeeze his penis through his trousers and popped his new eyelids open. Sharon's hand retreated.

'Well, looks like the eyes and the trouser brain work, even if nothing else does,' she said.

Joshua tried to breathe. No problem. He looked down,

counted his legs and arms; all fine. 'What the fuck happened?' He shook his arms to make sure that they were reconnected.

'I guarantee all the physical parts are present and correct. In fact usually, the lifting away of the bodily worries makes every-thing act much better. A bit like turning back the clock. You may even feel a bit frisky?' she asked and laughed.

For some reason Joshua laughed as well. He wouldn't normally have done. He'd probably have been very angry but he simply felt relieved.

'This deal, this arrangement with me, you said I'd paid my share. What did I do?' he asked, confused.

'Don't you worry, Mr Parnell. You solicitors and the small print! Always trying to renegotiate! Just enjoy life. You will remember soon. I will do my part at our meeting next week. Same time?' she asked.

'And erm... just what is your part?' replied Joshua.

'Oh come on Mr Parnell. You wanted me to kiss you. I've done that. You wanted to kiss my bottom and maybe more? We'll see how brave you are. Remember, you can't shut your eyes and hide. I'll know what you want,' she laughed. 'Seriously now, enjoy this week. You'll feel different, be lucky. Enjoy the bargain that we made.'

Joshua laughed again. 'I actually do feel very happy. Ok, well it's been very nice to meet you and I look forward to next week Sharon. I'll just get some forms for you to sign. Maybe we can go over your will or something next week. You can't be too careful. Never know when we might meet our maker.'

When he turned away from the cabinet drawer, papers in hand, she had gone. The door stood slightly ajar but it usually creaked when it moved. It seemed as if she'd turned into a spirit and drifted out, instantly, through a tiny gap.

'Hmm, able to open any door, she said...' he said out loud.

'Miss Hendrick. I bet you didn't see Ms Ryding leave, did you?' he asked, as he leaned towards the intercom.

'Oh that's strange. I didn't but you cannot always hear from the stationery cupboard,' came back the crackly reply.

'That's fine. Just book her in at the same time next week and try to leave the rest of that afternoon open. I may have plans... '

* * *

'Finger you? I hardly know you,' said Joshua, thoroughly enjoying the hot flesh under his palms.

'I bet you've been a little devil all week, after I lifted away your burden of inhibitions,' replied Sharon. 'Undo my bows, Josh.'

The solicitor reluctantly took his hands from out of the silky knickers. He reached to the sides one at a time and pulled at the bows, which easily came apart. He watched the back part fall down, exposing her delicious peach of a bum. The fabric remained trapped between the top of her thighs.

'Pull it through, slowly,' she encouraged.

Joshua did as ordered and his reward became the sight of her womanly bits wobbling between her thighs and gasps of enjoyment from Sharon, as the fabric tickled her innermost sensitive parts. He dropped the knickers to the floor and waited for further directions.

'Go on then. You wanted to kiss a woman's bottom,' she said.

'How on earth did you know? Apart from being able to read my mind?' he asked, as he took hold of her right buttock and sank his teeth gently into it.

'Ow... Oh you lovely boy. Do that again. Hurt me. Get your money's worth, Josh,' encouraged Sharon. 'Bite the other side as well and then kiss it better.'

'You're crazy,' he replied, kneading her left cheek like dough before nipping it viciously with his teeth.

'Jeez, that stung. Now spank me. I'll lean over your desk.' Sharon stepped over her discarded trousers and bent over. With two sweeps of her arms, most of his books, pens and files were on the floor.

'Aw Sharon...' he protested, until she laid face down on the table with her behind sticking out at him.

'Whack me,' she commanded. 'Use that ruler still on the desk.'

Joshua got the idea. He gave her six of the best. She screamed at every stinging blow and it wasn't until he'd stopped that he noticed the wet puddle on the floor between her legs.

She turned towards him. 'Sorry about that. You solicitors get me all excited. Anyway it'll be more fun for you fingering me, while I'm wet. Then you can lick me. I bet you can't wait for that and neither can I...'

'How do you know so much?' he asked the heavenly, desk bent, wet legged, brunette in front of him.

'Get on your knees again. Tell me your next wish,' she commanded and reached around to part her buttocks.

Joshua gently touched the delicately wrinkled skin of her womanly fold before slipping a finger inside her. His wife would never let him do this. She said it felt dirty. He soon found his target, the area of slightly roughened skin just inside and rubbed gently. Sharon gyrated her hips and moaned softly. He'd never seen between a woman's legs in close up and gazed at the darkened skin around her unmentionable area and the little puckered opening.

'Unmentionable...' she laughed. 'Say it Joshua. Be a man. Say I want to lick your pretty little asshole.'

'Well, erm... I couldn't, I shouldn't,' he stammered.

'Wifey says no; devil's daughter says yes. Sounds like it's more fun in hell, Josh,' replied Sharon.

Joshua pressed his face between her buttocks to lick at her womanly bits and didn't fight as she lowered her derriere until he carried out the she-devil's bidding.

The scent of her warm flesh almost covering his face seemed overpowering. It became difficult to breathe and lap at her bits, because she pressed back so firmly. It reminded him of their first kiss only with more derriere thrown in... He finally leant back for some air and she rose up from the desk. He watched as she took off her top and bra, to release a gravity defying pair of pointy-nippled breasts.

'I guess you want to fuck me now but you're not sure where, are you Josh? Choice of three places now, you're thinking. That's more than you hoped for, certainly two more than your wife ever offers. Trouble is we're even now. Our contract didn't include your penis,' said Sharon, cupping her breasts before pulling at both nipples simultaneously.

Joshua then recalled that when he hid in his stomach, Sharon had grabbed his soul but left his penis.

He looked at her silently for a few seconds as she toyed with her nipples. 'I get it; temptation. You are genuinely some lady devil or Old Nick himself in disguise. Have I given you my soul already?' he asked.

'Spot on. You're doing better than the other four solicitors. Nick's still below stoking the fires. I fell for his charms a hundred years ago. He's kept me looking young all that time. I had been due to go downstairs, as we call it, but we made a deal and he said he'd give me another hundred if I get him five solicitors. I don't know if I trust him though.'

'But you were only able to get my soul. I reckon I'm ok till I die in what, another forty years? Until then I have my body, penis and all,' he said. 'However, you're right. I'd really like to make love to you. Renegotiate maybe?'

'Oh, I'm ok too. My deal is for souls. Nick's happy to wait. I can earn more, if all five solicitors die today but it must be accidental or by their own hands. I'm not allowed to Kalashnikov you all down. That's against God's rules,' she explained.

'You have a pact with God?' he asked, looking baffled.

'Indeed. Not personally of course but Nick and Austin signed one, eons ago,' she replied.

'You mean God's name is really Austin?' laughed Joshua.

'It gets worse. Austin Rover and he never liked it. He got it whilst playing Scrabble with Nick years ago and the loser had to rename themselves with the remaining letters. The choice ended up as either: Dog, Gdo, Odg, Dgo, Ogd or God. They were all taken by various future languages apart from God,' she explained.

'Even Gdo?' replied Joshua, smiling.

'Ant's asshole in ancient Sanscript,' replied Sharon. 'Anyway, in a similar vein, do you still fancy a fuck?'

'What's the deal?' asked Joshua, biting his lip whilst watching her walking over to the empty hat-stand and pretending to pole dance.

'Simple. Attend Sarah's party. The other four solicitors are going,' she smiled.

'And then you're mine? Do I know them?' he asked.

'You may do all those naughty things that are running through your mind at the moment. Even the one with my bum pressed against the office window. I like that one. I bet no-one will look up if we're quick...' Sharon answered. 'The chaps are from Watkins Solicitors, the other side of town. You probably heard that their business went up for sale a couple of weeks ago.'

'I did. Word is they won the lottery. Did you pay them off?' asked Joshua, 'and fuck them?'

'It got a bit complicated. Two were gay and a third initially celibate. The senior partner made me cover him in yoghurt and lick it off. I didn't enjoy that too much but a girl has to earn a crust. Sarah worked for them when she first started so that's why they're attending her party. I gather they're off to various corners of the world on holiday, tomorrow. If you're wondering why I didn't offer you cash, it's because I judged that you'd prefer to keep working and have a long-term girlfriend who lets you do anything you want. Riding Ms Ryding, possibly?' she then bent over and wiggled her bottom at him. 'Deal then?'

Joshua dropped his trousers and mentally wrote his signature on her right bum cheek.

* * *

Half an hour and several positions later, the driver of a brand new BMW 7 series, distracted by the sight of a naked woman's bottom pressed against a top floor window, missed a red light and ploughed into a lorry at the road junction near Isaacs, Parnell and Payne. Joshua didn't hear because his ears were muffled by Sharon's thighs, which tightly gripped his head. She looked around from her naked window seat and tutted, 'Hope they're ok,' before letting Joshua loose from her grip for some air.

'God, you taste good, Sharon,' he exclaimed, wiping their combined juices from his face. 'So the deal is that we can do this regularly and all I have to do is go to this party?'

'Spot on Josh but less of the God stuff. This is pure devil.' She hopped off the windowsill and pulled him up by his tender penis.

'This is mine now along with your soul and you can have me whenever you want.' Sharon gave it another painful tweak before walking around the room to pick up her clothes. 'There's been some car accident a couple of minutes ago out the front. I can't stand the sight of any blood so I hope we can leave out the back way to go to the pub?'

'Ok. That's a nasty junction out there. Do you mind if I wash my face in the washroom before we go? I look like I've been through a hedge backwards,' asked Joshua.

'There's plenty of time. May I use your phone for a minute while you're in there? I forgot my mobile,' she replied.

'Phoning Nick with an update, eh? How his future tenant performed?' he joked, as he walked out of the office. He wore nothing but an ear-to-ear grin at the thought of his new life.

* * *

Suitably tidied up, ten minutes later, he pushed open the door to the lounge bar of the pub.

'Oh my God, Mr Parnell, There's been a terrible accident,' said Miss Hendrick running up to him. Before he could answer, Sharon had her arms around his neck hugging him.

'Everything's ok darling,' she said and planted a smacker on his lips before lowering her arms and grabbing his buttocks.

Joshua couldn't help respond and held onto the kiss before turning to Miss Hendrick.

'You bastard, you lying, cheating scumbag; that phone call is true. How the hell could you fancy a tart like this bitch?' The voice from the other side of the bar filled him with hair curlers and terror. He looked at Sharon who muttered, 'Oops,' before taking a few quick steps away from him.

His eyes focussed on his angry wife, owner of the shouty voice. She propelled herself at speed, on her short fat legs, waving two empty beer bottles in his direction. He guessed instantly that she wasn't gesticulating for another round.

As he ran out of the pub, he passed Sharon and wondered why she smiled as she waved at him or did she just hold up five digits?

He didn't see the ambulance that ran him over, causing fatal head injuries, and of course didn't know that the two rear passengers, who had survived a car crash in their partner's new BMW, may have lived if they'd made it straight to the hospital.

A brunette punched the air as soon as she walked around the corner from the Trumpeter's Arms. 'Nick Five, Dgo Nil,' she shouted. 'Two hundred, here we come.' She walked across to a chemist and started looking at the hair dyes. 'Honey Blonde, I think and possibly the name Colette.'

She then picked out a well-worn diary from her handbag, opened it up and drew a line with an equally used old pencil, through the words: *'Five Solicitors'*. Collette couldn't help laughing at the next words on her list. 'Gonna be tough,' she said and pulled a face.

'Five Priests'...

Be Prepared

Steve gazed at the multi-coloured sky in the distance.

The reds and blues, interlaced with streaks of purple, were fighting for his visual attention, as the small, bright yellow autumn sun struggled to avoid being locked away in God's document box for another night. He wondered which colours the Almighty would put on the agenda, for the next day of his holiday.

Solus finally flickered out, like a dying torch, and a minute or so later, the remaining few attractive parts of the spectrum reverted to a dark grey-blue.

He'd wondered whether to go and find his digital camera to take some photographs of the spectacle. Apparently due to dust from the Sahara desert being sucked up into the atmosphere; the BBC weather-lady had said this, so it must be true. Steve liked television women with their deep knowledgeable voices and tight blouses. He often wished that he could get a similar girlfriend to share his success with, but every relationship over the last year had turned sour so quickly. He had begun to think that he'd be forced to spend the rest of his evenings alone with a copy of Penthouse. The latest issue sat open on his dining table, just inside the patio door where he stood watching the sunset. On page nine, Sophia seductively applied squirty cream to her prominent nipples. He closed it up and placed it in the waste bin, muttering, 'You're no weather-girl. Probably think high pressure is a kind of blow job... '

He went back and stood on the patio. The light dimmed rapidly and apart from a solitary seabird call, the only sound below had been the metallic ping-pinging of rigging on tall yacht masts, bobbing in the harbour below.

After thinking just how amazing it seemed that he could effec-tively see the Sahara from this little seaside Welsh harbour, Steve slid the glass door into the closed position and walked over to the television. He pressed the set top on/off button, picked up the remote control and sat on the sofa ready for a night of soap.

The T.V. greeted him with a bright blue screen and some red writing.

A couple of minutes ago, he'd been marvelling at the combination in the heavens but the colourful replacement on the goggle box just didn't cut it for him.

'Bitch,' he uttered as he read the writing, 'SATELLITE SIGNAL NOT AVAILABLE'.

The man on the reception desk had warned him, when he'd picked up the room keys, that the engineer needed to attend today. An intermittent fuzzy picture fault had occurred. They thought it might be the booster amplifier that served the complex. Steve decided that the chap wouldn't still be working at this time of night and must have gone off for some spare parts.

'No telly, then,' he muttered, looking around and contemplating renewing his relationship with Sophie. 'Hang on... '

Steve went into the kitchen area. He might have seen something else there...

'Yes,' he shouted in triumph as he discovered a small radio next to the microwave.

He picked up the white plastic object and fiddled with the dials. It occurred to him that it might have been months, no, even years, since he'd last used one. The screen stared blankly back at him. Maybe the battery's flat?

Plan B, then. Violence, he thought. He gave it a vicious shaking and finally the little machine got scared before crackling into life, with a burst of Kenny Ball and his Jazzmen.

Jazz didn't rock his boat but when he tried to turn the control knob to change channels, it refused to respond. Steve picked up a dinner knife from the kitchen drawer and attempted to force it when a man's voice started speaking. 'Thank you to Kenny for opening the show. As usual we will have a variety of music over the next hour before the sports programme. We will also be having an interview with a new lady author, who has set her first book in this lovely part of the world... '

Steve decided against his forced Hari-Kari job on the squawk-box and tossed the knife back in the drawer. He picked up the radio, along with a packet of custard creams from the worktop, and retired to the lounge. Maybe the music wouldn't be too bad, he thought, and there might be the promise of some football later, or possibly rugby, as he presently holidayed in Wales.

He perched his entertainment machine on the sofa arm next to him and munched a couple of biscuits, as he closed his eyes and nodded to a track from Simple Minds. It reminded him of his last serious girlfriend. He'd done the dirty on her in a business deal and hidden abroad for six months before sneaking back and setting up again in another part of the country, under a different name.

As the music faded, the disc jockey came back on the mic. 'Many thanks to Jim Kerr there, one of my favourite performers and apparently one of the lady author, who's sitting opposite me, because she chose the track.

The radio signal faded out at this point and Steve missed the next few sentences. He took the opportunity to extract a few more custard creams from the packet and greedily stuffed two into his mouth. The sound suddenly came back and he avoided crunching them straight away as he tried to listen for the title of the next song. He hated listening to music and not knowing or remembering the name of the performer.

'Now tell me, my dear, a little about this book and why you chose to set the action in this locality,' asked the man's voice.

'Well, my motto is *Be Prepared for the Unexpected,* and that's why it's the title,' replied the low female voice.

Steve's mouthful of biscuits cleared the coffee table in front of him, splattering on the posh wooden flooring as he tried to get his breath.

'Shit,' he said as his arm sent the radio clattering to the floor and he tried to stop coughing.

He reached over quickly, picked it up and turned the volume knob to maximum.

'In the novel, the baddie character Stephan... every novel should have a baddie, by the way... well, Stephan is involved in a complicated business deal with Alison but manages to get away with all the proceeds. The story's about her financial recovery over the next year and of course, revenge. She slipped up and lowered her guard with Stephan. Previously, she'd stuck by her motto of *Be Prepared*...

'Fuck,' said Steve at the sound of the phrase. The voice, the story, the motto... 'Florence,' he said followed again by, 'Fuck.'

* * *

Almost fourteen months previously, Steven Morden had been sitting alongside his fiancée Florence Copping, at a shiny black table opposite three Oriental looking gentlemen.

An older man in a tailored suit spoke and then walked over to the man in the middle, holding out a pen. 'Thank you Mr Nagasaki. If you will sign first on behalf of your firm and then I will obtain the signature of Mrs Copping.'

The ledger passed over and the older man made his way around the table with the fountain pen and presented it to the lady.

'And so you are now business partners in *Always Geisha Limited*, ladies and gentleman,' said the man, having retrieved his pen and placing the gold plated object carefully into his top pocket. 'Congratulations from Black's Solicitors.'

'Bringing the best quality Japanese designed underwear to the unsuspecting British market,' said Mr Nagasaki smiling.

'The sexy Geisha look to every woman's bottom drawer,' replied Florence Copping, smiling before adding, 'and every woman's bottom.'

'Let us toast the moment,' shouted the man next to Mr Nagasaki and clicked his fingers.

'Ah, excellent Yamoto,' replied Nagasaki.

A set of double doors opened.

Steve Morden's eyes opened nearly as wide as the double doors, when he clocked the scantily clad dark haired waitresses trotting out from the doorway, carrying silver trays covered in small glasses full of clear liquid.

'We have Saki, my English friends. We will drink the nectar of the Japanese gods,' said Yamoto.

Steve took a glass from one of the beautiful little Oriental-eyed, smiling waitresses and sniffed at it while she turned around to offer some to Florence, sitting next to him.

He'd never drunk Saki before and his nose wrinkled a little at the smell. He enjoyed the sight of the trim behind just leaning over in front of him, as the waitress talked to Florence. The cream embroidered knickers barely covered the young lady's tiny buttocks and contrasted beautifully with her off white Asian skin. He tried to take in the fact that her slim thighs had a large gap in between, compared to chubby British ladies, when he felt a gentle slap on his back just as Florence got up to walk over towards the solicitors across the room.

'Mr Morden... Steven... I see you are admiring the company wares. What British lady would not wish to have an ass like that?'

Steve turned around. Nagasaki continued quietly speaking, 'Drink up. In fact as you British say, bottoms up,' and he gave the waitress a resounding slap on her backside. Steve watched as he downed three Sakis, one after each other. 'Don't sip, the taste is in the throat not on the tongue,' instructed the Jap.

The giggling waitress wiggled her smacked ass in front of Steve's face, before offering her drinks tray to him again. Steve looked at the full glass in his hand before saying, 'Here goes,' and downing it in one as Nagasaki had done.

After coughing a few times, he placed the empty glass on the tray and took two more.

'Good stuff,' he whispered hoarsely.

'Imported of course, from the main island. I take it that you agree with the quality of the design?' asked Nagasaki as his fingers went into the tiny cleavage of the smiling servant to pinch the cup material and pulled both waitress and bra down closer to the Englishman.

Steve caught a glimpse of a dark brown nipple as Nagasaki rolled the fabric back and forth between his fingers. The captured waitress smiled as broad as her tiny mouth would go and batted her brown eyes at him, in that peculiar Japanese way.

Steve knocked back the two Sakis that he held in his hands.

'If you find the merchandise pleasing, I'm sure the young lady will be pleased to arrange a personal viewing. In Japan, a director of a successful firm is allowed pleasures other than the wife… ' Nagasaki continued, 'Are you married, Steven?'

'Erm, no,' replied Steve, looking over to see where Florence Copping, his fiancée of two months, had got to.

Florence had moved away from the table. She stood by the double doors, talking animatedly to the older gold pen chap and the other two Japanese men. Two waitresses of similar build to his own, but in red and pale blue underwear, were circling them with trays of Saki.

'Wait here. I'll just have a word with Florence,' said Steve and hurried over to the other side of the room before returning a minute later.

'She's having a lift back with Mr Black the solicitor. I've told her that I'm staying around a little longer to chat about supplies.' He looked back and Florence waved a cheery goodbye. Steve followed suit and the double doors closed, leaving just the three of them in the room.

'Excellent. There is a room upstairs where Tora may show the full range. She is fluent in English and French. She has a degree in Computing and Economics from Tokyo University,' explained Nagasaki. 'Before you ask why she is here, working for an old man like me… it's simple: I pay well and on time.'

Tora gave one of her wide smiles again before straightening her bra and knickers.

'Cool,' answered Steve. 'And cute,' looking her up and down as he followed her out of the rear door to the lift.

* * *

Steve moved over to the table from the sofa and placed the radio in the middle to the accompaniment of the sound of Slade.

'Come on Noddy, get on with it,' he mumbled, as he impatiently waited for the 1970s hero to finish belting out an old favourite.

The DJ started speaking as soon as the track faded. 'And here I am again with Florence Copping whose book has been causing a stir in the area. Tell us a little more about the plot without actually giving away the ending, Florence.'

'Ha! I've been asked about the book so many times and sometimes when I'm nervous… as I am now… I think I say too much. So listeners, thanks firstly for giving me the chance. As I said earlier, it's about a business woman cheated by her partner in their relationship and also during a deal. After this he runs off with the money, leaving her virtually penniless and with child. The stress leads to an abortion, a breakdown and a gritty recovery,' explains Florence.

'Sounds intriguing,' replies the disc jockey. 'I gather that she gets her own back in the end? Murder, by any chance?'

'Ha! Maybe she does or maybe she doesn't. You'll have to buy the book. It's a complicated plot but suffice to say that the final chapter is set in the old fishing port of Haven on Sea,' replied Florence.

The blood drained from Steve's face at this point. He presently holidayed in that same village.

'And you have a book signing in the bookstore there, this Wednesday?' prompted the DJ

'Indeed I do and everyone's welcome to attend for a signed printed copy. It's at the Harbour Word bookshop on the new quay near the middle of the little line of shops. Great view of the marina yachts from there,' said Florence.

'Well, thank you Florence Copping and we all hope that the only murders on the marina that day, are on the pages of the novels, in the Harbour Word bookshop...'

'I can't believe the coincidence,' mumbled Steve as he turned the radio off. He started thinking. He'd only booked the trip three weeks ago. Even if Florence had found out he'd travelled to Haven on Sea for a break, she'd never have sorted out all this in that time to trap him. Write a book, arrange a radio interview, get printed copies etc... not possible. There cannot be a chance that she knows he's here.

Steve had a coffee and decided that he had to get hold of a copy of the book ASAP. He concluded that there existed a real chance that she'd want to kill him, based on what he did to her. The book may contain a clue or method and he could protect himself or even go to the police. He wasn't sure about the cops though, because he didn't know exactly what happened after he left, regarding his previous business dealings. Suffice to say, maybe it wasn't reported because of some kind of Japanese 'saving face'.

Steve seemed torn between running and finding out just what had happened. He had a brainwave and decided to search for links on his laptop regarding the book. After half an hour's slow searching using a plug-in dongle, because no fast broadband existed at the flats, he came to the conclusion that the only info let out by the publishers mirrored what he already knew, plus the book signing in two days at the nearby quayside shop.

Another mental flash led him to attempt a download of an e-book copy that he could read on his computer. After searching on Amazon, he concluded that it wouldn't be issued in the near future. That left only one option: Harbour Word, the bookshop base for the signing...

Steve went over to the bathroom to look in the mirror. He felt certain that he'd had a trimmed beard whilst going out with Florence. He'd only known her a few months and although he found her reasonably attractive, he fancied her money more so.

The tanned man that looked back had medium length fair hair. After stroking his stubble a few times, he concluded that a really close shave coupled with a number three haircut, should do the trick... and maybe dyeing the remaining shortened hair. Yes, he thought and some sunglasses... Try not to say anything as well... Who knows, he might just be able to pick up a copy and not see her? Of course, take a leaf out of her book and *be prepared*... He smiled to himself in the mirror. Out prepare her, again...

* * *

Steve sat on a comfy black chair, as he watched the slim Japanese girl wiggle her way out from behind the folding sides of the dressing area, for the sixth time. This time the outfit consisted of animal print underwear. The first couple of times were fun and a bit of a turn on as she posed in front of him, but he began to want for something more. He was forced to actually check out the merchandise instead of her body.

'I hope you liked the show. I saved these for last. They match me. What do you think?' asked Tora.

Steve looked her up and down.

'You're a beautiful young lady and the underwear's very you. I'm sure you'll look even nicer with less on though,' he hinted.

Tora laughed. 'You directors are all the same. Just want to put your hands inside my underwear... 'She pouted and turned her back to him.

'Erm, I'm sorry' said Steve. 'I didn't mean to upset you. Maybe I should…'

'Well go on then because I like it.' The Japanese girl bent over with her arms crossed and pushed her stripy behind out at him.

Steve didn't need a second invitation and leaned forward to push his palms inside the animal print to grasp her tight buttocks.

'Do you know what my name means in English?' she asked.

'No idea. Named after a pop star from the seventies?' he suggested.

'You've just had your hands inside one clue. I'll give you another,' and she straddled him on the chair before nuzzling into his neck.

'That's it?' asked Steve as she gently rubbed herself against him.

'Jesus…' he shouted, suddenly. 'What's with you? That bite hurt me.'

'Rrrawgh,' roared Tora. 'Third and last clue…'

'An animal?' he tried.

'Closer. Ok, another half clue.' She reached around her back and undid the bra clasp before holding a cup in front of him. 'Would any self-respecting Dalmatian, Toucan or Crocodile be happy in this?'

Steve looked at the stripy print before she rubbed it softly against his nose and then blindfolded him with it.

'Tora the Japanese Tiger,' he announced, triumphantly.

'Cool. You win first prize. That's a kiss,' she answered and gave him a long, drawn-out wet smacker.

'Anything else on offer?' he asked mischievously.

'I checked you out before the contract signing and got the idea that you were on the make, even though you're engaged. You're a naughty boy, Steven,' she answered.

'I don't reckon that you're any angel, either, Tiger girl,' he answered, as he moved his hands up her ribcage to find her pert breasts.

She grabbed his hands and pressed them hard onto her chest so that he couldn't move his fingers to feel anything. 'I'm in control of sending the first Nagasaki instalment of £20K to the joint account tomorrow.'

'Really? Florence's going up north to see another potential investor and I have to move £80K from her personal account first thing. She's given me the details,' he replied.

'I hoped you were going to be able to say something like that. How about you undress this Tiger now and in two days we go on a long holiday to see the real Tigers of the world?' she suggested.

'Might cost a bit; just where would we find the money?' he asked and smiled.

'Take your clothes off and Tora Tiger will help your memory,' she replied, before loosening her tight grip on his hands.

As soon as the blood returned to his hands, he felt her nipples harden under his touch and pinched them gently, between the sides of his fingers.

He wondered how much better could life get? Hmm, he thought, as Tora first pulled off his makeshift blindfold before starting to undo his shirt, he reasoned that he might be able to make one little improvement on the deal.

Two minutes later, he lay naked with his back on the carpet, getting a close up of the gap in between her legs that he'd been wondering about earlier. Maybe the more slightly built Japanese woman didn't need the chunky European thigh muscles? She teased him by rotating her nude nether region just out of reach above his face. Her legs had pinned his arms down. 'I didn't know Tigers shaved,' he joked, as he watched her.

She had the prettiest fanny he'd ever seen. Perfectly symmetrical and unlike any local girl's that he'd been privileged to get this close to. The usual pink or pale edged labial lips were beautifully crinkled and coloured dark brown. He'd never have expected it and guessed that he looked at another Japanese characteristic. He also noticed her nipples, which were a very dark brown as well. Steve could have watched her bits gyrating for longer but suddenly they arrived on his face, forcing their way into his mouth and grinding unexpectedly hard on his upper lip. Her small muscular calves crushed against his ears and somewhere in the distance a woman shouted, 'And Tigers suck as well.'

Five minutes later, he'd been well and truly milked. He watched her roll off him and sit open legged on the floor to his side. She licked her lips before leaning over and wiping his sodden face with her bra. She kissed him and then hovered over him, her hard nipples pointing at him and holding his common sense hostage.

'It's a deal then fanny face? You can fuck me for real after we see our first tiger but if you mess with me I'll cut you up.' She assumed a claws-out, cat pose.

'Ok, cock breath. Write me the account details down for tomorrow,' he replied, feeling certain that he could cheat this sexy paper tiger without getting his paintwork scratched.

* * *

Wednesday came and Steve got up by 7.30am. He avoided having a shower, in case he washed away some of the hair dye that he'd applied the previous day to his trimmed bonce. He walked over to the patio door and leant over the balcony. He could see the small group of ground floor shops, which contained the Harbour Word premises, from his third floor holiday flat. The shop seemed closed but there were a few cars and people wandering about in the adjacent car park. He wondered if one might be Florence. At one point, someone in a blue coat seemed to be looking up in his direction and he nipped inside like a guilty schoolboy and peeped around the uPvc frame.

Steve listened to the local radio for the next hour, wondering if there'd be any mention of the book signing in the morning lists of local activities. His reward had been a short recording from the programme that he'd accidentally caught earlier and the sound of Florence's voice for the second time in well over a year. He'd missed the actual start time of the event in the first programme but managed to glean from the second advert that it commenced at 10.00am and ran until 4.00pm. During breakfast, he decided over his cup of tea that he wouldn't go in straight away, even though he desperately wanted to read the last chapter. Customers might have dwindled by 3.00pm plus, so about 11.30am seemed right.

Five minutes before the appointed time, he put on his new coat and locked the flat before entering the lift. He looked down at his equally new trousers and shiny shoes. He'd picked some clothes of a type that he'd not normally wear and had no intention of ever doing so again. They'd go straight in the bin, once he'd obtained a copy of *Be Prepared for the Unexpected*.

When he started getting closer, he stopped and leant on the rail overlooking the marina for a few minutes. He looked down towards the shop and although the front door stood open, it seemed deserted. An A-board sat outside, partly blocking the pavement and advertising the book signing, so at least he knew that he'd found the correct venue.

His eyes wandered to the harbour below. The impressive yacht berthed just opposite and below the Harbour Word had just started its engine. The stainless steel fittings sparkled in the sun and he couldn't help watching the little woman who came out of the wheelhouse, as she bent over to fiddle with a coil of rope on the rear deck. She wore a white skipper's cap with gold trim and large sunglasses. To his surprise, she gave him a wave before going back inside. He watched her trim, tight denim-jeaned ass disappear and made a mental note that if he acquired a book without mishap, he'd ask her for a sail. Who knows, maybe his luck had turned?

Steve gazed again in the direction of the shop, happy to see a few people outside it now. He moved from the quayside over to the parade, lingering and pretending to window shop at adjacent premises. A minute later, he felt grateful to see an old couple go inside. After taking a deep breath, he marched quickly towards the entrance of the shop, trying not to think too much and hoping that he could quickly pick up a copy, pay and leave. He smiled as it reminded him of buying illicit over 18 porn mags as a kid.

As he went in, he faced wall to wall bookshelves. He then noticed a hand-written poster with an arrow and instructions saying *Florence Copping book signing to rear*. He couldn't see the back of the L shaped shop. He felt a little like a rat going into a trap. Steve shook his head at the thought. There can't possibly be any police here waiting to arrest him and what could Florence do if she recognised him? Stab him in the hand with a biro? His heart raced so he deliberately slowed down his breathing for a minute, whilst leafing through some Sci-Fi novels.

Happily, he overheard the couple next to him say, 'look, she's finished now. Let's get our copies.' He waited and a woman passed him, on her way out, holding a book whilst looking inside. He just caught the words *Be Prepared...* in gold print on the front-cover.

Steve looked around the corner and could see Florence sitting sideways at a small desk with several books piled in front of her. She chatted to the couple and seemed to know them; her hair had been dyed blonde instead of the highlighted brown that he remembered. He pushed his sunglasses more firmly onto the bridge of his nose and stood behind the talkative couple, fingering the ten pound note in his pocket. He'd noted that the book had been advertised at £9.99. He didn't want to get found out for a penny. Hopefully, he could just put the tenner on the table and turn away…

He started to sweat a little, as three more people came and queued behind him. Two weather beaten fisherman types and a large uniformed man with the words *Dock Security* on his jacket made up the trio.

Mentally telling himself to keep calm, he took his place next to Florence as the couple squeezed past him. 'Good luck with the book, Florence. Can't wait to see what happens to Stephan,' shouted the woman as she went.

'I've heard he gets shot,' answers the dock guard, laughing and adding, 'On my dock, of all places.'

'Shush, you have to read the novel first and then keep quiet,' replied Florence, holding a finger to her lips and smiling.

Steve felt like his head might explode. He almost prayed to get out of there in one piece. Surely she'd recognise him at this distance? He could smell her perfume; still the same one as before. He could see down her blouse, from his angle standing next to her. Florence always seemed to have a button too many undone. The dark heart shaped mole on her left bosom looked up at him accusingly. It knew that he had arrived and had wronged its owner. The multi coloured necklace centre piece, nestling in her deep pale cleavage, glittered as it sentenced him to death…

'Is 'best wishes, Florence Copping' ok or do you want to get personal?' giggled a woman's voice, speaking to him.

Steve woke up from his trial by jewellery and mumbled in as low a voice as he could manage, 'that's fine, cheers,' and placed the tenner on the desk.

Florence picked up a fresh copy from a pile and opened the cover and began to write on the inside page, before stopping and shaking her pen.

'Damn, it's run out. Do you want to wait here with the others, while I go get another pen or would you be happy with one from the pre-signed lot?' She indicated another pile to her left.

'Be fine,' replied the deep voice, holding out an open hand.

Her jewels were sparkling like crazy, attempting to tell everyone about the major criminal in their midst. Even her dangly earrings were joining in...

Steve took the offered copy and nodded, before turning around to find the security guard blocking his way. He turned desperately to look for a back door as the man's large hands landed on his shoulders. He knew now that he'd been nabbed...

'Hey,' said the uniformed man, 'we can't all fit in this small space. How about you help me turn Florence's desk around and then people can circulate?'

Steve looked at him with his mouth open. It took a split second to realise that he wasn't being arrested but being roped in as a helper.

'The desk?' prompted the guard. 'I know that accent. You must be off one of those Spanish ships in the harbour. Listen mate... please help me turn the desk...' he said slowly and put his large hands at one end to demonstrate.

The Spanish sailor mumbled, 'Si, Si,' and went to the other end to help.

Florence had stood up and continued chatting to the two other customers, totally oblivious to the man on trial, even though the books were now chanting in a thin papery voice, 'Crook, crook.'

'Cheers mate,' said the guard, slapping him on the back. 'I'll be around your boat later for some cheap cod.'

'Cheat. Sod,' echoed the books.

A woman grabbed his hand. He looked up; Florence stood there. He looked back down and saw her fingers place a small cake in his hand. 'A thank you,' she explained, still not listening to the wedding ring on her finger that twinkly-pointed at him and silently shouted, 'Get the bastard.'

Steve read the writing in the icing on the top of the cup cake, *Be prepared*. He could take this no longer and rushed for the door.

The fresh air hit him like a hammer. He wanted to get back to his flat but felt dizzy so he headed for the railings opposite and caught his breath. Everything spun around for a few seconds but finally his eyes focussed on the yacht below.

The little lady in the sailor's hat had stripped off and had been sunning herself on the deck below. She waved at him as the sun glinted off her Ray-bans.

He remembered his plan. If he got out in one piece, he'd go and chat her up but first he had to read the end of the book. He looked in his hand... a cake. 'Shit,' he uttered, wondering if he'd left the novel in the shop before finding it in his jacket pocket, where he'd placed it whilst moving the table.

His sense of humour began to return as he fingered the pages and thought about being nearly trapped, 'Si, si, Signorina... '

It disappeared instantly as he read the writing on the inside page, 'Got you, Flop'. He quickly found the final chapter and folded the spine of the book back, to lean it on the railings. As he did so he noticed the last page fall out and flutter towards the quay edge. It had been stopped from blowing into the dock by a coil of rope. He trapped it, by standing on it and then reached under the single metal rail to retrieve it.

A woman's low voice made him bang his head as he got up.

'Thought you'd got away, didn't you?' it said.

He stood up to see Florence standing a few feet away from him, reaching into her handbag.

'How'd you find me, Flop?' he asked, as the colour drained from his face.

'Don't you want to read the end?' she replied.

Steve dropped both the book and cake to the floor. He started to read out aloud the last paragraph, from the remaining page in his hand. 'The small revolver spat flame three times and Stephan slumped to the floor, dead.'

He looked back at her. 'You wouldn't,' and then noticed what she'd taken out of her handbag, the hand hidden by a scarf. Underneath, she held a dark hard-edged object, which rather obviously pointed in his direction.

Steve backed up against the railings. 'You can't shoot me here. There are witnesses in the shop. There's a girl in the boat below. Please Flop...'

'You deserve everything that you've got coming to you, Stevie. I'm happy now. I married Mr Nagasaki and want for nothing. Your theft means nothing to his company. You did take my personal funds, which is nasty and something else, now what did you do? Oh yes, a certain Japanese lady, from whom you obtained information and then scammed her as well. Bad boy, I reckon the noise from the boat engine will drown out any gunshot,' said Florence, putting both hands under the scarf and raising them towards his chest.

'But Florence, Flop... you always said that you were a forgiving type,' pleaded Steve.

Florence walked closer to him and he took a step back, tight against the guard rail.

'You're sweating, Stevie but maybe you're right,' said Florence and lowered her hands. 'Maybe I can forgive.'

Her last sentence became nearly lost in the noise emanating from the waterside below, as the yacht started to pull away from her berth.

Steve blew a sigh of relief and turned around to see the young lady skipper waving at him. The young lady Japanese skipper...

He had a good view of the Oriental Tiger painted on the stern of the boat, just after the rope coiled around his ankle and yanked him into the water.

'I know a lady who cannot forgive, though,' added Florence.

The yacht had stopped moving forward now and Tora waved at Flop as she gunned the throttle and the bronze propellers turned the water scarlet.

Florence took the water pistol out from under her scarf and shot at the coloured bubbles. 'Now this would have been a good ending to the story...'

Your Credit or Your Life

Randolf picked up the unopened mail from the glass coffee table in the lounge. It seemed strange for Silhouette to have left it there. She usually acted like a model of robot efficiency.

More than a little excited at the thought of opening a letter for the first time in months, he cautiously listened for signs of Silhouette having woken up. At first everything seemed quiet; then he heard the squeak of the shower knob being turned on and a reassuring splashing of water hitting the fibreglass tray.

Feeling like a thief, he grabbed the three envelopes and rushed outside to the balcony, trying not to spill his beer. He settled down on the black mesh chair and even looked around at the other apartments to see if anyone watched him.

'The coast is clear,' he muttered to himself as he jabbed his finger into the first brown envelope flap and eagerly tore away at it. He then realised that he hadn't even looked at the addressee. Quickly flipping to the front, he checked his name and repeated this with the other two.

Satisfied that none were for Silhouette, he unfolded the contents to find an invitation to the opening of a new bistro.

'Huh,' he muttered and made a similar sound when he checked the second envelope, which revealed a request from a dog charity.

'Woof, woof, woof. One left then,' he said, beginning to lose his enthusiasm.

Randolf had left this one because he'd recognised it as simply one of his monthly credit card statements. Silhouette dealt with all of this boring stuff, sorted out the banking and communicated with his accountants.

He nearly left it when he spotted the return address on the rear of the envelope. It happened to be for his Gold Card. The very card that had saved his life and helped pay for the apartment in the sun where he now sat on the balcony, resplendent in his bathers.

Randolf smiled and thought how nice it would be to look at that line on the statement that said 'Credit Limit - £100K', a worthy reward after years of financial struggle.

* * *

Nearly six months earlier, Randolf Johnson had been sitting alone in a Southampton restaurant. His long-term girlfriend had left him five days previously, when he'd informed her that he'd been laid off work, with little prospect of returning in today's austere climate.

He'd booked a table a couple of weeks before, to celebrate being together five years. The menu had been ordered and food paid for in advance. As a final flourish, a violinist would appear and play as he planned to get down on one knee in front of his lady.

Randolf flicked open the lid of the blue velvet covered box and gazed at the sparkly diamond on the gold ring inside.

He wasn't sure why he'd turned up at the restaurant on his own, apart from the fact that the food had been already paid for. In his current financial situation, he'd decided not to waste anything and so would eat his celebration meal, anyway. In fact, if he could manage it, he'd eat his ex's share as well.

Randolf coughed a little as he tried to hold back a few tears. He felt his throat tighten. Calmly, he began to breathe slowly and deeply through his nose. For several months now, he'd been having similar problems and been diagnosed with panic attacks. Stressful situations seemed to bring these on and the Prozac that he'd been prescribed hadn't helped.

A waiter came over to ask if he felt ok and Randolf pointed at his empty glass and made a drinking gesture. Within a minute, he gently sipped some water and the colour returned to his face.

The concerned manager had come over from behind the bar

and said, 'Are you ok, Mr Johnson? We haven't lost a customer yet, before they've eaten.'

Randolf laughed. 'Sorry Miguel. It's these damn coughing attacks that I keep getting. I'll be ok now.'

'I'm so sorry about Rachel. You were a good couple. I will only charge you half for this,' said Miguel.

'No worries, Miguel. I know that you ordered fresh stuff in especially and it's already paid for. Just bring it on and I'll see how far I can get with it,' replied Randolf, clearing his throat and feeling a little better.

Up until now, he'd been the only one in the restaurant and felt a little concerned that it would stay like that. He looked relieved to hear the small bell above the door tinkle and see two other women come in. Miguel waved a greeting hand and led them to a table across the room.

Randolf began to feel sorry for himself when Miguel appeared with the wine. He perked up when he remembered that he'd ordered a 2002 Rioja. He watched as Miguel used his shiny Waiter's Friend to cut away the wrapping and with a flick of a wrist, the extracted cork sat in the man's hand. He passed it to Randolf who took a deep sniff at the soft woody material that hadn't seen the light of day for years, to inhale the dark forest fruit aroma. Miguel saw him looking at the writing on the cork. 'It is genuine, yes?' asked the manager.

'It's just fine. Don't worry about a tasting; fill it up, please,' replied Randolf.

'Would you like the Spanish salad first or with the Tapas, signor?' asked Miguel.

Randolf took two large mouthfuls of the red before answering. 'That's lovely wine and perfectly aged. I'd like the salad with the Tapas dishes. Don't wait for me to finish each one. Just bring them out as they're ready, please.'

'Si, signor,' the manager replied and Miguel waved to the waiter standing by the kitchen entrance, before pulling in his stomach and walking over to the two ladies at the other occupied table.

Randolf watched him as he stroked back his black hair and flirted with them. One lady looked oriental and the other seemed of African descent. Her features had a mixed race look and seemed to combine the best of both. At this distance, she looked as though she could be a model.

His attention moved away from the two women by the arrival of his food. He watched a salad being carefully placed next to a dish containing Serrano Ham and Melon.

Randolf hadn't eaten all day and had greedily devoured the tasty combination, when the waiter reappeared with Blue Cheese stuffed Aubergine covered in Herbs and Pine Nuts.

He became so engrossed in the food and was half way through the next course of *Albondigas con salsa de Tomates* that he jumped, when he heard a woman's voice next to him.

'Isn't this food wonderful? We've just had those meatballs in tomato sauce,' she said.

Randolf turned to her with tomato juice dripping down his chin. The pretty African lady stood next to him.

'Yes, yes,' he stammered. 'I've been here lots with my girlfriend, erm... ex-girlfriend.' He could see her looking at the open ring case.

'Oh, I'm so sorry. I wasn't being nosy. It's a lovely ring. I adore jewellery. I'm sure another lucky lady will come along soon,' she said and waved before walking towards the ladies' loo.

Randolf watched her trim behind wiggling out of sight. 'Maybe, but you'll do just fine,' he said quietly to himself.

The Tapas list seemed endless. Randolf had nearly forgotten how many he'd ordered. He ploughed through *Patatas a la Brava*, *Manchego* Cheese with *Membrillo Quince* and into his second bottle of Rioja. He sent some garlic mushrooms and spicy sausage over to the ladies' table and they waved back in appreciation. The waiter came back and said, 'They thank you. They asked for your name and I have told them. They are called May Su and Silhouette.' He moved closer to Randolf's ear. 'That Silhouette, the one with the dark hair, I think she fancies you.'

Those words cheered Randolf up, no end. He looked down at the ring and took it out of the case. 'Time to move on,' he said, before popping it in his mouth and taking a large swig of Rioja.

The wine went down but the ring didn't seem too interested in moving on. Randolf knew that he'd made a bad decision as soon as he felt his throat muscles go rigid once more. He tried to swallow more wine but to no avail. As he got up to signal for help, he sent his wine glass crashing to the floor and his chair tipped over backwards. He staggered to his feet as the manager ran over.

'Signor Randolf. What shall I do? Is there something stuck in your mouth?' said Miguel, steadying him by the shoulders.

'He's choking,' shouted a woman's voice. 'Let me get to him. I'm a nurse.'

Silhouette ran over. She pushed Miguel to one side and thrust her arms around his waist and linked her wrists, before bringing then up sharply under his sternum.

Randolf made a loud forced grunt and the ring popped out into his Paella. They pushed him into a chair and Silhouette moved closer to Randolf's face and peered inside his mouth. He still desperately struggled to breathe.

'That Heimlich has removed the blockage but his windpipe is in spasm and has closed up. I'm going to have to make an emergency airway.' She looked around. 'Is that his wallet on the table? Get me a credit card out, and you, waiter, get me a clean straw from the kitchen quickly.'

May Su passed her a gold coloured plastic card and Silhouette picked up a piece of broken wine glass. She scored the card twice before snapping a pointed triangle from it. By now, the waiter had returned from the kitchen with a container of gaily coloured straws and decorative umbrellas.

'God, we're not making a cocktail, man.' she shouted. 'Miguel. Stand behind the chair and hold his head back tightly. This is going to hurt.'

The manager did as instructed but had to look away. Silhouette felt the shape of Randolf's neck with her fingertips, before jabbing the pointed end of the sharply cut card, deep into the tissues.

Randolf had almost passed out but the pain and the sound of a violin brought him back around into consciousness and he flinched.

'Tighter, Miguel. Pass me that red straw, May Su,' she ordered, 'and get that crazy violinist out of here.'

The musician who had turned up at nine o'clock, as booked, screeched out a D flat before standing at the doorway, opened mouthed.

'This is called a Cricothyrotomy, Randolf. Sorry if I hurt you but you'll thank me later,' she said softly, as she pushed the plastic straw into the small slit in his neck.

Almost immediately, air could be heard passing through the straw.

'Call an ambulance, Miguel. I'll take over holding his head,' and she replaced the Spanish manager's rigid grip with her tummy and soft brown hands.

'It'll take a minute or two for your lungs to fill up again, Randolf but I'm sure you'll be ok now. It's a hospital visit for you, next. I'm afraid that I've used up the balance on your credit card but what price is a life?' she laughed.

Randolf couldn't talk but felt conscious enough now to appreciate what she'd done and nodded.

The ambulance arrived a few minutes later and the paramedics took over from Silhouette. His throat had relaxed a little by now and they were able to place a small oxygen mask over his face with one of them holding the supply. As they helped him up out of the dining chair, Randolf reached into his

Paella and placed the garlic, fishy, diamond ring into Silhouette's palm.

'I joked about the jewellery. You know that I can't take this. I will clean it up and visit you in hospital, Randolf,' she laughed.

Randolf nodded. He felt glad to be alive and had met the woman of his dreams but made an absolute fool of himself, all in the last twenty five minutes. Good going, even by his standards.

* * *

Randolf's throat collapsed twice in the ambulance and the paramedics had to repeat Silhouette's treatment but with more suitable equipment. He underwent a tracheostomy operation that evening to place a permanent fixture in his neck.

He awoke the next morning to find Silhouette at his bedside.

'Visiting time already?' he mumbled, hoarsely.

'Try not to talk yet. The consultant has decided that it's too much of a risk to try to cure your panic attacks with medicines and has fitted a permanent valve in your throat. If you have trouble, you can pop out the bung and breathe freely. It's called a Montgomery or Monty for short. Is there someone that I can contact, a relative maybe?' she asked.

Randolf shook his head. 'Not close,' he whispered.

'Stuck with me then; here's your ring back.' She placed it in the drawer in the bedside cabinet. 'I'll be back this afternoon after my shift. Try and rest, now.'

Randolf watched her walk out of the ward. Only now had he noticed that she wore her hospital uniform. He began to hope that he would need some nursing.

He relapsed several times over the next few days and had great difficulty learning to eat again with his life saving device in place. He spent a month in the place, overall, undergoing various tests, both medical and psychological in order to discover the underlying cause of his airway problem. At the hint of a throat closure, he would pop open the cap covering the valve and try to sit down somewhere for a few minutes.

His only other visitor had been a reporter from the local newspaper, eager to do a piece on the helpful nurse, Silhouette. Randolf had his picture taken with her sitting on his bed.

On the day of his discharge, the consultant came around and spoke to him. 'Basically, we can't find anything wrong. The Monty will have to stay in your neck. Your condition may improve with time. We can't tell but even if it did, we wouldn't recommend the removal of the device. They last up to six months and are easily replaced. I remind you again about how important it is to keep it clean. I understand that one of the nurses here is a neighbour of yours and will keep an eye on you, at first. Oh, and you may want to see this.' He passed a newspaper over to him.

Randolf looked at the tabloid. Not really his thing. He preferred the broadsheets but took it anyway.

'Page seven,' added the consultant.

Randolf turned the pages to find a picture of himself under the heading It's a Plastic Life. Would you Credit It?

'There have been a couple of journalists at the hospital. We sent them away. I suppose that they'll be waiting outside your house. Good luck, Mr Johnson.' The consultant smiled and walked away just as Silhouette appeared.

'Have you seen this?' asked Randolf.

'I have. The girls showed me. It looks as though they've raised the hemline of my skirt and added a credit card to your hand as well,' she laughed.

Randolf looked more closely. 'Well, well. So they have, and your boss says that the press are sniffing around after a story. Is there any chance of a lift home, when you finish, Silhouette? I owe you dinner at least.'

'I thought you'd never ask. I'm at the end of my shift now. I'll fetch your clothes and get changed myself. I know where you live,' she laughed.

Silhouette knew because Randolf had given her a key to get some of his things during the stay and feed his goldfish. He noted that she hadn't offered to give it back and hoped that looked a good sign.

The hospital stay had taken a lot out of Randolf. He hadn't enjoyed the food and had lost some weight although that wasn't a bad thing. Increasing his exercise over the next few days produced an increase in coughing and he had to use his Monty a few times. This meant that he had to call on Silhouette several times and so, two days later, she moved into the spare bedroom.

The next day, there were two reporters at the door asking to come in. Over tea and biscuits, they explained that they wanted to do a piece on the couple and were willing to pay good money. After the discussion, Randolf said that they'd think about it and their story offer fee doubled at the door.

Later in the afternoon, Randolf received a call from a credit card company. After he'd explained that he'd been in hospital and said sorry to have missed a payment, he thought it might be a hoax call when the woman on the phone insisted that they wanted to 'give him' money. 'Star in an advert...' he said. 'How ridiculous!'

Silhouette grabbed the phone off him, just before he could put it down. 'Yes, I'm Silhouette, the nurse in the picture. Of course you can come and see us. Yes... Yes... Friday at ten will be fine. Bye.'

'Randolf! Don't you see? This is big bucks. Let's play them against each other. They want our story.' She went over to him and gave him a long kiss.

She'd never done that before and her next sentence surprised him.

'Let me try on that ring. We could say we're engaged now,' she said, putting her arm around him.

* * *

Over the next week, they talked with three tabloids, one broadsheet, two mainstream magazines, breakfast TV and Randolf's credit card company.

Silhouette turned out to be a skilled negotiator and arranged an 'exclusive first interview' with the highest bidding tabloid, appearances on nationwide TV and a deal with the credit company. All in, it totalled £170k and if they featured in some U.S. advertising, it could double.

'We could get married, if you like,' she said, after telling him the total.

Randolf felt too shell-shocked to say anything other than, 'Ok.'

She pounced on him that night. He'd gone to bed in his own room and nearly fell asleep when the bedroom door creaked open.

Although they'd kissed and cuddled, since she'd moved in, he hadn't pushed their relationship any further. He still had old fashioned ways. He wondered why, when he felt the warmth of her naked body press against him under the duvet.

'You've been very kind to me Randolf, I will be a good wife although I do like fine things,' said Silhouette.

'Sounds ominous,' he replied, as she stroked the hairs on his chest.

'In my mother's country, it is the duty of a good wife to attend to her husband's every need,' and she disappeared under the bedclothes.

Seconds later he felt her warm mouth kiss his manhood followed by her fingers stroking at the base. Her lips enveloped the tip and the fingers continued their sensual dance, moving, pushing, pulling, tickling, teasing...

'God, Silhouette. Ooo,' he shuddered. 'Where on earth did you learn to do this?' From memory, a woman's blow job seemed just a load of uncomfortable tugging, he thought to himself.

'It is passed on from one generation to the next in my family.

Do you like it or shall I stop? For some men, it is too sensitive,' said a slightly muffled voice from under the sheets. She came up for air and her face appeared, before he could answer.

'It is hot under there,' she laughed.

'Make it hotter' he ordered, laughing back.

'Yes, master,' and she disappeared.

When Randolf finally climaxed he felt like he wasn't going to stop. They were simply the strongest contractions that he'd ever had. She carried on with her lips until he had to beg her to stop.

Silhouette appeared wiping her mouth with the back of her hand.

'You didn't? Not all of it?' he laughed.

She leaned over and gave him a very man-salty kiss. 'Will you marry me then, Randolf, even though I will spend all your money?'

'If you do that once a week, it'll be worth it,' he answered.

'I will do it until the day you die, my master,' she replied and kissed him again.

Three weeks later, they were standing at the register office with Miguel and May Su as witnesses and a dozen photographers flashing away.

Silhouette's plan came to fruition over the next two months. The money had come piling in, as had lines of credit. He had purchased an apartment in Spain overlooking the sea. She reckoned that interest in them, as a couple, would wane quickly over the next month and they could quietly disappear abroad. They'd discussed opening a bar and their future. She didn't want children and Randolf agreed because of the large age difference.

'What do you see in me?' he'd ask. 'I'm too old.'

'Your money,' she'd reply.

'All I want is you,' he would say,' lifting up her top to hold her braless boobs.

'All I want is your money, master,' she'd reply and they'd both laugh.

After they moved to Spain, the panic attacks stopped. Silhouette would sometimes ask about them and he wondered if she looked a little disappointed, when he answered in the negative. He had almost considered faking one, in case she missed her old nursing duties.

Randolf quickly let her run his life because she seemed to be happier with a pile of things to sort out. His contact with the U.K. rapidly diminished and he began to spend his time serving behind their little bar and laying in the sun feeling every inch, a genuine ex-pat.

The highlight of his life became his weekly meeting with Silhouette's mouth and true to her word, she always left husband feeling the luckiest man in the world. She turned out to be a hard worker, a true friend, organised all of his paperwork, looked half his age and had a figure to die for.

* * *

Randolf glanced at the patio door to see if Silhouette had emerged from the shower. He hoped to see her walking about naked, across the lounge again. Her dark wet hair trailing limply over her brown shoulders and her young jutting breasts pointing at him.

He couldn't see her anywhere, so eventually he opened the last envelope and took a good glug from the glass of ice cold beer in his right hand. He flipped the Gold Card statement open with his left, to look at the glorious credit limit.

'One hundred thousand pounds; flipping brilliant,' he said out loud.

A little piece of writing attracted his attention just as he nearly tossed it onto his balcony 'out-tray' with the dog letter and bistro invite. Randolf's eyes squinted in the bright sunlight as he read it twice.

'Account Over Limit'.

He felt his throat tighten on the beer he nearly swallowed.

Under the warning, it said 'No payment received for last month'. He quickly looked at the entries above. '*Cash withdrawal £15000, Cash withdrawal £9000, Tiffany Jewellers £22195...*'

Randolf started to choke and couldn't get his breath. The panic attacks had returned. He clutched at the life-saving device in his neck, desperately trying to get the cap off. His frantic efforts were in vain and he tried to think of something to prise it open.

He remembered his wallet and as he clawed it from his back pocket, he knocked over his drink in the process. The container smashed to the floor with a loud crack, scattering glass and liquid in all directions. He felt a shard of the exploding glass impale his bare thigh.

The patio door flew open. A horrified Silhouette shouted 'Randolf, oh my God!'

Randolf ineffectually tried to open his emergency airway with the blunt corner of a credit card.

Silhouette looked at the desperate scene of her choking, bleeding lover pleading with his eyes for help, as he turned bluer by the second.

'Let me, Randolf,' she said and pulled the Gold Card from his weakening grip. 'It's too blunt. We need to cut it. I'll use the broken glass.'

Randolf's semi-conscious mind prayed that his angel wouldn't cut herself. How could he repay her a second time for saving his life?

He felt a sharp pain, as she pulled the pointed piece of glass from his thigh and watched as her bloodied fingers deftly cut the plastic rectangle into two sharp pointed triangles.

His body had started to go numb. He could only just feel the warmth of the blood trickling down his thigh. He closed his eyes, in anticipation of the life giving flow of oxygen through the open airway.

Randolf never felt the two points of plastic as they pierced both eyelids, let alone saw the smiling Silhouette starting to mop up the blood on the floor with his credit card bill...

Virtual Virgin

'So you're quite certain that you've never had sex with or without your knowledge, Mr Harding?' asked the blonde in the white coat, looking over her thick-rimmed glasses.

'I'm totally positive about that. Like I said, I've had offers but the timing didn't seem right. I guess that, by the odds, some of us are always left on the shelf,' replied the slightly embarrassed man, trying to avoid the penetrating gaze of her green eyes peeping over the spectacles.

'And never been raped whilst drunk, for instance?' she queried.

'I think I'd have spotted that one,' he answered, looking mystified. 'I'm a man.'

'It's completely possible. Slip three Viagra and a date rape drug into your vodka and orange. No taste, everything's buzzing, you're dancing and chatting away, then bang. You wake up a day later with part of your life missing and a sore cock,' explained the attractive interviewer, leaning closer to him to check his response.

'Look really. What can I say? Most definitely not, Zandra; I rarely drink alcohol. In fact sometimes I wish I could just be somebody else. I have no luck with women,' he replied, holding her gaze for a split second before looking down at the floor.

'My, you are shy aren't you? I think the fact that I'm a woman is really getting to you, Mr Harding. Your psychological report appears to show an inbuilt fear of the fairer sex. It's ok. You can look up now. You've got the job, Peter. Congratulations.'

* * *

A week earlier, Peter Harding had been scanning the classified ads in the local paper. He felt quite despondent. The business that he'd worked in for several years had gone into receivership without warning and he'd turned up last Tuesday to find the main gate padlocked.

He found a printed note in an A4 poly-pocket tied to the metal structure, stating that an offence would be committed if the premises were entered or any items removed without permission, signed by an insolvency firm. There were several of his colleagues standing outside. His immediate boss currently harangued a man wearing a black security uniform, standing the other side of the gate.

'No good shouting at me, mate. I'm only here to make sure there's no trouble,' the guard shouted back to the gathering crowd.

'But we've still got our things in there. My leather jacket, my laptop and my plants,' protested Peter's boss.

'I need my reading glasses as well,' added a middle aged woman.

The uniformed man laughed. 'Should have gone to Specsavers love, then you'd have a spare set.'

'Listen. Won't you open up just to let one of us in? We could make a list and you could check it,' suggested one of the younger men, who had just turned up.

'That's more than my job's worth, son. I've been on security in a few of these close-downs in the last few months. You can't do anything until the assessor's been in and looked around. It may be later today or could be next week. They're a law unto themselves,' explained the guard.

He felt a hand on his arm. A quiet voice said, 'This is terrible Peter.'

Pete looked down at his coat sleeve to see the pale ringless fingers of a lady's hand grasping his forearm. He froze as he recognised the bright red nail polish. The pretty young lady from along the corridor in the sales division had spoken to him...

'I... I... Erm, well... ' he stammered.

'Oh, I... I... didn't mean to startle you, Mr Harding. Is it ok if I call you P-Peter?' she stammered back.

Pete caught her gaze for a second before lowering it to her chest. 'Oh. Yes, yes of course. Erm...call me Teat... No, no. I mean Pete. Please... It's Amanda, isn't it?'

She unconsciously pulled her coat front tighter together. 'Yes it is. We've only spoken once before; several months ago but you remember my name.'

'Amanda Pullins, payroll number 6969, employed 14 months, etcetera. I have that kind of brain. Guess that's why I've run the payroll for a few years. Erm... correction, used to...' he explained. 'You were in sales. Did you have any inkling of this close-down? Looks like the firm's gone bankrupt.'

'Sales of the old range of tools were dropping considerably towards the end of last year but the new range sourced in China sold a lot cheaper with a bigger margin, I think. We seemed to be obtaining orders for those. Ah well. Lucky I didn't put a deposit on one of those new-build flats in the High Street,' she answered. 'In fact, the estate agents are looking for a part-timer. Think I'll get over there now before anyone else does. There are sixty people working here. That'll hit the job market in the town.'

'Sixty two, including us to be precise, Amanda. I'm good with figures.' Yet again, his eyes let him down as he checked out the outline of her trim waist. As he looked up, her eyes told him that she'd noticed.

'Oh, I don't mean that I think you are just a figure. Well, no, you do have a nice payroll number 69 69, I mean you have good assets... What am I saying?' he closed his eyes and tried to calm down.

'Don't get so flustered, Peter. I don't bite,' said Amanda.

'Oi, Pete. We're making a list of our stuff in case the assessors turn up. What about those dirty mags that you've got hidden behind the toilet cistern?' shouted Chris, the young man who'd asked the guard earlier and had persisted with his idea of being let in to pick stuff up.

'Can't remember those... Oh I see... Joke. No, no, I've nothing of any value to take away from the old place, thanks Chris,' replied Pete.

'Not even Amanda?' said Chris, nudging his free arm.

'Yes, erm... Gotta go now, Chris. Look, Amanda, estate agents? I- I don't suppose that I could accompany you that way? You're still h-holding my arm, anyway,' he asked.

'Oh my God, I'm sorry,' and her hand flew away into her pocket. 'This is such a shock and... and I don't usually chat with many people at work. I'd be delighted if you'd come along with me.'

'So we're going now? There's not much point in staying here. Why don't we just ask Chris how long he's going to hang around, maybe he can give us a ring if anything happens later?' suggested Pete.

'Go on then. It'll have to be your mobile, I won't give mine out to strange men,' she replied.

Pete went back over to talk to Chris, by the gates. His colleague agreed and took his contact details. As he went back to Amanda, he kept his phone in his hand.

'How about we swap numbers if we're both job hunting? Maybe I might find something useful for you or vice versa?' he asked, feeling suddenly brave. He'd never asked a girl for such a thing and this seemed like a legitimate excuse.

'Oh, erm... of course, the thing is I can't actually remember it. Maybe if you give me yours, I can ring it and you'll get it in your received call list?' she suggested.

'Sounds like a plan,' he said. He used a line that he had heard in a thriller last week on the TV, and he'd been dying for the right situation in which to try it.

'Sounds like a phone... actually,' the girl part repeated, after he'd used her mobile to ring his own and she giggled.

He laughed at her little joke.

'Did you get it?' asked Amanda. 'The number I meant.'

'Yes, yes, that's fine,' he answered, pleased at his little act of subterfuge.

'Right, we'd better get along to the job shop. Shall we take the walk along the river?' she suggested.

'That'll be nice. Quite romantic down there...' Pete stopped as he realised what he'd just said.

'Are you asking me on a date, Mr Harding?' inquired Amanda, with a cheeky grin.

'Oh erm, no, no, I meant the scenery, I think...' he stammered, thinking, oh shit; it had been going so well.

'Ok, I accept, Peter. I haven't had a date for ages,' she said loudly, so that Chris, who had been watching, overheard her.

About twenty yards further along the road, she whispered to Pete, 'Actually I've never had a boyfriend before or a date. I hope you don't mind pretending.'

Pete almost let out a sign of relief. 'That's no problem Amanda. I haven't had many girls either,' he lied. There were no notches on his bedstead.

'Are you seeing anyone at the moment, then?' she asked.

'No one in particular, busy with hobbies, catching up on TV etc., you know how time flies,' he replied.

'Same here, it's not that I don't want a boyfriend. I just never seem to be asked,' said Amanda, wiping the corner of her eye.

Pete stopped walking and she did likewise. He looked at the side of her face.

'You're crying, aren't you, what's wrong Amanda?' he inquired.

She threw her hands around his neck. 'I'm sorry Pete. It's the pressure of losing my job, I guess and now walking along here with you. I don't want to sound desperate but will you really go out with me? I don't mean sex and stuff, at least not for a while. You shouldn't do that before you're married.'

He felt a little taken aback at the sudden outburst. 'No, no, of course it's not right to open your box too early... I mean... did I just say that? Sorry, I mean you're completely right and I'd be delighted to call you my girlfriend.'

She punched him playfully in the arm. 'Thanks, Pete. What do you mean by my box? No wait, I think I can guess,' and her head looked down, at the front of her skirt.

Pete laughed at her frown.

'Have you been in many boxes?' she asked, unexpectedly.

'Well erm...' he stopped and looked into her soft brown eyes and couldn't lie. 'I'm a virgin and I guess that makes two of us?'

The smile on her face as she took his hand and started walking again answered his question.

* * *

After all of the activity in the virtual laboratory, Pete felt dog tired. After disengaging all the leads from his head visor and carefully placing the *Tactile Tendrils* back on their cushioned table, he slumped back in the padded armchair, just behind the exercise area.

A few minutes later, he'd almost regained his breath when he heard a firm knock at the door.

'I'm coming in now Pete. Have you turned everything off and left the *TTs* safe?' asked Zandra from the other side of the door.

'All done, I'm having a rest in the chair,' replied Pete.

The door opened, a head looked around the edge, and green eyes peeped over black spectacles.

'Everything ok, Pete?' Zandra walked in, looked at him flopped across the chair and wrote something on her clipboard.

'Not very fit, eh? That's what you're writing,' asked Pete.

'We have to keep full records on anything we observe in these first tests. I'm sure it won't affect the result, if I tell you that you seem to be less flustered after exercise. It's almost as if, being fully rested, your shyness and inhibitions regarding women come to the fore. Did you use to find yourself more relaxed later at night, if you were at a party for instance?' she asked.

'Maybe that's true, come to think of it. I put it down to the alcohol but thinking about it, I hardly ever drink a lot,' answered Pete.

'Interesting...' said Zandra.

'Really?' asked Pete, 'In what way, exactly?'

'I want to test you further tonight. Rather than going home now, I want you to use the research bathroom facilities and talk to you afterwards. Maybe a relaxing shower will bring back your inhibitions and fear of women. Like I said, it'll be interesting,' said Zandra.

'Overtime, eh? Double pay, I assume,' said Pete.

'We get our perks, Mr Harding,' and she winked at him. 'I'll show you to the bathroom. You might want to consider staying tonight, if you're really tired. We want to start again at 8 a.m. sharp so it'd save you travelling home. There's always a member of staff here for security reasons so there's always a couple of fresh beds.'

'You're not staying over by any chance?' asked Pete and then wondered why he'd asked.

'Is that wishful thinking, maybe? Have a shower and we'll see,' she laughed.

Pete watched her turn on her heel and strut out of the door. He smiled to himself, as he scanned below her white coat and watched her slim calves work against the unnatural female posture of the black high-heeled shoes. Maybe I'm scared to look her in the eye but when her back's turned... Very nice legs, he thought, as got up from his chair and followed her down the corridor.

* * *

Pete rose early the next day. At first, as he looked around, baffled at the unfamiliar surroundings, he wondered if he'd been drunk and got lucky, but his mind quickly realised where he'd slept, when he felt the aching in his muscles.

He thought back to the recent job interview and the odd questions. None of it made sense yet but he should be paid handsomely to take part in this psychological research and the money soothed his pain.

'Wanted... Shy young men', the advert had said and he now sat with Zandra Ludwig as she described the position. The research firm developed new gaming technology. A few more steps up from a plastic box plugged into a computer; their ideas would actually put the player in the action and all possible sensations would be available; hot, cold, taste, touch, fear etc., everything but pain...

She'd explained that the potential market would be huge; male teenagers huddled in their bedrooms in front of their laptops awaiting their first girlfriend and failed Lotharios the world over, being able to engage in passionate erotic sessions with beautiful women, in the privacy of their own home.

'You mean like a virtual blow up doll?' he asked, unbelievingly.

'Exactly, we're still testing everything and once you've passed the health computer generated testing side of things, we can progress you to *Virto*. That's the experimental device that generates an artificial reality around you, such as a bedroom with the woman of your dreams...' she explained.

'Why me, then?' he asked.

Zandra replied, 'As a virgin, your feelings are completely unblemished and you will be able to truthfully report back to us regarding the true effects of our design work on a man.'

'Are you using other people?' replied Pete.

'Yes, of course. You are our virgin. We will be running other tests for sports games, such as tennis and football etc. The possibilities are endless, Peter. We are hoping for a medical therapy usage, as well, to encourage people over their shyness regarding sex...' Zandra explained. 'Who knows, perhaps you might fancy an older woman like me after finishing the program?'

Pete suddenly regained his shyness and peered at the floor. He really hoped that the latter would happen but didn't think his new girlfriend would particularly like his new job, if she found out...

* * *

Pete blinked a few times as his eyes adjusted to the sunlight. He'd just been to see a Sci-Fi film with Amanda in which a man had been miniaturised and fed into the internals of a computer. As they walked out of the cinema into the street, she said to him, 'I don't know why you picked that film, Pete. It looked so stupid; the idea of running around in another imaginary world is just so scary. And then that bit where he fell in love with a robot; I'd kill you, if you did that to me, honey. Who waved to you as we came out? I didn't recognise him from the factory.'

'Oh, that's Steven. He works at my new place, writing software,' answered Pete.

'So how is the new job going? You don't say much about it. I know that it's government stuff and top secret but being as you're in accounts, surely there's something interesting that you can tell me?' Amanda asked.

'Oh well, it's tiring and boring. I manage; there's a fair bit of computer work and stuff like that,' he vaguely replied.

'Do you get any time to play any of those online games? I remember you telling me about a poker den at the old place,' she asked.

'Erm, yeah... a few but nothing involving money, I'm not going into debt or anything like that,' he laughed.

'That's good. I'm safe as your girlfriend then? No floozies at the firm and you're still keeping yourself for me? Another year and we might be able to afford our first flat and get married. It'll help if I get a job. You were lucky with yours. Shame they're not recruiting because we could work together,' she said.

'Shame, yes. Anyway you wouldn't want to be here. I'm sure something will turn up elsewhere soon. Didn't you say you had an interview?' he asked.

'Yes, in two days. Apparently the firm needs someone quick, as a volunteer has dropped out. Details are sketchy at the job centre so I'll find out more, just before, I guess,' Amanda answered. 'I'm so happy you don't think I'm strange, waiting until we're married. I love you, Peter,' and she gave him a big kiss on the cheek.

'It's no problem,' answered Peter, looking forward to his first session on the *Virto*...

* * *

Two weeks later he sat in a laboratory being given final instructions, before linking up with the '*Ultimate Virterience*', as Zandra pronounced the full title.

He had spent the last few days on the basic computer training machine and genuinely felt fitter and stronger as the unaccustomed exercise worked its magic on his flabby muscles. A doctor had only yesterday checked his heart and reflexes, before giving him the all clear to engage in his first *Virto* session, as the techies called it.

Zandra had explained that the annoying sticky pads on his head and chest muscles plus the connecting wires of the so called *Tactile Tendrils* that attached him to the trainer had been combined and built into a visored helmet, similar to that of a motorcyclist. Forward vision though didn't exist, like in training, because the wearer didn't need to move. The virtual game took place lying down on a comfortably padded couch. The inside of the visor had become the monitor, which fed visual input to the eyeballs. Circuits inside the helmet, connected by electromagnetic touch with the relevant areas of the brain, completed the illusion of being elsewhere, such as in another room. The details of the scene that unfolded before the wearer were a product of the software and the user's imagination.

'Do I really need to have the tranquilliser?' asked Pete, as he lay down on the padded lounger. 'Surely that won't be possible for general usage?'

Zandra stood back as a doctor carrying a syringe came closer.

'It'll be necessary the first few times, to get you to relax and let your mind combine with the visual and cortical output of *Virto*. We hope that you will quickly begin to recognise it and not need help. It's a bit like riding a bike for the first time. Soon, keeping your balance becomes second nature. We are developing a pill for home use and also hope to construct a hypnotic element inside future headsets, for the general public. I'm afraid though, you get the needle. I remind you again that we will always use your virtual name Trepe to converse with you as an avatar in order to avoid generating confusion inside your brain. Other volunteers will have different names so that if you meet them in future competitive programs, you will not recognise them in real life, a kind of privacy code. Anyway, good luck and sweet dreams, Trepe, your new lady friend will do anything you want...' instructed Zandra.

Trepe didn't have chance to reply as the fast acting tranquiliser flooded into his veins and his head filled with impossible colours, not of his own world.

* * *

'Trepe,' shouted a voice through a kaleidoscopic rainbow.

Pete watched a pair of eyeballs, connected by a piece of loudspeaker wire, roll along a young, multi coloured girl's tummy and stop when one of them landed in her navel, whilst the other rolled around to a standstill, like two balls in a snooker match.

'Trepe, you're connected. She's in front of you. Say hello,' instructed the voice, from another world.

Virtual hands solidified in front of him, resting on the girl's legs.

They were strange hands, of a different multicolour from the female torso on the pot black table; so weird that they moved at the same time as his own hands...

'Trepe, answer me...' the female voice said, spoiling his restful dream.

Pete became Trepe as he finally realised that he had arrived inside *Virto*. The experiment had worked and as the colours reorganised into the standard human spectrum, he could see a heavenly, partly clothed young lady, lying on a bed, just in front of him.

'Fuck,' he said to no one in particular.

'Wow, your whole repertoire, Trepe; all you can say? Or is that the comment of a typical male mind, when confronted by beauty?' Zandra asked. 'Don't forget about the virtual controller box that should be under the bed. We may use this later to try to play games in the scenario, so don't break it. I know it's virtual but it's still part of the program.'

'I'm so sorry, Zandra. This is really weird and incredible. The detail is fantastic, just like HD in 3D. It's better than real life,' he replied. 'All my limbs move, I can walk around and I feel great. Who is this girl? I think she's sleeping,' said Trepe.

'The program brought her out of your mind, so her name is anything you want, Trepe. Say the first girl's name that comes into your head and see if she responds,' advised Zandra.

Trepe thought for a second. 'Marlene,' he said quietly to himself. 'She reminds me of a girl in school,' he explained.

The girl stirred and stretched her arms. She turned her head towards him, yawning, and suddenly realised that someone watched her.

'Oh, sorry,' she exclaimed, putting her hand to her mouth. 'I didn't mean to be rude. You're not boring me...'

Trepe then remembered his one and only conversation with Marlene. It ended something like, *'surely you don't think I'd go out with a sad boring git like you, Peter...'*

'Men like you turn me on. Your biceps look so muscular in that tight jumper, Trepe. Why don't you take it off to let me see you properly? You must have been working out loads, since I last saw you a few years back,' she said and smiled.

Trepe turned around to look for the male hunk that must be standing behind him but found no one. He looked back at her, pointing at his chest. 'You mean me?' he asked, closely scanning her features.

It had been several years since he had last seen Marlene. This woman looked similar to how he remembered her but the hair had grown and gained highlights; gone were the school skirt and blouse and her body now had womanly curves.

'Of course I mean you, silly. I know that I ignored you in school but just think 'girly phase.' I'm a woman now, a quite experienced one at that and I need to say sorry in the only way that you want...' she said, standing up from the bed with arms akimbo.

'You look like you mean business. It's Marlene, isn't it?' he asked and then suddenly remembering his shyness, looking back down at the floor.

'In the flesh,' answered the girl. 'Still as shy as the last time we met, eh?'

Trepe raised his head, 'Marlene, do you know where we are?'

'In my bedroom, Trepe and you're about to lose your virginity,' she answered, turning away from him and starting to unhook her orange bra.

'And I'm Trepe, someone you know? And I'm erm... muscular?' he asked.

'Stop asking stupid questions and get under the duvet. Clothes off first,' she answered.

Trepe watched her as she tossed her bra to one side. Marlene's back had a faint horizontal pale line drawn onto the almost flawless, tanned skin and as she bent over to drop her matching orange knickers, a similar white G string mark performed a sexy T-trail across her derriere.

The detail of the *Virto* experience amazed him. Zandra seemed to be correct, in that this lady had been concocted from his memories and wishful thoughts. Looking down at his arms, he now realised, though, that his own body still appeared as a multi-coloured, slightly shimmering form; quite unlike the female figure that had just pulled back the quilt on the bed and had started to climb underneath.

'Come on in, the water's fine,' Marlene encouraged, pulling up the duvet to hide her boobs, as she leaned against the headrest.

Trepe's promises to remain a virgin floated to the top of his 'things to do list' in his mind. It was quickly sat on and squashed many places below, by the sight of Marlene's bottom as she rolled over onto her side. The duvet appeared to be clasped between her legs and she playfully rubbed herself against the lucky material.

'This is how you wanted to do it the first time isn't it?' Marlene asked. 'Anyone would think I'm a mind reader,' she giggled. 'Get your clothes off then, stud.'

Trepe could feel his shimmering body shaking, as he loosened his trouser belt. He turned his head away from Marlene and whispered, 'Zandra, are you there? She wants to make love to me...'

The answer swiftly spoke out of his earpieces, 'we promise that we won't watch...'

'I didn't think of that. I couldn't perform in public, Zandra. What happens if I don't get a... well, virtual hard on?' he asked.

'Just imagine and you'll find a way. Marlene sees a hunk, so be one,' encouraged Zandra. 'We'll keep the helmet-camera feed recorded but unseen, until you return to the lab. Your vital signs will continue to be monitored but I'm afraid we have to keep audio, Trepe. I'm sure you'll soon forget us...'

'Ok,' Trepe replied quietly and turned to face Marlene who still seemed to be making love to the duvet. He started to remove his clothes and became pleased to see that his body had lost its multi-coloured sheen. Pete's arms, legs and most importantly his male member were all pumped up and ready for action.

Marlene flung the imprisoned quilt to one side and continued to lie on her left side. As the naked Trepe approached wondering what to do first, she put her right leg out at an angle and kept her left one straight. Trepe could see the dark hair covering her nether regions, his first real woman in close up, or at least she seemed completely real to him.

Marlene grabbed his arm and pulled him towards her and pursed her lips. As he went in for the first kiss, he remembered the helmet at the last moment and thought for a split second that he may nut her, before closing his eyes to wait for the protesting scream.

Warm, wet lips met his and a soft tongue licked the worried thought into submission. He felt his hand being pulled and landing on something soft. Trepe opened his eyes to see a brown nipple teat poking between his fingers. He moved his hand to squeeze the tender, motherly softness of the dark chunky point that contrasted so beautifully with Marlene's pale breasts. Her kissing became more urgent, the harder he squeezed. Her hands guided him into a sitting position, on her left thigh.

This had been something that he'd dreamt about; the only picture that he'd found in the sex manual from the library that meant all of the lady's body would be in reach, during inter-course. He gazed down at his willing partner below his engorged shaft. Her bottom, boobs, shoulder, leg and mouth were all available to touch, stroke and caress…

A hand grabbed his penis. 'Do it now while I'm wet,' commanded the owner's voice and pulled him towards hairy haven.

Seconds later, he had become a man and his latent urges to thrust madly were calmed and guided by a hand on his balls. He quickly learned that a painful nip equalled slow it down.

'Trepe, you are so good at this. I hope this is how you imagined your first time,' Marlene said, her breasts shuddering at each deep push.

Trepe reached his right hand over to steady the tender boob flesh and cleared her hair away from the straining ligaments of her neck to kiss the hot flesh. His left hand then pressed down along her back, fingertips dancing against the bony tips of her spine and then back up to grasp her shoulder. He could feel her buttock muscles tensing against his tummy as he drove deeper and faster along the last few feet of his virgin path.

A second later his vision exploded into a crescendo of coloured fireworks as his orgasm seemed to overload *Virto's* visual effects. Sprays of incandescent sparks blasted out from Roman candles, in tune to his pulsing shaft.

He heard Marlene's voice a few seconds later and again felt her hot sweating body underneath him as the helmet vision kicked back into life.

'Wow, who's a clever boy, then? Ten out of ten on the first go. Better not tell the little Mrs,' she said.

Trepe pulled out and Amanda's face superimposed itself on Marlene's for a second.

'What do you mean? This isn't real,' he answered.

Marlene grabbed his penis before licking her palm. 'What is this salty stuff, you dirty dog?'

'Zandra, is everything ok? Are you listening?' he asked out loud.

'Don't worry Trepe. Although we didn't expect those

comments, it's just the program self-generating the scenario by linking into your deeper thoughts. That's why we're testing *Virto* in different ways. At present we have another volunteer playing a game of tennis, in the other laboratory. The software now has to separate two individual's thoughts during periods of intense activity and is coping well, although I believe that you had a little interference at your climax,' she answered.

'I see. I thought that *Virto* had only one user during testing. There's another thing; your voice has become a little crackly and also I think that at one time, I saw my girlfriend's face,' he said. 'How do I close this thing down; we never discussed it properly? I'm looking at Marlene now and I think she wants second helpings...' he queried.

A loud bang in his ears made him jump and the room went dark. Trepe stood still and waited, his heart pounding almost as much as a couple of minutes earlier. He'd been warned that there may be the chance of a loss of transmission and to remain calm whilst the techies at the lab sorted the fault.

Five minutes later, he began to become a little worried. Trepe actually started to feel cold and remembered that the last time he looked, he had no clothes on. He tried crawling about on the floor to get the things that he'd discarded earlier but found nothing; no clothes, no bed and no Marlene. Even if he'd found her naked, they could have cuddled up together under the duvet in the dark, whilst waiting for the virtual cavalry.

A sudden crackle in his helmet speakers preceded bright lights being switched on in his room, and he had to initially close his eyes, due to the glare. When he opened them, he found himself back in the bedroom but minus the soft lighting, bed, Marlene and even the other furniture that he'd paid little attention to.

'What's happening, Zandra, the walls are back but not much else?' he queried.

Still no reply; he started to become even more bothered.

'Ok, so we're not talking. I guess there's still a communication problem. Well just in case you can still hear me, I'll start speaking the 'making love' report. To be honest, it's a bit spooky standing here alone. At least I seem to be wearing some fuzzy clothes at the moment rather than being completely naked.

Trepe started describing his transition from Pete to his virtual avatar and kept stopping every few sentences, hoping for a reply that seemed a long time coming.

Suddenly the wall to his left side shook violently. It appeared as if something heavy had hit it. He went closer to look and put his hand against the backdrop to feel for any clues. It didn't make sense why this virtual structure, which existed only in his mind, should behave like that.

A few seconds later, Trepe jumped back in alarm as something unexpectedly came through the wall. It moved in and out of his room and seemed to be depositing something which fell to the floor underneath.

The activity stopped after a few seconds so he moved closer and could now see the point of a little toothed saw. A small sprinkling of dust had appeared on the floor. It looked familiar to him but, before he could identify it, the tool started moving again quite quickly and he then realised that a hole seemed to be being cut from the other side.

Trepe remembered where he'd seen something similar. When he'd laboured for a builder, the chap had used one to cut holes in plasterboard for light fittings and similar things. It had a handle and the saw simply pushed through the material and any shape could be cut out.

It made no sense. He couldn't remember making his virtual room out of the stuff and there definitely shouldn't be anyone living 'next door'. He watched as the saw made a vertically downwards cut over a foot long, before slowly turning and heading off in a horizontal direction. The amount of dust on the floor definitely increased and he bent down to dip his finger in it. After gingerly smelling and then tasting it, he spat out the remains and confirmed his assumption of plasterboard. Pete wondered if this might be the start of another virtual game that they'd kept quiet; maybe a test?

He started to wish for a companion with him, such as Zandra. Even Amanda would have been ok at a pinch, although she would probably be screaming by now.

As the saw took another turn upwards, his only conclusion could be that someone had started cutting a hatch into his daydream. It sounded incredible but no other answer seemed feasible.

Feeling brave and he wasn't sure why, he knocked twice at the wall, 'hello, is there anybody there?'

After he'd spoken, he realised how stupid that would have sounded. 'Who are you?' would have sounded much better.

The saw stopped for a couple of seconds. There were two taps back from the other side, before the saw redoubled its efforts and turned a fourth corner; the cut now heading for the start point.

'Shit,' he said. He started looking around for a weapon but being as most of the room contents had disappeared earlier, all he found was the game control unit. He stood to one side of the opening to be, holding the incredibly dangerous weapon above his head, just in case a monster's head suddenly appeared through the hole.

The saw finished its cut and withdrew. A few seconds later, he heard a series of taps, repeated over and over; it seemed like a warning, an SOS maybe.

His thoughts were correct about the plasterboard wall. Part of it fell down, but not the bit he watched...

The hatch remained suspended in mid-air and the whole remaining wall crashed on top of him, knocking Pete to the ground. Its weight and flimsiness cracked it into several pieces, as it hit his head and shoulder. Even so, it almost looked like the lights had been turned out, from his forced lying down position on the floor under the debris.

'Sorry, are you ok? That wasn't the plan,' shouted a woman's voice through the board over his head.

Trepe wiggled his limbs, fingers and toes before answering, 'fine, I think. Could you lift it off me? I'm stuck.'

He heard a cracking sound as though more wall pieces may fall on him so he braced himself, but the weight actually became lighter and he assumed that whoever had come through had started to remove his prison a piece at a time. The sudden burst of light came as a relief, when the final section slid slowly off him.

'I couldn't be any quicker because I'm not a man,' said a figure, through the floating dust around him. 'I thought maybe all this game exercise would toughen me up but it obviously hasn't.'

He'd heard the voice before but it sounded a little muffled. As he stood up, he could see why. His rescuer wore an identical helmet to his own.

'I'm Daanma,' said the yellow lid and held out a gloved hand.

'Oh hi, I'm Trepe. Did we meet in the practice games, last week? I couldn't work out if my opponents were real or not. Nice to put a face to a name,' he joked, tapping the side of his own yellow helmet. 'Lucky I had this on when the wall came down.'

He wondered what Daanma why stared behind him and then realised the cut out hatch still hung in space.

'I cut this out to try to escape and to kick it through, but the rest of the wall caved in. This place doesn't obey the rules of nature. How did you get into my little universe?' she asked.

'I could say the same thing. As far as I thought, my scenario existed alone and I certainly didn't expect neighbours,' he answered. 'I thought my space ended at the wall, nothing more; I never thought it could be plasterboard. Why did you come through?'

'Judging by your lack of furniture, I have the same problem as you; the helmet seems to have packed up and I'm stuck in this machine or whatever it is,' said Daanma, 'Any ideas?'

'Not really. There's nothing here. Where'd you get the saw from?' he asked, looking over into her side of the now extended ex-bedroom. The main difference seemed to be a pale orange colour on the walls and ceiling rather than the pale blue of his.

'There's a tool box and some paint near one of the corners. I found it behind one of the virtual cupboards which disappeared. I wouldn't have known otherwise. Maybe someone started making some repairs' she suggested.

'Why repair something that's like a dream?' he asked, rubbing some dust from his visor. 'What did your game do, Daanma? Maybe we can pool some information to get us out of here?'

'It wasn't really a game as such. I had been presented with a set of problem situations and how I would cope. The first one being a locked door in front of me, and I had a set of keys. I had to get through and close it before a virtual dog reached me,' she answered. 'In the second one, I had to rescue a cat from a high windowsill.'

'How'd you get on?' he asked.

'The dogs pretended to bite me but it didn't hurt. I threw a chair up at the cat and it fell onto a railing underneath but simply pulled itself off the spike and run away,' she answered. 'I then started playing a game of tennis.'

'That'll be those safety protocols at work. Nothing is supposed to get hurt here,' he explained.

Daanma held out her finger. 'What's this then?' she asked.

Trepe looked at the blood congealing from a cut on the side of her digit and frowned.

'I slashed it on the sharp saw teeth. Did that wall hurt, when it fell on you?' asked Daanma.

'Certainly did, especially my shoulder,' he answered and rubbed it through his shirt.

'So it looks like we can be hurt in here. How weird,' said

Daanma. 'I wish I could see properly. This helmet restricts my movement and view. We might be missing something; mine has a tinted visor. What were you doing?'

'You'd never believe it, I...' he stopped in mid-sentence.

Their surroundings flashed a little and some furniture came into soft focus. The bedroom had partly returned. A pale Marlene lay on the bed, with her legs apart and indicated with her finger for him to come closer. He realised that his own body had also become naked again and he grasped his todger hoping that Daanma hadn't seen it. The scene flashed a little and he heard Marlene's voice speaking at a very low volume, saying, 'Fuck me again, you...' before fading out, as did the bedroom and contents.

When the walls reappeared, he saw Daanma looking down at his hands.

'No need to hide it or say what your project is,' she laughed.

Zandra's voice crackled loudly into his ears, 'there's been a glitch as you've probably noticed, Trepe. We're working on it and think the fault is at your end. I know we said that it may be dangerous to remove the helmet but our expert consensus is that there is no choice. We suspect that something must have come adrift inside during the lovemaking and need you to check.'

'What about the failsafe system? You said that there wasn't any way a man could become stuck here, in this virtual place,' he replied.

'I'm afraid that we seem to be still learning the rules, Trepe' said Zandra.

'So I don't suppose you know that the walls are actually plasterboard and my body can get hurt?' he asked.

'Wait and don't do anything. I'll get back,' said Zandra and the crackly voice link ceased.

'What did she say?' Daanma asked. 'I could only hear your half of the conversation. It didn't sound good. Hold on, she's trying to talk to me, now.'

Trepe watched her nodding her helmet and heard her say 'yes', twice as she turned around and twisted her head a few times, as though trying to improve a bad signal.

'Lost her,' she finally said. 'She wants me to take my helmet off in a few minutes to check for damage. I think they seem worried. Did they ask you to do that?'

'More or less, Zandra had to get her team to check something first. I guess we're guinea pigs,' he replied.

'I really don't understand this and I'm scared, Trepe. Let's do it both at once, if we have too. I don't want to see your head blow up or anything like that,' she suggested.

'If we explode, we both go together? Weird, but I reckon we'll be fine,' he agreed.

Trepe's headphones made him jump as they emitted a loud feedback. 'Shit,' he said, holding useless hands over his fully covered ears.

'Sorry about that, Trepe, just testing a new link. My voice should be clearer now. The first noise had been a test ping designed to bounce back to us, and make sure we had a clear pathway. If you find damage inside the helmet, we may be able to upload a reparative patch and bypass the fault,' she said.

'Daanma's isn't working either. How can both sets of headgear have gone wrong?' he asked.

'Daanma? Do you mean that you are not alone? That's impossible,' said Zandra.

'She's here, complete with helmet, in fact she nearly saw both of mine...' he replied, adding, 'she cut a hole through my blue wall and don't bother saying that's impossible again... Her room is orange inside if you don't believe me.'

Zandra replied, 'everyone here is shaking their heads. We have no idea of the wall material, or the fact that the virtual units could be next door to one another. Your experiences should be totally separate, although the results are fed into the same control room. Part of the program is self-generating, alive in a sense;

designed to learn and overcome barriers or problems. My guess is that part of the software made the surroundings from the mind of the person who fed the original material data into it.'

'You mean the programmer used to be a plasterer? Bloody cowboy, if you ask me,' commented Trepe.

'Something as complicated as this had input from many people, and it's not unheard of for little jokes or much more serious elements to pop up in a program when least expected. We obviously try to sieve out this stuff but it looks like a rogue element has crashed a large part of the system. Now that you know Daanma is also in there, I will have to give you her instructions as well, because that link has completely failed,' explained Zandra.

Trepe relayed the missing half of the communication to Daanma, who nodded before replying, 'Ask if we are in danger. Are our bodies ok, back at the lab?'

Trepe asked the question and received the reply that both of them were still unconscious, with occasional motor movement, as usual. Their vital signs had showed a few spikes consistent with shock but otherwise stayed within expected parameters.

'Ok, I guess that two blips were when the wall fell on me and Daanma cut her finger,' he said.

'Indeed. I've been told that her body in the lab is gently grasping one of her hands and apparently yours brushed your right shoulder several times, according to the medical observers,' replied Zandra.

'Well, I used to feel very tired after the initial virtual training scenarios...' said Trepe.

'I know but that felt quite different. You were physically walking and jumping etc. during those. In the *Virto*, you shouldn't even break sweat. There should be no direct link to your bodies, whatsoever. The firewall settings built into the operator safety mechanism have changed. The tech director thinks that we may be able to reset it, by getting you to take the helmets off. That will break any signal exchange between your real and virtual brains. There's an adjustment keypad inside, and the speaker volume should be just loud enough to for you to hear us. The settings can then be changed with your fingers,' explained Zandra.

'I thought that the helmets made us exist in the virtual scenario. Surely we can't be separated? I must speak to Daanma,' said Trepe.

She spoke before he could. 'I think I got the gist. We're in the unknown here, just like we said earlier. No one knows what has happened to our little world, do they? If it's already part gone, because of an apparent helmet fault, maybe it all goes if we take them off?'

'Or maybe we fix it and save the day? Not much choice. Do it together as agreed? Maybe if we get through this we could hook up one night in the real world? We'll have a near death experience in common,' he asked.

'Thanks but no thanks, I gotta boyfriend waiting and I saw earlier the stuff you get up to,' she laughed.

'Cool, anyway only asking. Real life relationships can sometimes suck. Hold on, Zandra's speaking again; asking if we're ready to take the helmets off' he asked Daanma.

'On the count of three, Trepe... One, two and three...' She closed her eyes and lifted the electronic headgear up by holding the sides.

'Fuck,' said Trepe as his helmet lifted.

'Bastard,' replied Daamna, adding, 'you evil lying devious bastard, Peter.'

'Erm, yes... I certainly didn't expect to see you here, Amanda...' he replied, worriedly.

'And you think saving your virginity just for me allows you to fuck machine made blow up dolls? We're finished, you tosser. Just get Zandra to tell us what buttons to press and I'm gone,' she shouted.

'Maybe we can speak about it back in the lab? Listen, Zandra's talking; she says look at the left side by the earpiece loudspeaker and prise open the small blue plastic flap. The buttons are underneath,' he said.

'Mine's open,' she said. 'I used my fingernail.'

'This one's stuck. Can you see the buttons? Zandra says to press four, two, nine, nine and replace the cover. Put the helmet straight back on and they should be able to reboot the drive inside.' He watched as Daanma carried out the instructions.

'I'll do yours now, you prick. Let me try my nails on it,' and she held her hand out for the headgear.

After a few seconds, she said, 'It's no good. The clip is engaged too tight. I need something to prise it open. Pass me that tool from over by the wall.'

Peter fetched it and Amanda asked him to hold the helmet steady against his chest, whilst she prodded the edge of the plastic flap that had become stuck fast.

As she did so, Zandra's welcome voice returned in her headset, 'it's worked; we'll bring you out in one minute, Daanma. Sort out Trepe and prepare for debrief with a hot cup of coffee...'

* * *

Ten minutes later, as promised, she sat on her laboratory couch, warming her hands on a cup of cappuccino and looking over at Peter, lying on the couch next to her.

For some reason, her feelings of anger at seeing him naked with another woman had subsided. The doctor in charge of the medical team said that she may still be in shock, after her virtual escape. She turned away from Peter as someone approached.

'We've tried everything. His life signs suddenly failed before you came out of the program, Amanda. Did you see anything odd?' asked a worried Zandra.

'Everything seemed hunky dory. Pete's avatar Trepe had said

that I'm the only one for him and we're going to marry soon,' answered Amanda, with a tear in her eye. 'I really haven't a clue what's gone wrong.'

Zandra shouted into the microphone, 'Pete, Mr Harding... Trepe, we've lost all input and visual from you. If you can hear me, check all the connections for a problem. We can't bring you back until you do.'

Trepe couldn't hear, the severing of his aorta with a plaster-board knife might have been the problem...

Mer-Maiden

Dylan looked down in disbelief at the silver stopwatch in his hand.

'Do it again,' he ordered the bedraggled, long haired blonde, who had just pulled herself up onto the blue tiled edge of the swimming pool.

'I could go even faster, if someone tied my hair back tightly and I took my cossie off,' the dripping lady answered, as she flung the sodden hair back out of her eyes, with a flick of her head.

'There's something wrong with this counter. You're six seconds faster than the last record set in the London Olympics' said Dylan.

'Only six? I'm getting out of shape then. Just use the time on your phone for a rough estimate, then. It can't lie. I'll do another ten lengths when you're ready. Look. I'll even sit on the side of the pool and slide in, to slow it down,' and he watched, as she effortlessly hauled herself out of the water to sit on the edge.

He noticed that the water seemed to run off her tall, curvy body really quickly and, within seconds, she appeared dry apart from her long hair flipped over her right shoulder.

'You've got that hungry look in your eye again, Dylan. See anything that you fancy?' queried the lady, looking up at him through big green eyes.

Dylan realised that his gaze must have been almost crossed-eyed, as he tried to unglue it from the orange swim-suited figure, half-turned towards him. One eyeball wandered down her cleavage whilst the other caressed her ample thighs.

'Oh, erm… just thinking, Morgan,' he replied, as he rubbed them back into place with the back of his hands and refocused on her forehead.

'I'm ready for you,' she gently reminded him.

He rummaged in his pocket, found his phone and began pressing the buttons.

'Hate these damn menus,' he muttered. 'I know there's a race timer facility on here somewhere…'

'Don't bother looking, Dylan. Just read off the time clock. It'll be accurate enough to show the difference. I predict eight seconds for this swim,' she said.

'Ok,' he replied. 'You're tiring then, I guess. Eight seconds slower than the record's still pretty good, though. Ready then… go.'

'Ha… ' she said and disappeared with a small splash.

* * *

A week earlier, the clock had turned midnight and Dylan felt tired. He had nearly closed up his laptop and felt ready to go to bed, when he heard a beep. A message popped up, saying that he'd received an email.

He would normally have left it but he'd just spent an hour clearing out his junk mail and felt that he had to keep it in order for one night, at least.

He opened up his in-box and looked at the sender, with one finger already poised over the delete button.

From: *DateMate*. Subject: *Message from SeaFilly*.

Hmm, he thought. *DateMate* is an online dating agency that he'd signed onto for a free month, a while ago. He'd chatted to a few ladies and even met one but the cost to join for a year seemed prohibitive. They'd kept sending emails encouraging him to join and he'd eventually blocked communications from them.

Dylan clicked on the email. He'd never actually received an introductory one from a lady on the website; it always seemed to be him who'd done all the chasing. He clicked the link to the site and logged in to read the message.

A 'Welcome Back Welshboy69' message appeared and

Mer-Maiden

continued, 'Thank You for signing in to *Datemate* once again. Please accept a free week and we hope that you will reconsider a subscription. Over fifty percent of our users find happi...'

He skipped the rest and clicked to see what SeaFilly wanted.

It read, 'Hi, I've seen your profile and you seem an intriguing man. I too, am very interested in the sea. I have a degree in ocean biology and currently run my own marine orientated gift-shop, in Haven on Sea. If you fancy a chat, feel free to message me. No limpets attached, X Morgan.'

Hmm, here's a girl with a sense of humour and a degree. Might be worth a few minutes of his time, he thought and sent a reply.

'Love the joke. I'm not actually subscribed to this dating site and only have a free week on here. My name's Dylan. I'd love to see your shop. Haven on Sea is about fifty miles away. Are you open Saturdays? I could pop over in a few days. Maybe we could have a coffee nearby or a bite to eat? Don't let the barnacles grow under your feet, Dyl X.'

The reply came back seconds later; almost as if SeaFilly sat waiting by the computer.

'Hi Dylan! So glad you replied. I love your name. Did you know it has links with the sea? My shop's on the little parade by the quay. It's called *Shingle Tingle* after that feeling you get, when you first take off your sandals and scrunch your toes into the warm dry sand. How about 11.30 on Friday and we could have a pub lunch at the *Mariners* nearby? XX Morgan.'

Two kisses that time, he thought as he read it and then sent a reply agreeing to the rendezvous.

Dylan then closed the laptop and went to bed in an unexpectedly good mood, feeling quite excited at the prospect of meeting Morgan.

* * *

151

Déjà vu, thought Dylan. He had the same disbelieving look on his face that he'd had a few minutes ago. Morgan hauled herself out of the pool smiling. The only difference being that he stared at his mobile phone.

First he shook his head and then he shook the phone.

'Are you going to shake me next?' asked Morgan now stood up in front of him.

'You, you... you're magnificent,' he said.

'I'll take that as a compliment on my physique,' answered Morgan, moving closer to him. 'You should see my six sisters.'

'Seven of you? Ah, I see. Joke. The Magnificent Seven. I'd love to time them,' he laughed.

'That would make you a seven-timer. That's a lot worse than a two-timer. It's the death penalty. I'll have to eat you,' she replied and opened her mouth wide in front of him, baring her scariest fangs before kissing him firmly on the lips.

Dylan yet again felt that chemical high run around in his veins and that curiously salty taste left on his tongue after Morgan kissed him. He closed his eyes to enjoy the moment and felt her arms close around him to draw him closer.

'Try and get away, weakling, or face the love of the SeaFilly,' she said, linking her hands behind his back.

He wiggled this way and that before finally giving up the struggle and saying, 'Ok, I give in. You are incredibly strong and super fit, especially in the water. I don't understand why you're not a professional sportswoman and similarly why you're interested in a nerd like me.'

'Ok, Dylan. I'm not supposed to but I'll come clean and tell you my background over lunch. I warn you now; you probably won't believe me at first. I'll get changed and see you in the foyer,' she replied.

Dylan watched her speedo-suited body walk away to the changing room. The rise and fall of her wide hips in the orange swimsuit cried out for his attention. He noted that she had the broad shoulders of a professional swimmer. Her calves and thighs were also quite large, as were her feet. If he'd read this description on her *DateMate* advert he wouldn't have bothered, but in real life she looked incredibly alluring.

Five minutes later, she met him near the reception desk, at the entrance to the leisure centre.

'So... Any ideas how I did it, Dylan? I didn't cheat,' she beamed at him.

'Not at all sure; you're somehow different. Hopefully you'll enlighten me at lunch. Shall I carry your bag?' he asked.

'What a gentleman I've found. I can manage it easily but since you've offered...' She held out her kitbag to him, with one hand.

Dylan took hold of the bag and a second later it crashed to the floor. A metallic clang echoed around the high ceilinged room.

'What the heck's in there? It weighed a ton,' he said, looking shocked.

'Well, I usually carry weights to strap to my arms and ankles when I swim to give myself a good workout. Still want to carry the bag?' she queried.

Dylan picked it up from the floor with both hands and lifted it up and down a couple of times.

'Must be a good ten kilos here; that's like tying a couple of bags of sugar to each limb and you can still swim?' he asked. 'I'd just sink.'

'Women are naturally more buoyant than men,' she answered, pulling the front of her blouse down a little lower and raising an eyebrow.

Dylan grunted as he took the weight with his right hand and walked through the automatic doors.

'How far is the lunch date?' he asked unhappily.

'Just a street away; we'll soon be there.' She linked arms with his left side. 'Your reward will be like a fairy-tale come true.'

Morgan started humming a tune, just a few seconds after they started walking. The load in Dylan's arm seemed to lighten. The notes contrived to carry him along the pavement with her.

'What's that song? I don't recognise it but I like it. It's really catchy but sounds old-fashioned,' he asked.

'It's been in my family for generations. My mother used to sing me to sleep with it. It's not a lullaby; it's a traditional song asking for a good harvest. I'll sing you the words,' answered Morgan.

She started softly singing in a style and language that Dylan didn't recognise. He stopped in his tracks still holding the bag and unaware of the burden. After looking at him in the eye for a few seconds, she turned and walked on towards their destination and resumed singing.

Dylan followed, unable to look away. His mind filled itself with her beautiful face, sexy movements, the strange foreign words and a story... such a strange story of shipwrecks, with drowning yet smiling sailors and hunger satisfied at a very special feast.

Morgan stopped singing outside a pub.

'Here we are, Dylan. Don't think I'd better sing in here. Might get chucked out,' she said.

Dylan snapped out of his trance. 'I, erm... What? Flip, this bag is heavy, Morgan.' He wondered for a second how he'd not noticed the hard work before unceremoniously dumping it on a wooden chair.

The crash made several customers turn around to look at the pair. An old lady tutted before she turned her attention back to her fish and mushy peas. Her husband, who wore a sailor's cap and old yachting blazer, seemed to eye them with a little suspicion.

'Quiet, Dylan, you're upsetting the natives,' she hushed.

'That bloke keeps staring at us. Do you know him?' asked Dylan.

'No, but sometimes I find that men of the sea are wary of me. Seems to run in the family according to my mother,' she replied.

Dylan pulled a non-understanding face and then looked around inside the pub.

'The walls of this place are covered with sea orientated stuff. There are nets, anchors, ropes, and oars; all sorts of things. What's it called? For some reason, I forgot to look on the way in,' he asked.

'*Seafarer's Arms,* and it's quite quaint. I always get a buzz when I come in here,' she answered.

'Even if the customers don't like you?' he laughed.

'Ignore him. Come over to the bar with me, to order drinks and look at the menu,' she said.

Dylan did as told and followed her, as she walked past the nosey couple's table with her head held high, looking as if she owned the place.

The bar-lady greeted her. 'Hello Morgan. I haven't seen you and the girls for a few months. How are you and who's this dark stranger? He's gorgeous.' She fluttered her eyelashes at him.

'Hands off SeaVixen, this land-lubber's my boyfriend. His name's Dylan,' replied Morgan.

'Ah, it's time, then. Hello lubber Dylan. What's your poison?' asked the bar-lady.

'I'll have a Scotch, Glenfiddich if you have it, on the rocks, please,' replied Dylan.

'Hush now. You must never say that phrase in a sailors pub. We'll be found out,' said SeaVixen. 'You can have ice.' She looked at him closer in the eye. 'You haven't told him yet have you, Morgan?'

'Just about to prise the clam open and allow him to see the pearl that he's wooing, Adriana. How's the little one, by the way? She must be over a year old now,' asked Morgan.

'At a kind lubber neighbour, when I work, Morgan. That's something you may have to arrange unless you find someone to mind the shop,' replied the bar-lady. 'Anyway, being as you're about to get spliced, may I suggest some special food to get you in the mood?'

'Why, yes please, Adriana. I'll leave it to you. Give me a pint of Mariner's Hitch and we'll be over at that table near the fireplace,' said Morgan.

She looked at Dylan. 'You have that mystified look again.'

'SeaVixens, land-lubbers and getting spliced? I feel like I'm in some pantomime. The Loch Ness monster will slide through the door, in a minute,' he said.

'No, no. Never been south of Grimsby,' replied Morgan, with a knowing face...

* * *

Dylan looked at the satnav for a second and laughed when a computerised woman's voice said, 'arrived at destination. Why Sy Op More Gans.'

'That's 'Y Siop Morgans', you English tart,' he replied. Dylan had entered a name for the end of his journey and had no idea that the voice would attempt to pronounce it. 'It means Morgan's Shop in Welsh,' he explained to the machine.

The map on the screen stared back at him silently and appeared totally unimpressed with his linguistic ability. It simply turned itself off with a bleep when he stopped the engine.

'Right then Morgan, time to see what you look like,' he said quietly, under his breath, as he took off his seatbelt. He realised as it sprung back up to his side that his hands were shaking a little.

'Go away nerves,' he said much louder and shook his hands in front of him, above the steering wheel. Dates always wound him up a little inside. 'I'm sure she's not a deep sea monster. Hopefully she's quite pretty,' he added softly, noting as he wiggled his fingers that they were now behaving.

Dylan looked at his mobile phone. Five minutes to go. He decided not to wait any longer and walk straight into the shop.

There may be customers in there anyway, he decided, so he'd be able to check out the surroundings and get a peek at her serving, before making first contact.

He laughed to himself as he walked along the short parade of shops. *'First contact'*... More monster or alien thoughts...

The window front appeared full of sea related gifts, as expected. He couldn't see through into the shop, past the display. As Dylan lingered for a few seconds looking at the pretty arrangement, with its shades of blue and green, he concluded that Morgan must be a creative type. Some of the things were maybe not quite the right size or shape but their positioning worked very well, from his perspective outside.

Tall shelves blocked his view to the rear of the premises, as he opened the door. A little 'ding' from a brass bell announced his arrival. He closed the door quietly and looked around. The shop seemed deserted with no customers about. There seemed no sign of Morgan either. In fact, it just occurred to him that if there'd been two women of similar age standing there, he wouldn't have known which one to talk to.

His ears were massaged by soft unidentifiable music playing from some hidden loudspeakers. His nostrils were filled with air containing a lovely scent, similar to that found in a candle or soap shop but more subtle. His eyes swallowed the blue-green theme from outside, which now had soft sunny orange mood lighting and gifts added to the display. He felt safe here, in a weird baby-like way. There was only one thing missing, a mother...

Something touched his cheek and he reached up to see what it might be, without thinking. He found soft fingers and quickly turned around to look straight into the eyes of a woman slightly taller than himself.

'You must be Dylan. Your skin's a little dry. I have a lovely seaweed based moisturiser that would suit you,' and she then ran her fingers through his hair. 'Maybe a little *Essence of Shark* conditioner would tidy this lot up. Nice dark, thick locks, by the way. Looks like good Welsh stock, boyo.'

'Well erm, thanks. I'm English born but my parents are both Welsh. They both had black hair,' he answered, trying hard to think of something to say. He'd been practising chat up lines on the drive over but hadn't planned for anything like this scenario. Dylan felt a little taken aback by this early invasion of his private space. He wasn't angry because it seemed very pleasant, just unexpected.

'May I have my hand back now, Dylan?' asked the blonde.

He looked down and realised that she'd stroked his hair with her right hand but he still clung onto her left fingers that she'd used to touch his cheek. It felt gorgeously warm and as he apologised and quickly let go, he felt a lovely sensation that ran up his fingers, kicked his funny bone, clicked his spine and made a tiny blue-green explosion just behind his eyeballs.

'Whoa,' he said. 'That felt weird,' and shook his head.

'Ah, that's the *Shingle Tingle*. Like it? I think that my shoes must build up static or something. In case you're wondering, I'm Morgan, by the way,' she explained.

'Well hello Morgan. I'm pleased to meet you. Nice shop, I have to say,' he answered, at last beginning to string a few words together. 'It's very welcoming, homely, feels safe and also feminine,' he added, 'I can't quite think of the word.'

'Well spotted. Your marine degree is telling you that life began in the sea and for many, it ends in the sea. It's a continual cycle with the ocean environment being home to the creation of so many living species. I call this effect Sea-Womb Chic. Imagine being conceived and developing inside a fellow mammal such as a dolphin,' explained Morgan.

'Oh I see,' said Dylan. 'I guess inside a fish would be quite different.'

'Most certainly; they don't have the same range of feelings or colour co-ordination at all. Apart from squids, that is, but they're so argumentative. Just like piranhas,' she replied with a straight face.

'Really?' answered Dylan. 'My course didn't do much deep sea creature psychology. It sounds fascinating.'

'It is. I once met a porpoise with premature para-psychotic pseudo-pigmentation caused by being thrown back four times by trawler-men. Even the sharks wouldn't eat her,' said Morgan, giggling.

Dylan laughed at her last comment, not sure if it could be a joke or she might be a clam short of a pearl necklace.

'Come on then, you must be hungry. I'll close the shop for dinner and we can go over to the pub nearby for a pint of grog.' She gently brushed past him, again invading his personal space, giving him another little tingle before walking to the back of the shop. His eyes scanned her body as she did so.

She stood a little taller than him and he checked for heels but she wore flat, black, sensible court shoes. Her clothes were layered and a little unusual but suited her. She seemed either a little overweight or possibly just well-built underneath the fabric. Morgan had a purposeful walk, kept her back straight and looked quite fit. He remembered she'd liked swimming in her *DateMate* resumé. She seemed nice but he wasn't quite sure about the fishy craziness bit, just yet. He tried to get a better look at her face, as she came back with the shop keys, but she spotted his gaze and stopped to assume a hand on hip, pouting model-like pose.

'Will I do? Have I cast out the first line, caught the first tiddler and earned my sea-legs?' She lifted up her skirt to show a shapely muscular calf.

Dylan liked what he saw. She had started growing on him, and fast...

'You're a lovely girl, Morgan. Maybe you can tell me more about yourself over dinner?' he replied.

'Ok boyo. Off to the *Sea Horse Pub* we go,' and she gave Dylan a firm slap on the behind to encourage him out of the shop door.

* * *

Morgan's view of all-things marine seemed much more hands on and from the heart than Dylan's scientific, evidence led, view of things. It didn't bother him at all and he always enjoyed a good debate. She had been shaping up to be great company and he felt glad that he hadn't just deleted her email.

He'd finally had the chance to see her close up and look at her face properly. Dylan hadn't wanted to stare before; he felt too much of a gentleman or maybe just a little shy. Things were different across the table though. He'd avoided the usual pitfalls of shaking the top off the salt pot, drinking beer with the mat stuck to the glass bottom and spraying hot juice from his Chicken Kiev down Morgan's cleavage.

Her features were far from perfect. The mouth looked a little too wide, the lips a bit too prominent, her nostrils appeared too flared and one eye seemed a little higher than the other or maybe her jawline skewed a little off to one side? Dylan wasn't sure. Each item taken in isolation could have come from a police identikit. It almost looked like the slightly mismatched set, had been thrown at a blank face and landed in approximate places. The end result though, appeared fantastic. There could be no doubt about it. He'd fallen for SeaFilly with her womb-chic and fishy ways but couldn't put his finger on exactly why. Neither could he understand what she saw in him. He shrugged his shoulders and decided that love really does swim in mysterious ways.

Dylan settled in his seat first and watched Morgan as she changed her wobbly chair for one from the next table. She sat down opposite him, with her elbows on the table, cupped her face and said, 'Yes, you have a question?'

This had been the second time that he'd sat in a pub with

Morgan. On the first occasion, a week ago, in the *Mariners* near the quay, he'd learnt a lot about her that day, or so he thought. She sounded highly intelligent and undoubtedly had a genuine degree because he'd tossed in a few queries and made some deliberate errors, in their conversation about long term protection of endangered sea species that she'd corrected. This second meeting allowed him to probe deeper.

'There's more than one question, Morgan. I've begun to really like you but there are a few odd things. The bar-maid at this pub, SeaVixen or Adrian... Adriana who obviously knows you, seems to think we're getting married. This is only the second time that we've met. You both seem to like me or my Welshness and why did Adriana ask if you'd told me about something?' he queried.

'Ok,' replied Morgan. 'Think of a lady to do with the sea.'

'Sea? Erm, Pamela Anderson in Baywatch,' suggested Dylan.

Morgan shook her head.

'Queen Elizabeth?' he asked.

She raised an eyebrow.

'The ship. No? How about Neptune's wife, whatever the name is? You know, with the trident?' he tried.

'That was Salacia. A bit of a loose nymph, if ever one lived. You're getting closer, much closer. Keep traditional. Think fishtails... ' and she gave a swimming impression with her hands.

'Hmm, mermaids?' he guessed.

She smiled her widest smile.

'No way; you're not a mermaid. You've got no tail, anyhow,' he laughed.

'Ah, you spotted my legs then, Dylan? That's good because I didn't have you down as a scaly-tail man. Look, here comes the Adriana special combo. I'll convince you as we tuck in,' she replied.

Dylan looked at the steaming rice dish placed on the middle of the table and said, 'Wow.'

Adriana gave them a serviette each containing wrapped cutlery and simply said, 'Food of Love.' She lit a scented candle on a small plate, made several silent magician-like gestures with her hands and then bowed to them.

'Is she casting a spell?' asked Dylan, as she walked away.

'An ancient sea blessing,' answered Morgan. 'What do you think of the food? Rice from the water fields of Thailand mixed with scampi, mussels, king prawns and of course, oysters with a Welsh cheese sauce. You will be mine after this,' she laughed.

'And that is mermaid food?' he queried, as he forked out a huge prawn.

'Well… actually mermaids are fiction. Just stories made and mixed up by sea-riders and land-lubbers over the centuries then passed down by the side of a roaring fire in a pub. I'm a Mer-Maiden. We have legs, swim like dolphins and have our own traditions. Adriana's another one but you must swear never to ever tell anyone,' explained Morgan.

Dylan looked at her serious face as she carried on eating. The fragrance of the candle reminded him of her shop. He felt relaxed, even though he seemed to be getting involved with a very strange woman, whom he found immensely attractive.

'So where are the Mer-Men? Why do you need a 'lubber' as you call them? How about a sea-rider, a sailor, I presume?' he asked.

'For Mer-Men, read Mer-Masters. They died out over a century ago, partly due to our traditions and partly due to in-fighting. We're genetically very similar to lubbers and riders. Oops, I've dropped a prawn down my front. My hands are messy after that oyster. Would you fish it out, please?' asked Morgan.

Dylan leaned over without thinking and hooked the slippery object out of her soft cleavage. He felt that *Shingle Tingle* run up his arm again. 'Flip, are sure you're not an electric eel?' he asked.

'It's a Mer-Maiden thing. We give off this aura when it's time to mate. Hope it doesn't hurt,' she explained.

Dylan eyes opened wider at the word 'mate'.

'Adding more to the story, I'm from the Mid-Welsh coast Mer-Maiden stock. I never met my father but mother told me he used to be a boat-builder. My name Morgan means 'From the Foreshore'. Did you know Dylan means 'A Son Born by the Sea'? You have a strong marine interest, with a degree in the subject, so do you understand why I've chosen you now?' she asked, continuing with, 'You handled my cleavage pretty well.'

Dylan laughed. 'Your swimming ability is so impressive and I noted that water seems to dry off you so quickly, like you have a slippery skin. I should have checked for webbed feet earlier.'

'Well spotted. We have slight differences. Generally hairless apart from our heads, green eyed, webbed feet when young but wearing shoes eventually breaks the connecting fibres, and waterproof oiled skin with an underlying fatty insulation layer, yet dry and warm to the touch. Plus of course the speed of a dolphin, underwater,' she said.

'And that song; you're singing in a language that I don't recognise? It nearly hypnotised me. Wasn't there some kind of mermaid who sang to encourage sailing ships onto the rocks? You mentioned a harvest song. Harvesting shipwrecks, maybe?' he asked.

'Clever boy; Sirens, they were called. They died out. We had a bad press in those days,' she replied.

'Well ok. Like I said, I'm listening and you may be a Mer-Maiden. What I do know, but I'm not sure if it's the food or the scented candle spell working, is that I really fancy you and I've definitely not fallen for a lubber woman this quickly.'

'That's good. You're starting to believe. After lunch, we're heading back to my flat on the quay. We'll continue your education in the bedroom. You can be Neptune and I'll be Demeter, one of his lovers. It's said that she tried to hide from him by turning herself into a filly and hiding at the centre of a herd of horses. I'm SeaFilly, so do you fancy your chances as

SeaStallion?' she asked, winking.

* * *

'I call this the Queen scallop, my lord Neptune.'

The SeaStallion looked up at the firmly muscled Mer-Maiden's naked behind that hovered over him.

'I will open the shell, so you may see the pearl, my king. I suggest that you use your royal tongue to tease and please my inner gem,' said the lady to the waiting pseudo Mer-Master.

Dylan watched, as the kneeling Morgan reached around to part her nether lips and reveal her lady assets. He wanted to reach up but she'd pinned his arms down with her legs. She held her shell-like soft frilly lips open, to unveil an engorged pink fun button just above her moist pink slit. He could hardly wait as the object of his desire came down closer to the tip of his outstretched licker.

The *Shingle Tingle* shot through his mouth at first contact and ran straight through the roof to his brain, before flying along his limbic system, direct to his penis. He then felt Demeter's hand on his shaft and jumped as the feeling ran back in the other direction, like a massive peripheral nerve short circuit.

'Ha, the stallion awakes,' shouted Morgan before forcing her mound hard down onto Dylan's face. Her powerful thighs pushed his head from side to side, as she controlled the direction and position of his lapping action. After a few minutes, he found it almost impossible to breathe, as her ample buttocks and thighs enveloped his face and nostrils. His pinned back arms couldn't throw off the fit filly, even if he'd needed to do. If ever he wanted to die during sex, now must be the breathlessly happy time.

Morgan's body finally tightened and she screamed out, 'Fuck... ' before letting out a deep sigh and lifting her rear end away from him.

She gently rocked above him for a few seconds and dripped

onto his face, softly mumbling, 'fuck, fuck, fuck...' before spinning around and climbing on top of him, face to face.

'Thank you Neppy. I enjoyed. Your turn now; this is the 'Breast Stroke'.

She lifted herself up slightly and with one hand deftly slipped his erect organ into her wet fanny and began to move up and down.

Dylan tried to push up to meet her but Morgan's size and position kept her firmly in charge of the action. She put both hands on his chest and began to pinch his nipples between her fingers, alternating with a soft circular motion around the areolae.

He began to squirm with delight underneath her. She spotted his enjoyment and increased her speed and force.

'Caress my boobs as well,' she ordered, slowing for a second.

Dylan managed to get his hands on her pendulous assets, without disturbing her grip on his own partying nipples. Morgan sighed again, as he pinched SeaFilly's teats and within minutes she viciously rode her SeaStallion, to the culmination of the undersea union.

Although his eyes were open watching the beautiful lady of the sea ride him, she swiftly merged into a vision full of tempests, leaping dolphins and flying fish. Iridescent clam shells and orange pink conches fell from the skies, to be scooped up by the crests of stormy sea waves and tossed in equal amounts onto dark sinister rocks and soft black volcanic sand. A solitary woman's voice sang an enticing song. The grey tide rolled back miles from the shore, forming a rock hard pillar on the horizon which just held there in mid- air, gathering intensity...

And when he could hold back the dream no longer, the Tsunami released, the valves opened and the ocean seed surged into the hungry womb of the sweating Mer-Maiden, jostling for position to be the first, the strongest, the Welsh champion and fertilise the awaiting ovum.

Another 'fuck,' issued from Morgan's mouth as she lay flopped on top of Dylan.

'Sorry about the swearing but undoubtedly good sex...' she commented, raising herself up on her arms and looking down on him. Her blond hair hung all around his face like a tent, tickling his cheeks. She moved back further into an upright position, where he could see a rivulet of sweat running between the cleavage of her curvy breasts. She held them in both hands pointing at him. 'Did you feel the ocean during the fuck? I'm like that inside all the time. It's the call of the waves. Mer-Maidens can pass on their feelings to lubbers whenever they like. Are you a believer now, Dylan?'

'I think you've convinced me now, SeaFilly. That felt awesome,' answered Dylan, nodding in an affirmative fashion.

'I'll know in a few days if I'm pregnant with a test but I can tell now, that I am. I can sense the mother/baby bond. It's a Mer-Maiden thing... '

'Erm, you're not protected? I...' stammered Dylan, trying to focus on the real world.

'Don't panic. For generations the Mer-Maidens have brought up their girls without the help of men. Quite Amazonian, we are,' she said.

'Aren't there any boys?' asked Dylan.

'Like I said, the Mer-Masters died out because of fighting and tradition. Lubber/sea rider genes only beget girls for some reason,' she explained. 'They're always cute though, like me. Don't suppose you fancy another boat ride?' Morgan started moving again on his extremely sensitive organ and then laughed as he pulled a face.

'No worries,' she said, as she plopped him out. 'You've filled me with an admirable lubber ocean. I have to go down to reopen the shop for a few hours now. Feel free to have a shower and we can meet again for a celebration in a week's time at Adriana's house. She's having a few Mer-Maiden friends around and cooking. We always celebrate a consummation. You just have to attend. It's a tradition and you'll be the centre of attention at the dinner table.'

'Well, ok then. I'll try. Seafood again?' he laughed.

'Funny you should mention that. Traditionally it's a special cooked meat.' She came back over to him, lying on the bed and stroked his cheek. The Mer-Masters never really understood. I'm definitely thinking of breaking the rules for you, Dylan, next week. How'd you fancy Asian or maybe Thai or Japanese?'

* * *

A week later, Morgan collected some of the empty plates from the dining table and took them into the kitchen. A sudden warm feeling in her lower abdomen made her touch her tummy.

'I know little one. Tradition is sometimes hard to digest. You've hardly been there a week and you're already complaining.' She put a pile of bones from the kitchen top into the waste-bin and washed her hands before looking around for something else to tidy up. There were several items of clothing thrown on the floor so she picked them up and folded each one before putting them in a large carrier bag.

SeaFilly went back into the room and looked at the happy, chatty, smiling, slightly drunk faces of her Mer-Maiden friends. Morgan asked Adriana if she'd like some more dinner.

'Why thank you Morg. I'll have another rib and some of the sweetmeat. You know I just love that new boyfriend of yours. Welsh did you say? I so love a Welshman, they're kind and so tender-hearted,' answered SeaVixen.

'So true about the heart,' replied Morgan, picking up Adriana's baby girl and tickling her little webbed feet until she smiled. 'I hope little Mari-Anna finds herself such a lovely man, one day.'

'I used to quite fancy having a child with a strapping German lad,' giggled Adriana. 'We all have our fantasies but I've heard the large ones can be very fat and cleaning out the oven after the consummation feast is terrible…'

Morgan looked out of the open French windows at the waves crashing onto the nearby beach, thinking about Dylan. She felt an urge to throw off her lubber attire and run naked into the ocean but resisted the temptation. She turned back to Adriana.

'You know that conversation we had about giving up the Mer-Maiden ways? I'm glad that I didn't and stuck to tradition, Adriana. And your fantasy? Fun, yes, but German men's clothes? They probably wouldn't take them at the charity shop,' replied Morgan, laughing and picking at some meat stuck between her teeth with a splinter of Dylan's jawbone…

Scent Sleuth

Jason stood with his mouth open. He waited with baited breath as he stared patiently at the pale skin between the shoulder blades of the brunette, who had just stopped jogging on the noisy treadmill.

The ensuing silence from the throb of the rotating rubber belt and the repetitive thud of the lady's trainers came as a relief to his ears and allowed his other senses to come to the fore.

The object of his desire, a growing bead of perspiration, gathered from the sweat covering the muscles of her soft neck. He could see that the dampness extended into the small forest of fine hair that had escaped being gathered up by the black bobble, around her high pony tail.

Jason moved closer to the brunette, who had now dismounted from the exercise machine. The loudest noise in the room became the heavy breathing of the tall curvy lady in front of him. He stood six foot tall and she seemed only a little shorter in her pink trainers.

As her breathing began to slow, he noticed that the fascinating globule had enlarged to the point where it could no longer disobey gravity and had started trickling a wobbly pathway along her spine.

He placed a hand on each of her shoulders. She smelt warm and sexy. Her back muscles tightened momentarily at his touch.

'Are you going to do it?' she asked in a low expectant whisper.

'In a few seconds, Liz,' he replied quietly. His senses were swimming in the close proximity of the attractive lady. The feel of her back under his palms fought for victory, over the odour of her exercise and the sultry sound of her voice and fast breathing.

Jason started getting impatient but there remained one more sensory input to add; the human built-in chemical laboratory.

He watched the rivulet travel downwards under the black

plastic clip of her bra, along the spinal valley underneath. She had well-formed vertebra; his mind's eye tried to ski a slalom between each miniature pink alpine peak.

A split second earlier, he had debated whether to loosen the bra strap, just in case it interfered with the bead's travel. A momentary thought of holding her large boobs from behind became extinguished by the sound of the lady speaking again, louder this time.

'Please do it now, it tickles,' she pleaded.

Jason didn't reply. He felt like a hawk perched on a high ridge, watching a solitary pigeon fluttering in the valley below.

A second later, he closed his eyes and pounced...

Liz gasped as Jason's tongue caught the advancing drip and she wriggled as he licked up her back.

'Oh my God!' she exclaimed. 'That's beautiful. Tell me what you taste, what you see in your mind and what you will write about me...'

* * *

A week earlier, Jason Hargreaves had been summoned to an urgent meeting at his departmental headquarters. Usually found in a laboratory with various animals, his job entailed analysing chemicals in what seemed to him to be a vain attempt to save humanity from itself.

As he sat in the waiting room, his mind wandered over the events of the previous day.

'Another fancy perfume that's reacted with a load of posh ladies,' he had said, describing aloud the light pink contents of a test tube, while he gently heated it in the crackling flame of a Bunsen burner. He then took it away from the heat, added a few drops of liquid from a plastic container and shook the mixture as it fizzed.

'We ladies like to smell nice,' said the woman in the white

laboratory coat, on the adjacent bench.

'I know, Sally,' answered Jason, 'but I can't see why these firms keep producing new scents. Each one ends up getting more bad reactions than the previous formula. Why can't we just use the ones that we know? There have been hundreds manufactured over the years.'

'Profit, dear boy,' answered Sally, 'and of course we women like to be different from each other.'

'Different is the word,' replied Jason. 'According to my report sheet, this scent gave one woman 'a neck like a lizard's skin' and another said, 'her earrings turned green.'

'Maybe the jewellery shop cheated her on the 24 carat?' laughed Sally. 'Ok, possibly you're right; there are too many chemicals. I'm working on a tablet that's supposed to cure a reaction to an emergency drug but this one has now been found to react badly with a third drug.'

'Maybe if she wore some of this Eau de Chameleon, she'd be protected?' suggested Jason.

One of their colleagues interrupted their banter by leading in a young chap in leathers, with a motorcycle helmet under his arm. 'Messenger for you, Jason; he says it's urgent.'

'Don't suppose when you've finished with him, you could send him around to my flat, Jason? He's quite cute,' said Sally.

'Jason Hargreaves?' asked the biker, slightly blushing at Sally's comment. 'I'm instructed to tell you to attend with a departmental director at nine hundred hours sharp, tomorrow morning.'

'But I'm on leave tomorrow. Who sent you?' protested Jason.

'Only Irene Bowden would use the phrase 'Nine hundred hours sharp'. Thinks she's still in the army,' said Sally. 'Bet you they've found another mystery for you. Can't wait to hear what you find.'

'Another one that's got some forensic scientists baffled, I suppose, like that Welsh guy who drank aftershave. Why me?

The staff members are already calling me 'The Scent Sleuth', replied a downhearted Jason. 'I'm going skiing tomorrow.'

'Just do as you're told Jason. There's going to be another round of redundancies next month, so be grateful. You usually seem to disappear for a week across the country, doing these investigations, so you'd better have the rest of the day off to cancel your holiday and pack a case. There's a fully loaded chemical testing kit in the attaché case by the fume cupboard. I checked it and replenished out of date contents last week so it's ready to go,' instructed Sally.

'Cheers, Sally. If I quickly write up what I've done on the Lizard Liqueur, will you carry on?' asked Jason.

'No problem, Jason. Hope you get a live one this time. They're usually dead,' laughed Sally.

'I wish,' replied Jason. 'Be even better if to investigate a pretty lady,' he added hopefully.

'And you can trap her with your overpowering knowledge of perfume,' said Sally.

The messenger smiled and said, 'I assume that you know the address. If you have no more questions, I will leave.'

'Don't suppose you need someone to help you out of those tight leather trousers tonight?' asked Sally.

The red colour returned to the young man's face as he turned and silently walked away.

Jason looked at Sally's grinning face.

'Can't blame a girl for trying,' she said.

'You're at least twice his age,' he laughed, 'and you're married.'

'Go on Jason. Get your stuff sorted, before I grab you instead,' laughed Sally.

* * *

Irene Bowden's receptionist assured him that all of his cancelled holiday expenses would be refunded and, with luck, he would receive two week's leave in return for his cancelled week's skiing, shortly after the resolution of this urgent matter.

Jason took a seat by the window and looked out through the metal bars. The green hills in the distance were quite at odds with the modern secure building that he currently waited in. With its uniformed gate sentries and twelve-foot razor wire fence, it could be mistaken for a military or important governmental centre, not simply a privately funded research company. The extra security appeared a few years ago, after a raid by anti-vivisectionists. The firm provided top quality problem-solving services for food and cosmetic manufacturers and occasionally, the Police.

He'd been working there since studying chemistry and pathology at university. In his time, the business had grown and many bosses had come and gone. Jason had stayed in the background in the analysis department where there had been little chance of promotion but he enjoyed his work and because the annual pay rises were reasonable, he stuck at it. In his spare time, he had developed an interest in writing and always hoped that one day he would be able to devote his full attention to the subject.

In the meantime, though, as Sally said, 'he had to do as he was told'. He turned to the receptionist after hearing an electronic buzz.

'Mrs Bowden will see you now, Mr Hargreaves,' she said, looking up from her computer.

Jason nodded and straightened his silk tie as he stood up. He knocked twice on the varnished maple door before entering. A woman's voice shouted from inside, 'Come.'

The middle-aged lady sitting at a large black desk in the fluorescent-lit room waved him towards a chair facing her. As he sat down in the matching black comfy leather chair, he wondered whether to comment on the weather or be silent.

'A most odd case, this,' said Irene Bowden.

'An odd man for an odd job,' replied Jason, instantly wishing he'd stayed quiet.

'Ha! Your report said that you had a sense of humour. Well, as you probably know, I'm Irene Bowden, formerly Major in the WRAC. A lot of people think I've been put into a director's position to cut costs and slash jobs at random. Anyway, I have read every staff member's CV and history, including yours. The other directors brought me in because of my manpower skills. Everyone nowadays, in a business like this, must have a purpose, a skill and a reason to serve the department. Your folder, Mr Hargreaves or maybe I can call you Jason?' She didn't wait for a reply, 'made some interesting reading.'

'Erm, good,' had been all that Jason could think of as a reply.

'Two days ago, the company had a file passed over from the Police to investigate. A situation has developed involving a potential serial killer, which they and their forensic staff cannot nail. People have died; there seems to be a link to only one person but there's no evidence. Absolutely zilch,' said Bowden.

'Why pursue it then?' queried Jason.

'Because the Justice Minister wants an answer; news of this case has travelled up the ladder and those on high are watching us. The Ministry of Defence has also been sniffing around,' replied Bowden.

'The MOD? What on earth for? Do they think that someone has found an undetectable way of killing people? Might put them out of a job,' suggested Jason.

'I guess that's why. The forensics suspect poisoning but they cannot find any deadly chemical or method of application,' said Bowden.

'Undetectable poison; now that could be useful for the spooks. Remove a few unwanted dictators?' suggested Jason.

'Or in this case, a few unwanted relatives,' continued Bowden. 'The person concerned now stands to inherit a large amount of money. The death of two people has put the suspect at the front of the bank queue.'

'And does the suspected killer deny all knowledge? And just says he's lucky with money, I suppose?' asked Jason.

'On the contrary, Jason, firstly, it's a she and secondly she's asked several times to be investigated because of the unusual circumstances,' answered Bowden.

'Oh, I see. Could she be playing a double bluff, hoping if nothing's found early on, to prevent any long term investigation?' suggested Jason.

'Possibly, she's a clever lady. A qualified but non-practising solicitor, who now writes crime novels, believe it or not,' answered Bowden. 'And I know that you dabble with that kind of writing. It's in your file,' she added, tapping another folder on her desk.

'I've been picked on purpose to check her out, then?' asked Jason. 'Don't suppose I'm allowed to see what else you have on me?'

Irene Bowden smiled and shook her head. 'It's all relevant to the job. I cannot think of any other staff member who could improve on the police or forensics result. You, Hargreaves, think out of the box and I judge that talent is needed here.'

'She's been psychologically assessed, I assume. No sign of any killer traits?' queried Jason.

'Apart from a taste for killer heels, she seems almost too good to be true. Her name's Liz Thomas. She lives in West Wales. Another chance for you to practice your Yucky Da,' said Bowden.

'Who did she kill or should I say might have killed?' asked Jason.

'Two brothers. Both were unmarried. They lived for years with their mother. Liz had met them several years previously, when she worked as a partner in a Pembrokeshire based firm and had organised the old lady's will,' said Bowden.

'Anything suspicious in the paperwork?' asked Jason.

'Pretty standard stuff; when she died, everything ended up being split fifty/fifty in a written will,' answered Bowden.

'No favourite son, then, Mrs Bowden?' asked Jason.

'Under the circumstances, probably not; they were twins,' she replied.

'And they both died? How is Liz inheriting from them?' asked Jason.

'According to Liz, and the story's been corroborated by several acquaintances of hers, they contacted the woman after their mother's death to go through her will and later entered into a relationship with her, initially platonic. They both had previous wills, which left everything to each other. Several weeks before they died, these were changed, such that in the unlikely event of both their deaths, their assets went to Liz. All two million of it,' explained Bowden.

Jason let out a whistle. 'A bit of a coincidence, dying together like that. Car crash, maybe?'

'No,' replied Bowden. 'In the same bed.'

Jason raised an enquiring eyebrow.

'Apparently Liz Thomas woke up in the middle of them, after a steamy dinner party and they were both stone dead. Post mortem said heart attacks, probably within a few minutes of each other. It's a bit odd, because both chaps were fitness fanatics and only forty-five years old. Rob and Dave Jones were their names. They ran a butcher's shop. Their house contained a gym with every kind of apparatus you could think of. Liz lives there now, alone,' said Bowden.

'Did she make all the right noises? Crying, distress, etcetera, over the death of her er... lovers?' asked Jason.

'Indeed she did and as I said previously, insisted on a detailed investigation,' she answered.

'Just like you said, Mrs Bowden, very curious; any other leads?' asked Jason. 'What about the mother? How did she die?'

'By being run over by a lorry after stepping into the road; sad, but nothing suspicious. The only other odd thing that's turned up is something that happened to Liz Thomas, many years ago. When she turned eighteen, her first boyfriend ended up in intensive care, after spending a night together with her. Seems that he stopped breathing but she woke up a doctor who lived opposite. He gave him CPR until the ambulance arrived. The poor chap spent several weeks in hospital and suffered brain damage. He's never been able to tell the story of what happened that night. Tests for poisoning were carried out at the time, although not as sophisticated as those of today. Liz didn't volunteer this information. It came up when the Police were going through her records. When asked about it, Liz claimed that as it's such a traumatic experience, she automatically shuts it out of her head. She also claims that she has never had a boyfriend in the intervening years, before the twins,' explained Bowden.

'So where do I come into this, apart from being able to add another angle of thought?' asked Jason. 'My fields of expertise are chemistry and pathology. Unless I find a box of dead experimental rats in the shed, where's the poisoning element?'

'Apart from death by sheer coincidence and bad luck, the only answer must be poisoning. We have to look, therefore you have to look. Liz has agreed to any tests or medical examinations necessary, in addition to any samples and swabs that the forensics have taken of her, the twins and the house. It's all in this report.' And Bowden passed a folder across the desk to him. 'In the old days, I'd have offered you a cigarette or whisky at this point but that's all banned now. Apparently animal rights supporters could use them to make firebombs.'

'I wondered why the guard asked me,' replied Jason.

'Indeed,' said Bowden. 'I hope you enjoy reading the Police report, all sixty seven pages of it. Most of the science in it is beyond me but I'm sure that you'll find some of it interesting. We're going to tell Liz that we've found nothing wrong and that there are just a few more tests and questions to wrap up the investigation. I said that we're putting our top man on it to speed it up. That means you, Hargreaves. Hopefully, if she's hiding anything, she'll drop her guard, if she thinks it's nearly over. What we're not telling her is that you'll be approaching it from the love angle, Jason,' said Bowden seriously.

'Er... how do you mean?' he replied, wondering if he'd misheard.

'Do I have to spell it out? Seduction... Sleep with her or whatever's necessary to get a result. Get under her skin and make her open up. Her story, her cover, it's just too good. You're a handsome man, Jason. Unmarried, fit and you have an interest in writing. You should be just her type. She's a little overweight and uses the house exercise equipment with the twins. Your CV says that you know your way around a gym. Get close to her,' suggested Bowden.

'I've had a few short stories published; nothing major. Is she good?' asked Jason.

'No publishing deal but apparently promising, according to one of the coppers who went through her stuff. The twins were also budding writers; another factor that brought them together. I've seen some of her stuff. A bit er... raunchy, in places,' said Bowden, looking up to the ceiling.

'I thought that you said crime fiction,' replied Jason, followed by, 'ah, I suppose you mean there are a few bedroom scenes?'

'For a woman who apparently hasn't had many boyfriends, she has a vivid imagination. In fact, the Police think that their final night together may have been a trial run of a scene for a story but obviously something unexpected happened,' replied Bowden.

'How intriguing... So basically, you've given me licence to woo, wine and be wicked with our suspect. I'm allowed to do any tests, take any samples for analysis that I please, to either convict or prove her innocence. If I like her, do I get to marry her? She seems well off,' joked Jason.

'That's your look out,' answered Bowden, laughing. 'You'll have unlimited credit for the time being but no Ferraris please, and just don't get her pregnant during the investigation. She'll probably sue us. Oh and be careful. We don't want another unexplained death.'

'That thought had occurred to me, Mrs Bowden. She's either innocent or dangerous. How will I contact her?' asked Jason.

'You have an appointment at her house, tomorrow afternoon. It's all in the file. Get your plan written up on the computer and email it to me tonight. I'd like messages at least once a day if possible. If you go quiet for two days, the Police will send in an armed team to get you out. I want you to make a different spelling mistake in my name, in every message, so that we know it's you who's emailing,' ordered Bowden. 'If you crack this, it'll look great on your record and keep the Police business with the company. We've heard that the privatisation of all forensic services is on the cards. This government wants to spend their credit crunch cash on normal policing and outsource the rest.'

* * *

When he arrived home, Jason went through his previously packed skiing holiday suitcase and adjusted the contents ready for a week in - sunny or not - Wales. Out went the padded jackets and in went the waterproofs. Out went the ski-boots and in went the hiking footwear. He'd no idea just what he'd end up doing with Liz and so amongst his clothes, he put in a few of his 'pulling shirts' and, remembering Irene Bowden's advice, hid a packet of condoms in the wash-bag.

After a quick shower, Jason sat down in his dressing gown and went through the 'Thomas File' at his desk. Many years ago a file was just that: a folder full of pieces of paper and photos, some listed and some not. Quite often, things would go astray. The odd statement removed for a favour, the odd photo of a topless girlfriend ending up on a police locker room door etc. but this file had become like Liz Thomas herself: pristine and well ordered. Everything also came copied onto a memory stick and five minutes later, Jason had it downloaded onto his computer. He had decided to leave the Police evidence folder at home and just take a laptop over to Wales. He made a point of hiding the new computer document away amongst his laboratory work records. The organic poison list seemed a suitable place.

Jason preferred the old system of shuffling pieces of paper around on his own wooden desktop, rather than flicking backwards and forwards via computer screens, although both had their merits. At least on the laptop, you had Wikipedia and Google. He knew that you couldn't believe everything written online but generally they saved a lot of legwork. Even so, he thought, it still felt nice to spread everything out. After copying the contents of the memory stick to his laptop, he avoided opening the hidden computer poison folder and opted instead to randomly empty the real file, over his desk. He laughed out loud when the first piece of paper that he finally picked up contained a story written by one of the twins, starring a lady spread out on a desk. 'Entertaining,' he said out loud to himself as he read it over.

After making a mug of coffee, he returned to his laptop and typed out a few comments plus an initial plan of attack in an email to Bowden. Next, he opened the hidden file and looked at the photos of Liz and strangely found that the more he looked at her, the more attractive and interesting she became…

Jason had an idea and rummaged through the random papers on his desk, based on something that he'd seen on the screen. It took him a minute to find it. As soon as he did, he held the recent letter that she'd written to an officer up to his nose and inhaled deeply. Amazingly, there remained a trace of perfume on it. He then looked at the signature: Elizabeth Thomas. A little shudder went over him; expectation or fear? He hoped the former and read again the twin's short story of the lady on the desk. He wondered if Liz had been the inspiration for this and decided that might be a suitably sexy piece to re-enact with her. Jason read it one more time and committed it to memory...

* * *

Jason stood at the blue wooden door of the dark pennant sandstone cottage. The entrance stood at the centre of the double fronted building and the garden outside looked in full bloom. He looked around at the flowers and shrubs. Some were familiar but others were new to him. Apart from the colours, the most noticeable things to his trained nostrils were the scents. He had been born with an excellent sense of taste and smell, which he had honed over the years.

He hadn't noticed that Liz Thomas had opened the door and watched him as he sniffed the air.

'Hay fever or enjoying the garden?' she asked. 'Mr Hargreaves, I assume? I'm Liz,' and she held out an outstretched hand to greet him.

'Oh sorry... Hello, please call me Jason. I'm just taking in the bouquet of your lovely garden, I'm not much of a gardener myself but can appreciate other people's efforts,' he replied and lightly shook her hand. She had a firm grip, he noticed, as though challenging him...

'Come in. I've made a room up for you. I'm afraid that I cannot claim to have had much of a hand in all those beautiful flowers. As you know, the poor twins and their late mother owned this place for years and all I've done is water them,' she explained.

Jason caught a hint of another nice smell as he squeezed past her, whilst carrying in his overnight case. 'That faint perfume; it's very attractive, I don't recognise it.'

Liz laughed. 'You have a good nose. I never wear perfume but for some reason certain men seem to think that I smell nice. It's a little embarrassing,' she explained.

'Really, I... erm, it must be my hormones,' he stammered, looking at the attractive brunette in close up for the first time. She looked every inch an attractive woman and a far cry from his mind's idea of a serial killer.

'You go upstairs to the first room on the right while I put the kettle on. We can have a cup of tea while you take down my particulars,' and she laughed before winking at him.

Over the next few days, Jason went through the events leading up to the twins' death. He discussed their mother, the wills, their interests and hobbies. All the time searching for a link, maybe some unknown chemical that they had accumulated, which had led to their death. He couldn't believe that this attentive flirty lady in front of him could commit murder.

He remembered Irene Bowden's words. 'She's just too perfect'. Well maybe, he thought, and she sure smelt nice. His nightly emails to Bowden detailed his thoughts and results but all were negative. He had taken water, soil and various dust samples before sending them by fast courier back to Sally for urgent analysis, again with no suspicions raised.

The conversation turned to dieting and weight loss on the third day and, after Jason told her about his fitness regime, they ended up in the house gym.

The array of equipment impressed Jason and so did Liz's enthusiasm to try each one according to his strict instructions. By day five, she had lost a few pounds and gave him a big kiss on the cheek as she hopped off the scales.

On day six, the conversation in the evening turned to writing and she took him to the study, where he looked over some of her work. He didn't have time to read whole novels and had to satisfy himself with speed reading a few chapters. She second guessed his motives and produced her original crime plot notes, asking, 'Do you think I'd make a good killer?'

He laughed, 'to tell the truth, not really. I think I'll be wrapping up my side of this investigation tomorrow. I can't say if the police will want to investigate further. It'll depend on who's pushing them.'

'And obviously they'll be asking you lots of questions before bothering me again. I hoped that it would be all over by now. I want to go away after tomorrow, for a long break,' she said sadly. 'Anyway, if it's your last day tomorrow, I'll give you a special surprise. Something to die for,' she laughed, before kissing him goodnight.

On day seven, he awoke to a knock on the door. Liz entered his bedroom with a cooked breakfast and cup of tea on an old fashioned silver tray. She wore a much more revealing blouse than anything she had worn before and a cream skirt cut well above the knee. She seemed to linger deliberately, a little too long, as she bent down to put the tray on his lap. His eyes dived down into the pale valley of her deep cleavage.

'Have to build up your strength for later, Jason. Today is your last chance to crack my case. I'll be in the study waiting for you when you need me,' she said, winking as she walked out the door.

After she left, Jason wondered if yesterday's special promise had been this breakfast or something a bit more racy... After quickly scoffing down his bacon and egg, he dived into the shower and began wondering if he should say anything personal to her.

He'd really enjoyed her company but hated trying to catch her out for murder. He then remembered the desk in the study. Perhaps the one in the short story and maybe she planned a re-run? If so, he could tell her of his feelings towards her.

'Do you like my writing, Jason?' asked Liz, as soon as he walked in the door.

She sat on the end of the desk, facing him with her legs crossed, showing a pleasurable length of thigh. Liz held a notepad on her lap and she had been drawing with a pencil.

'From what I've seen it looks great. I'm only an amateur author myself but I can't see why you haven't tried to have your completed crime novels published,' he answered.

'Don't you think it's odd that I'm being investigated for murder and yet I write about the very same thing, Jason?' she asked, looking him straight in the eye. 'Have you worked out how I killed them yet?' and she leaned her shoulders forward a little, enhancing her cleavage.

Jason smiled. He had an idea what might be coming. 'I really don't think that you did. There's absolutely no evidence, Liz.' He watched her uncross her delightful thighs and pull a sad face as she twiddled a pencil in her fingers.

'What do you think of this for a book cover idea?' she asked and showed him her drawing.

He looked at the roughly sketched spiders, toads and creepy crawlies set amongst a background of flowers.

'Interesting subjects; wouldn't put them on the front of a romance,' he laughed. 'Horror or crime, maybe...'

'That's what I thought. They could be clues dangling in front of you.' Liz held up the pad and waved it hypnotically in front of him. 'Whoops, I've dropped my pencil.'

Jason bent down to pick it up. His earlier thought had been correct. As he straightened up, Liz grabbed him by the hair with her hand and pulled his head towards her. She simultaneously lifted her skirt with the other hand and opened her legs.

Jason gazed at the shaven area and the delicate pink flaps of skin, shyly hiding the next part of the twin's desk story.

'Do your stuff, Mr Police Bloodhound, and then tell me what you would write.' Liz then leant back, before placing a leg on each of his shoulders and wriggling closer to the edge of the desk.

Jason's hands reached under her legs and took hold of the soft padded sides of her hips. She urgently tugged his hair and guided his mouth to the target area. Liz screamed as his tongue lifted away the covering skin, to touch her fun button.

'Go doggy,' she shouted, as he lapped away.

The natural scent of her body and taste of her womanly juices mingled with the warmth of her skin and the heat of his passion for her. Foreplay had never been so good. During the next three minutes, he felt as though he'd been through a mangle, as she alternatively forced his head onto her and then gripped him so tightly between her legs. At times, he had difficulty breathing as her curvy thighs and excess tummy tried to envelop his face completely.

She screamed again at the final high. 'Well done, boy,' and patted him on the head, keeping up the doggy theme.

Jason felt a bit light headed as he stood up. She grinned at him as he extricated himself from her sweaty dangling limbs.

'No, no, naughty boy,' she said as he reached down to undo his trouser zip. 'We need to visit the gym first to finally solve the case.'

'Ah. Er... yes,' agreed Jason. He felt pretty wound up after that close encounter and wanted to finish the job. The twin's story had ended at this point so he hoped the next chapter would take place in the gym. All that equipment, all those positions, hmm... he thought and licked his lips.

Two minutes later, he watched her switch on the exercise treadmill. She had kicked off her shoes and put on some trainers. They didn't match her short skirt and neither did the orange bobble that she used to trap her locks in a pony-tail. He took a sudden interest when she took off her dark blue blouse to reveal a plunging lacy black bra.

Now that he could see Liz's bare shoulders, Jason could see now that her clothes had been kind to her and that Liz had been correct. She carried a few extra pounds but in a sexy pleasing way. She came closer and kissed him.

'I can taste myself,' she laughed. 'Very nice, I think...'

'Indeed,' he answered. 'What's the plan, Liz?'

The curvy brunette got up onto the treadmill in her ill matching attire and said, 'you can taste me again. Watch my back, Mr Clever Scientist, for another clue.'

Jason just laughed and looked at her from behind as the machine slowly accelerated. The rise and fall of each hip in the well-fitting skirt worked on his lusty thoughts. He could see her full boobs gently bouncing in the large mirror on the wall.

'Look at my back,' she shouted over the noise to refocus his thoughts.

Jason moved closer…

* * *

'So you really want to know what that your sexy sweat tastes like?' asked Jason, standing still with his eyes closed.

'Tell me, tell me… But don't look at me, keep those peepers tightly shut. You told me that you were special, that your mouth and nose could detect things that other men can't. Tell me about the flavour, the scent, the individual components, the volatility; does it linger, does it change, do you see anything?' Liz asked, looking anxiously at his face before kissing him on the lips.

'Wow, it's not what I expected; which is salty washed out urea. Granted, it's salty, but not like table salt. Another salt; not sodium or potassium, maybe chloride linked but more like sulphate. There's definitely a faint metallic tingle like putting the tip of your tongue onto the terminals of a PP3 battery,' he answered and closed his mouth, to roll his tongue around inside.

'What about the other taste of me that you had before?' she asked. 'You know, from down below.'

Jason laughed. 'Ha, so very enjoyable and I have to say that particular taste is still in my mouth as well.' He raised his fingers to his nose before licking the tips, 'and not surprisingly still on my hands mixed with your sweat. It's just such a high. You must be stacked with lady pheromones.'

'I guessed that I might be. Anything else? Your ears or eyes maybe?' she asked inquisitively.

'You sound like you know something, Liz. Actually I can now see colours floating about inside my eyelids and the taste in my mouth is constantly changing. The chemicals from between your legs must be reacting with your sweat to produce something else. This is just wonderful. Why didn't you tell anyone else about this?' He then staggered a little.

'Whoops, you nearly lost your balance, Jason. Just keep your eyes shut and sit on the floor with me. Enjoy the moment and the sensation. It's so nice to hear you describe what's happening. Please go on,' she pleaded as she guided him down.

'Well, I'm feeling a little warm in my mouth but cool in my extremities. The flavour is constantly evolving. I've tried LSD and several modern designer drugs under controlled conditions, as part of my training but this is completely different. There's no way that you slipped me a Mickey Finn because I've been watching you like a hawk,' he explained.

'What do you make of the changes?' she asked.

'Strange you should say that. The way it's going, it's almost alive. Organic, I'd say. That's the best word for it. Ah; now my mind's playing tricks. The colours are beginning to merge into shapes like toads, beetles, spiders and flowers. That's weird,' he said, beginning to lean on her.

'Clever boy; that fits in very well with my theory,' said Liz smiling.

'I'm feeling a bit tired now, Liz. You're just amazing but I guess like any chemical high there'll be a downside and a headache later,' he replied. 'What's your theory then? Tell me because I think I'm going to nod off. Sorry, I often do after sex but not before,' he laughed.

'It is a theory of mine, Jason, but your trained observations have to make it the truth. You will next start to feel sexy then go so sleep. Finally your heart will slow down and stop. I am the killer,' she said, still smiling.

'Bugger off,' he replied.

'Denial as well; I didn't expect that. Well, you said I seemed special. I worked it out after my first boyfriend ended up in hospital. I did lie, I'm sorry. There were a couple of other lovers who I practiced on, before the twins; a girl needs her jewellery after all. Animals usually know how to avoid poisonous prey but men don't. I'm like those toads in your vision or deadly night-shade or a bad tasting caterpillar. I produce secretions that combine to form an organic poison that breaks down quickly afterwards. Like a tarantula, I kill my lovers,' she said. 'Cue the sexy stage…'

Jason finally opened his eyes. 'Don't arse about Lizzy. Just squash me into those gorgeous boobs,' he whispered.

She tutted and undid her bra before suffocating the remaining spark of life out of the man who nearly solved the undetectable poison case…

Venus

Rob nuzzled his head between the new girl's pert breasts. He looked up at her face, to see if the expression had changed but she continued to stare fixedly at the wall behind him.

'Playing hard to get, eh?' he said softly and placed a hand over her hard left nipple and tweaked it.

The blonde remained cold and expressionless, so he persisted and put his hand between the topless woman's legs. She had no knickers on and he found her nether regions straight away, under her short tartan skirt.

'Don't worry, now, honey. Just relax. This is part of the interview,' soothed Rob and he pressed his fingers further into her perfectly formed, smooth crotch hoping for a response.

He heard a knock at the door and a blue uniformed woman entered.

'Bring her in now. I've found her clothes,' she said, grinning at him.

Rob carefully lifted his interviewee up over his shoulder and slowly walked towards the doorway. 'She's still not talking, Rose,' he said.

'I'd slap you, if you ever tried that with me, Rob,' replied Rose. 'I know you're the boss but that's no way to treat a lady, even if she is going to work here. What's her name?'

Rob carefully allowed the girl to stand on her feet in the next room. He noted that she still ignored his gaze. Rose pulled her skirt down to cover her naked bottom and picked up a red blouse from the floor.

The manager bent down and, as he did so, ran his hand over the girl's shapely calf.

'She's called Venus,' he said to Rose.

'How do you know?' she asked. 'You said that she wasn't talking, poor girl, she must be cold,' added Rose, helping her with the blouse.

'It's carved into her foot like all the mannequins,' he said laughing…

* * *

'It's ready now to check, boss,' shouted a chubby girl assistant, from across the shop floor.

The manager, Robert Mills, pressed a few buttons on the electronic till before taking out the master key and hooking it by the chain back into his pocket.

'Sorry about that, madam. The coat had been wrongly labelled. It'll show as a cancelled item on your till receipt. Carry on Tracey, and don't charge for the bag.'

He walked over quickly to the main entrance and waited on the mat under the hot air from the door curtain, before going outside and standing on the edge of the pavement. He looked to his side briefly, before crossing, to see Venus staring in his direction.

He smiled as he traversed the stationary traffic. 'Now she looks at me,' he said quietly to himself.

When he reached the other side, his view across to the shop had been blocked by a bus. He had to be content with a row of bored faces judging him and a cat-food advert saying, 'good for your pussy', on which someone had drawn a large erect penis.

As the well-endowed member pulled away, followed by a couple of cars, he began to see the shop front through the dissipating cloud of diesel fumes. Summer had arrived and the revised window display had been filled up with long legged, short skirted, female dummies.

Tartan had yet again made a fashion comeback, combined with strong reds. Rob wasn't too fond of the new look, when pictures of the range had appeared in his email box, sent from head office but, at this distance, he admitted to himself that it certainly looked an attention grabber.

The window dressers had come up with an attractive display but he felt a little sad that he'd had to avoid using his favourite mannequin Gloria. She had been in the window for three years, wearing everything from tennis gear to hacking jackets and jodhpurs. The problem being that she had become a permanent redhead since falling over and breaking her nose over a year ago. The trainee who had repaired her with superglue hadn't realised that the wigs were interchangeable and reattached her ginger bob on a long term basis. Her red hair looked a total colour clash with tartan.

Venus seemed to be watching him again. The girls must have moved her when the bus blocked his view, he thought, because she had faced to the side when he noticed her as he crossed the road.

Rob waved over to Rose standing in the window and pointed at the lady that he'd recently carried and motioned to turn her position sideways. He watched her lift up the model, wipe her nose with a tissue and place a small green beret on the blonde's head.

He gave the thumbs up sign from across the road and ran back through a gap in the traffic. A kid on a bike shot across in front of him so he had to stop quickly in his tracks as he reached the shop pavement. Rob had decided to go back inside and have his mid afternoon tea break, but after the near collision changed his mind and took the opportunity to have one more view of the summer range from outside.

The shop had its main entrance situated to the right, as looked at from the front. He would have preferred a central doorway as in his last shop, which gave two separate frontal display areas. The long display window in Alldroits meant that he either had to design a continuous theme, fine at Christmas, or carefully arrange two or three groups that didn't clash with one another. This time he had decided on a summer fashion show, running from one end to the other.

Rob went over to the left side of the shop and walked in the direction of the front door, with the poise of a sergeant major inspecting his assembled ranks, prior to a wartime campaign. He had his hands clasped behind his back, for fear he would attempt to reach through the glass to adjust a collar or sleeve on one of his female troops.

When satisfied that the display looked all in order, he took one more look at the new girl in her matching skirt and jacket, as she stood behind the glass by the entrance. He noted that her gaze seemed just right to catch a customer's eye. Rob blew the blonde a kiss. Venus had turned out to be a good buy from an Internet auction site. For some reason, she had been listed under astronomy. Rob laughed to himself and hoped that she'd help take his sales to the moon and back. The only thing that he didn't like had been the fact that the maker had designed her so that two fingers of her right hand almost looked crossed. He'd have a job fitting winter gloves on her in a few months but never mind, he thought, there's always mittens.

The afternoon passed quickly and he looked nicely surprised at cashing up time, when Rose informed him that takings were up, especially in the last few hours, and that several Venus-style jackets had sold.

'Good girl,' he said to Venus, on his rounds before locking up the premises. He always liked to be the last staff member to leave, unless it had been a holiday and the deputy sales manager stepped in. The usual routine consisted of a walk around each section of the two floored sales area in order to make sure non-essential electrical items were turned off, but leaving a few low wattage display bulbs lit up to tease passers-by. He would then set the alarm and drive home, sometimes via the local inn.

Rob always looked forward to his pub nights, especially since his last girlfriend had left him six months previously. There were usually a few stray women lurking in some corner of the hostelry and he kept hoping that he might find his next conquest sitting at one of the sticky wooden tables. The drinking night varied because of the shift pattern and this week's fell on a Saturday.

He stood at the rear exit and pressed the remote control to unlock his car doors. The bulb had blown in the security flood-light above the yard where he had parked, but doing this turned on the courtesy lamp inside the vehicle, making it easy to find because the car park turned pretty dark on a cloudy night.

A sound inside the shop made him stop. He listened for a second and heard it again. It reminded him of a woman's footsteps, a bit like heels on a tiled floor. Rob waited and the sound stopped. He debated whether the air conditioning heating system had made a noise whilst cooling down, but remembered that, on two previous occasions, there had been a lock in.

The first time, he had been greeted by a howling cat scooting out between his legs after crapping on the floor of the children's clothes section. For a few hours after opening, the staff had been giving every mother and toddler dirty looks until Rose had finally skidded on the problem. On the second occasion, he had been called in by the police late in the evening after two fourteen year olds had hidden in a camping display for a dare. He thought the mother would have been grateful for the rescue but he'd ended up being chased around the car park whilst she swung at him with her handbag, shouting, 'kidnapper.'

Rob didn't fancy meeting Tiddles or Mrs Thatcher again so, just in case, he turned on the first inner light and went back inside. As he reached the escalator, he shouted, 'if it's you two boys from last month, I've already called the police and they're taking you straight to the station as it's your second offence...'

He waited ten seconds, 'and if it's you Tiddles, I have a shotgun...'

A clatter by the exit drew his attention and he ran towards the door. He looked outside and everything appeared ok in the gloom. The car interior light had stayed on and he couldn't hear the sound of any escaping little boy's shoes.

'Bloody cat,' he cursed, and resumed his locking up routine. As he walked over to the car, jingling the shop keys, he wondered for a second about the car light still being on. Maybe he'd have to get it checked because it usually lit up for about a minute before fading out, he thought. This faffing about must have taken longer than that.

As he pulled away into the traffic, he drove past the window display and tried to look back over his shoulder, in order to see his prize mode, but left it too late. The other summer girls watched him drive by. 'I think we're going to be happy together, Venus,' he said, as he turned on the radio. The announcer continued, 'And the next track is *Turn to Stone* by ELO.'

Rob parked his car outside the house and had to run inside to go to the loo. As he relieved himself in the downstairs cloakroom, he heard a voice, 'Mr Mills... Robert... I took in a parcel for you.'

He zipped himself up, had a cursory hand-wash and looked out into the hall corridor. 'Hello, Mrs Sanders. You almost caught me short,' he laughed. 'It looks like the postman has delivered the book I ordered, whilst I went to work; just typical. Thanks for looking after it.'

'That's ok, erm... Robert. On your own?' she asked, trying to look past him, as she handed the parcel over.

'Yes, as usual. I'm going to nip around The Three Crowns for a couple or more pints now. Will your husband be over later?' he asked, slowly closing the door.

'I'll tell him you'll be there,' she replied, 'if you need any condoms, just knock.'

Rob closed the door and quietly said, 'phew,' before starting to open the brown paper wrapped box. He hesitated to guess as to why Mrs Sanders thought he might strike lucky tonight. The covering put up little resistance to a kitchen knife, neither did the cardboard underneath, and within a minute he leafed through a book about Roman mythology.

He'd had an interest in this subject since his schooldays and the discovery, plus winning, of the Venus mannequin in the Internet auction, made him look further so he had picked up a second-hand copy of an old guide.

The dusty old book seemed a relic in itself. He sat down at the kitchen table and turned to V for Venus. It read, 'Goddess of Love and Eroticism. She may present her true self in unexpected form. Listen to her words, for she will protect you from your own folly'.

'Huh,' Rob said to himself, 'maybe I should have asked her about going to the pub and getting stoned?' He locked up and walked the short distance *to The Three Crowns* and soon supped at his first pint of the night.

* * *

The next day, he woke with a very dry mouth. It always felt like that after a drinking session. The dryness seemed to be related to the number of packets of peanuts that he'd scoffed, as well as the units of alcohol.

Rob rolled over and hit his nose on something soft. He opened his eyes and felt surprised to find a woman lying next to him. Her eyes were closed and the mascara smudged. She snored gently.

He reached out with his left hand to touch her bare shoulder and moved his fingers along to her back. At first he thought he had been dreaming but the slight throb in his head told him that Sunday morning had arrived.

The woman felt so delicately soft. He took his hand away and stroked his right forearm. His own hairs felt so rough in comparison to her skin, he thought. She hadn't stirred and he just had to touch her again so he placed his palm on her shoulder blade.

He noticed that her back felt cool to the touch, yet he felt hot.

In fact, he'd probably woken up because he'd become a little too warm under the duvet.

The woman had pushed the duvet down to her lower back. She must have been sleeping on her tummy for a while, he decided. That's why her soft back felt so deliciously cool to his touch. Her face rested in the crook of her forearm with her left cheek looking a bit squashed. The nostrils moved a little as she quietly slumbered.

The temptation to touch her a little more became overwhelming. He moved his hand further across and felt the vertebrae in the dip of her spine. His fingers followed the track further down to the small of her back.

The duvet blocked his path here. He snuck under it and moved his fingers from side to side and found the paired dimples of the lower back. He rubbed the bones underneath. His touch went back to the middle and traced the centre path back down to the dip of her tail bone. They lingered here for a couple of seconds, gently massaging the hard bump under the soft skin. He loved this area of a lady. He lowered his palm onto the top of her right buttock. It felt much warmer than her back. He gave it a gentle squeeze.

A flicker of a smile crossed her face but the breathing remained the same. He moved his hand over, onto her left buttock and gave it the same treatment. The smile broadened and one eye opened. 'Hi,' mumbled a low voice.

'Pleased to meet you,' he said. 'I hope that I didn't do anything wrong just then...'

'Your touch is very nice and gentle,' she replied. 'Any chance of a drink? I feel like I've been asleep a few thousand years.'

'Ok. Just give me a few minutes to get a brew on. Hope you don't mind seeing me naked because I have to get out of the bed now?' he asked.

'I won't look,' she lied and laughed, keeping one eye open.

* * *

The kettle finally boiled and clicked itself off. Rob had busied himself by taking a couple of ibuprofen and drinking a glass of water. He racked his brains to remember who the blonde could be and just how he'd got her into bed. Her name remained a mystery as well as her face, although he'd only really seen one side of it earlier.

Now that the water had boiled, he reached up to a kitchen cupboard and opened the door to retrieve a couple of mugs. He dropped a spoonful of instant coffee into in each cup and, as he poured in the hot liquid, Rob received a reminder that he stood stark naked; a singeing splash landed on his todger.

'Shit,' he shouted and jumped. He quickly put the kettle down to examine himself and after a couple of prods and tugs decided it still had life left in it. His mind then wandered to the pretty lady upstairs and had he notched the bedpost...

'Nah,' he said to himself. He seemed to remember collapsing just inside the front door after closing it. One of the neighbours ended up having a fortieth birthday party celebration and he'd got into drinking rounds with a large group.

Rob sloshed some milk from a plastic carton into the coffee. He'd not had a visitor yet who'd drunk instant black so, with a mug in each hand and a teaspoon in his mouth, he padded up the stairs in his bare feet. He didn't need any sugar; his last girlfriend always kept some in the dressing table, on the grounds that Rob always forgot to bring some, for her cuppa in bed. As he passed the top of the stairs, he saw his clothes thrown on the bathroom floor along with some woman's things, which looked familiar. His mind must be starting to remember, he thought.

The blonde still lay face down on the mattress but had now turned towards the middle of the bed. He placed both cups on the single bedside cabinet on her side.

'That'll be my first cup of coffee in years,' she mumbled into her pillow.

'Oh, I could have made tea. You should have said,' he quietly replied and decided to push his luck and placed his hand on her bottom again. It still felt as warm to the touch as when he left her to make the hot drink.

'Did you sleep ok last night?' he asked, fishing for clues. 'My memory's a bit hazy; I guess it's too much beer.'

'It felt lovely to sleep in a bed again. Modern mattresses are so comfy,' she replied, wiggling her torso against the soft lower sheet.

'So erm... you are satisfied with last night, as it were...' he continued and stroked the soft skin on her inner thighs from knee level up to her butt.

'I haven't had a fuck for ages. I don't suppose that you could service me?' she asked.

Rob's mouth dropped open and the comment took a couple of seconds to sink in. He watched her pull her knees up and away from his touch and started thinking that she needed a TV or dishwasher fixing and this had all been a crazy mistake.

She settled into an all fours position and reached around to open her pussy lips. He just stared for a couple of seconds unable to believe his luck. The blonde seemed clean-shaven down below and her wonderfully symmetrical female anatomy simply beckoned him in.

'A thank you for waking me from my accursed slumber,' she said, partly looking around at him through her uncombed blonde fringe. 'Fill me with the magic of your Anglo Saxon seed.'

'Yeah sure, of course,' he stammered and assumed a kneeling position between her soft open calves. He felt his manhood brush her warm fingertips, as they kept her delicate lady-lips waiting for his entry. Her right hand grasped his shank with a thumb and forefinger to pull him in deeply. It retreated to join with her other one, in reaching around and clasping his buttocks to hold him fully inside the beauty.

'It's been such a long time. Ride me my young Robert, as hard as the warrior Bellerophon rides my steed Pegasus, in the heavens...' she shouted, lifting her head and placing her hands on the metal bedstead.

Rob needed no more encouragement and spurred on by the unusual but somehow appropriate language, took hold of her hips and began the most exciting, doggy style fuck of his life. A few minutes later he drove hard for the final time and reached around to grasp her firm, hard nippled breasts and became almost deafened by her scream of satisfaction.

'Venus is complete, once more,' she said and rose up fully to her knees, before turning around to face him. She reached down and squeeze wiped his sensitive cock with her right hand, making him jump at the sudden touch.

'Have you been reading my book downstairs?' he asked, pulling away from her grasp, 'or do you like to be called Venus really? *Men are from Mars* and all that?'

The blonde climbed off the bed and he noticed that her pubic hair had been shaved into a slender V, the base pointing to her clitoris.

'Goddess of love and eroticism,' she replied, quoting from his dusty book.

He followed her into the bathroom and watched her wipe away the escaping man juice. His eyes wandered onto the pile of discarded clothes that he'd passed earlier.

'Your jacket and skirt are the same as the new stuff that we put on display yesterday. You must have bought them in the afternoon. I thought I recognised your face.' He bent down to sort out her things from his and finally handed a pile to her.

'You're the same size as the model and her name is Venus. That's odd though, I'm sure that we had only one size eight jacket and we had to order more...'

He instantly looked back at her smiling face, as the weird conclusion dawned on him.

'Have I just fucked a dummy?'

* * *

'Look Venus, I just can't believe this,' said Rob, sitting naked on a wooden chair by the kitchen table. 'Zeus cursed you and a few others for millennia, when he found you teasing his dog, Sirius. That's a bit harsh, isn't it?' he asked.

'Well, we were encouraging Hercules to stretch him to twice his normal size…' admitted the blonde, now fully dressed, in Venus mannequin style.

'Huh, you are a dead ringer for my model. Shall we call her Venus A for the purpose of this conversation?' he asked. 'Have you any identification?'

She kicked off her shoe and pointed to her foot. Rob looked and noted that in the same spot as Venus A, this lady had the V word, albeit in a more ornate script. He licked his finger and rubbed the flesh attempting to remove it.

'That's a tattoo. It must have been there ages,' he said.

'Thousands of years…' she replied, 'may I at least be called Venus B, please?'

'Hmm… you have to admit that this is all pretty strange. Tell you what, I know that I'm always the last one in Alldroits at night and I still have the keys. If you came alive and nipped in my car when I wasn't looking, as you claim, Venus A will have disappeared from the window. Let's go right now,' he suggested.

Venus B answered, 'No problem, as you say nowadays.' She walked to the front door, opened it and stood outside. She patiently chewed at a crusty bread roll and waited.

Rob rummaged in a couple of drawers for the car and shop keys before joining her outside.

'This food, is it a bread?' she inquired.

'It's seeded batch. Now are you sure about this? You can tell me your real name and we can go back to bed,' he added,

hopefully.

'I'm quite sure, what about you? You've got no clothes on.' she replied.

'Shit, why didn't you say?' he shouted as he panicked a jammed the wrong key in the house lock.

Venus B slapped him on the ass after a few seconds watching him struggle and showed him the correct one. R rushed inside and ran straight upstairs.

'Hello, I'm Mrs Sanders,' shouted a woman's voice from o the hedge. 'Are you Rob's new girlfriend?'

'Greetings,' replied Venus B. 'He has filled me with his ba of seed.'

'Oh, I see... and you're happy with that?' she asked in re with a horrified look on her face.

'Of course, when he gets dressed, I will find my friends he can do the same to them,' replied Venus B.

'Well, erm... lucky man. I must go. You youngs nowadays...' and Mrs Sanders ran back into her house.

Rob came out of the house doing up his shirt buttons. 'I he most of that. Will you let me do the talking to people that I kr until I get to the bottom of this? Now get in the car, where I see you and we'll go the shop, Venus.'

'B,' she added, smiling.

* * *

The manager of Alldroit's face dropped, as he pulled up out the shop. The mannequin sized space in the window next to entrance confirmed his fears. Venus the summer model w there. He drove around to the rear car park and went in followed by Venus B. Rob told her to wait by the rear exit v he looked around upstairs.

When he came back down the escalator, he could see a Sunday shoppers outside, looking and pointing in the windo

must be down to the well-designed display, he thought, as his feet hit the metal grill of the ground floor and he became forced to walk again.

'Oh no,' he said, as he saw the reason for the small crowd. Venus B had reassumed Venus A's previous display window pose. Every now and then when the people turned, she would change her pose a little and he watched as she soon had the crowd in stitches of laughter.

'How am I doing, boss?' she shouted. 'Good publicity, here's the photographer.'

Rob immediately recognised Bill Trent from the local evening paper with his pocket camera. The man waved at him to get closer to the model and Rob reluctantly put his arm around her. After several flashes, Rob managed to pull the blonde from her stage.

'Venus with no A or B?' she asked.

'Seems like I'm wrong, you are Venus and we'll be in the paper. I'll have to think of a better story,' he replied.

'I can get you a new model, an even better one,' she suggested, 'if you save my friends...'

* * *

The next weekend, Rob parked his car in a small shopping centre in the next town.

'I can't believe that you're getting me to do this, Venus,' said Rob to the blonde sitting next to him in the passenger seat. 'How can you be sure it's her?' he asked.

'I've told you Rob, it's a goddess thing. We can sense one another up to fifteen leagues. That's maybe fifty of your modern miles. Zeus cursed twenty eight women and changed us into statues to display clothes, for ever. We automatically reformed to a newer form as fashions changed. Originally we were all together in one taberna but ended up being split up and sold. My

girls were transported to all corners of the Roman Empire,' Venus explained.

'I suppose taberna means a shop, maybe a Roman department store?' he asked.

Venus nodded, 'I'm the leader of the gang...'

'And you reckon that Bellona and Luna are really in this store and Med is in a window four miles away?' he asked.

'I pointed out Med to you on the way here, so you know she exists. I can feel their presence strongly and they're upstairs. I'll know them when I see them and their name is always on the foot. Zeus had us tattooed as a warning to others,' answered Venus.

'Warning... how do you mean?' he inquired, looking her in the eye.

'I'll be honest. Some of the myths are true. We can't all be trusted. There used to be a lot of debauchery, robbery and head chopping, back then. If you played your cards right, you'd end up in the stars, if not... well look at me,' she explained.

'I never asked, but how did I wake you up or somehow reverse the spell?' asked Rob.

'Although mannequins, we are completely aware of our surroundings. Hundreds of years, listening to shopper's chit chat, soon teaches you the language and customs. You had a very unusual aura that I could detect as soon as you came near me. Maybe it's your interest in mythology. I felt you at the first kiss and as for your phallus...' she replied. 'Oh, one other thing; I kept my fingers crossed when Zeus made the spell. Always do that if you're cursed; weakens the effect long term.'

'Ah ha, you had crossed fingers as a mannequin,' he smiled. 'Do you mean I might get to sleep with more gorgeous women?'

'It's compulsory,' she laughed. 'Are you sure that you'll be able to convince the store owners to sell?'

'It's either that or sex in the shop, with a live Saturday audience. I think it's time to live up to my sales manager title, Venus. Show me the dummies,' replied Rob.

Half an hour later, they were loading two lady models into the boot of his estate car. Both were brunettes, the slim one wore hot pants, tights and a T-shirt, the other somewhat larger figure had been purchased from the lingerie department and boasted a forty two inch set of puppies.

'Lucky I knew Martin the owner, from my old job. He owed me a favour and we got the girls for a song. Don't know why you insisted we bought the clothes as well, though, Venus. It's not as though they can feel the cold at the moment,' he said, about to close the rear hatch but for some reason felt a need to reach in and tickle the smaller dummy's bare feet.

'Even though they look like lumps of plastic on the exterior, my Roman friends all still have feelings inside and being naked is for the bedroom and bathing. They will be pleased that you paid extra to cover their modesty. You also sensed Luna's ticklishness, I noticed. You'll be starting to wake her up doing that,' laughed Venus, 'Luna is very sensitive.'

'Ah, so she's the slim one. That Bellona looks a big girl,' he commented as he climbed into the driver's seat.

'The goddess of war, and, between you and me, domestics, as your police force call them. Gave a few of her lovers a hard time...' whispered Venus.

'And you're going to tell me that Luna is the moon goddess and suffers from bad periods and lunacy?' he joked.

Venus didn't disagree. 'Quite a bunch, aren't we? I'd love to find Agenoria again, goddess of activity. Never still for a moment apart from Zeus' spell...'

Rob looked behind him, through the gap in the seats, at the two heads that seemed to be almost kissing one another.

'Don't even think about it, Rob...' warned Venus with a smile on her face. 'We'll wake them purely one at a time.'

Half an hour later, they were driving back and forth along a main road through a small village. The shops had been passed three times and as Rob slowed down to pull in by the side of the road he asked, 'Goddess sat nav not working, Venus?'

'It's difficult. Med always is. She's Greek you see. The Roman Empire absorbed various parts of the previous Greek civilisation, including some of their mythical stories and figures. She's like an adopted sister. My positioning sense is not so accurate with her, I'm afraid. We may have to leave her. I'm thirsty and hungry, is that a hostelry over there?' asked Venus.

'That's the *Caesar's Rest*, quite appropriate really. A Roman army camped here during the conquest of Britain. Would you like to try a bottle of Italian wine?' he asked.

'Nectar of the goddesses,' she replied. 'Will the slaves feed me grapes, like the old days?'

* * *

As Rob supped his beer, he watched Venus attempting to season her food by shaking a pepper grinder over it and looking mystified.

'You have to twist the top,' he advised and laughed as she showered grains into her wine.

'It's one thing learning languages and the ways of the English by standing in a shop and listening, but altogether another to live here,' she giggled and pulled a so-so face, after sipping her adulterated drink.

'I'll get you another glass,' he said and went back to the bar. As he stood there, he had a brainwave. Venus felt sure that Med seemed close and another use for dummies had crept into his head.

As he gave the correct change to the barmaid, he asked, 'is there anyone around here who does clothes alterations or designs costumes, maybe?'

'There's old Mrs Gosbert across the road. She's the person all the locals go to. Folk reckon she's a witch because of her collection of sewing dummies, they say some are real...' replied the woman, saying the last few words in a whisper and looking around the room.

Rob also looked around to see if anyone watched their conversation and then realised she had been partly joking. 'Oh, right, thanks for that,' he said, slightly embarrassed, and walked back to Venus with the good news.

'Med might be just over the road, according to the bar-lady, in the house of a seamstress. We can go over when we finish here.' He poured some wine from the bottle into the fresh glass and noticed that she'd drunk the peppered one anyway.

'How's the Italian?' he asked as he watched her down the new glassful.

'Refreshing, just like meeting a friend from eons ago,' she replied, motioning him to empty the remaining golden fluid into her empty glass.

'You know, I quite like you, Venus. Are you planning on staying around the area? I don't think Zeus and Hercules are around anymore and you'll need a roof over your head.' He could see Venus' eyes beginning to roll a little and from experience knew that propositions were best made drunk.

She put down her glass partly on a beermat and Rob had to catch the fragile item as it wobbled and attempted to escape onto the floor.

'This fermented potion is much stronger than I remember,' she slurred. 'I must have more Italian drink later, it is similar taste to the time my gang became drunk in Lambretta and we cast a spell to turn the villagers into little horses. I wonder if they still run freely around the countryside?' she asked.

'In a way, they do,' he replied. 'And your plans?' he reminded her.

'Roberto, your name has Roman origins. You have helped me greatly and still have the awakening of my two Roman friends to enjoy. I will have to leave you and I hope you understand that I have to keep our existence secret. You will be left two gifts. One is Med, who we will hopefully find and the other is the ability to stand guard over your shop for eternity,' she explained.

'Ok, so I get a new girlfriend and I eventually become a star above the shop?' he asked and smiled hopefully.

'That would spoil the surprise to tell you...' answered Venus, staggering as she got up. 'May I sleep a little in the chariot while you look for Med? She's easy to recognise, quite wild hair...' and she flopped to the floor.

Rob carried the drunken goddess to his car and lifted her in. He lifted up her skirt and did a quick check for the V, to reassure himself that he wasn't going mad.

The angry beep of a passing car as he nearly walked across the street without looking reminded him that he wasn't immortal just yet. One day, he thought, maybe there'd be a statue of him in Alldroits, to celebrate their best ever salesperson?

As he opened the gate to the cottage opposite, an old lady's head popped up from behind a gooseberry bush.

'Hello, my dear, have you come to fix my computer?' she asked. 'I'm hoping to see the transit of Venus that my grandson filmed in New Zealand.'

'Unfortunately not,' replied Rob and he introduced himself as a collector of mannequins and had been told that she may have some for sale.

'I don't usually sell them. There are more than twenty, I think. You're welcome to look. I'm eighty-two now and I can't take them with me. I've been waiting three weeks for the computer man, I keep ringing but he's so busy,' said Mrs Gosbert, sadly.

'Well I'll have a look at your machine first if you like. I used to be handy with electrics but I don't understand electronics,' he said.

Rob went into the room that the old lady pointed to and had to move a pile of stacked fabrics to get at the unit. He checked that the wall switch had been turned on and that all the wires looked connected but the grey metal box seemed dead and the screen blank.

'Looks like there's no power, Mrs Gosbert, 'maybe it's just a fuse, have you got a tiny screwdriver?' he asked, not really hopeful.

'There are two little ones in the sewing machine,' she replied and he watched her flip a lid open on its base, to reveal the said items.

'It's not a fuse problem but probably just a loose wire,' he said, after opening the plug. A few seconds later, the whirring noise of the hard drive confirmed his fix.

'You wonderful man, now I can talk to Kev in Christchurch on the internet. I'm so grateful. You can have one of the dummies for free, Mr Mills,' she said, excitedly.

'That's very kind of you. Is there one called Med by any chance?' he asked.

'Well, I do give them names, it's silly really. My old memory's not what it used to be…' she replied.

'Wild hair?' he added.

'Oh, wait a minute. There's one I used to call Me Dear or Madeira, with funny hair, think I named her after a word on her foot,' she suggested. 'I'll show you. Hmm, now when did I use her last?'

Fifteen minutes after sampling various homemade biscuits and promising that if he ever needed any trouser legs taking up, he'd come back, Rob carried the statuesque six foot lady back to the car. He awoke Venus as he clonked her on the head with Med's feet. The goddess turned around to view his prize.

'Bellona won't like that,' said Venus, pointing out the newcomer's feet next to the war-girl's nose. 'Our Med wasn't too fond of the Roman baths. Anyway nice to see you but I wouldn't want to be you, girl.'

'She's a pretty model and no mistake,' said Rob, as he got in next to Venus. 'She has a very dark complexion and quite spectacular hair. It seems attached unlike the others, which are obviously wigs. Just out of interest, were you always blonde?'

'Yes. Clever old Zeus and his curse made sure that if ever our wigs were changed, someone would soon swop us back to our natural colour. Med is different though; in real life, her hair seemed so alive that it became almost part of her,' she answered.

'And she's part of my reward. What's the catch?' he asked inquisitively.

'Kiss her at your own risk,' replied Venus. 'She will get you many sales in the shop. Back in the old taberna, the clothes that Med displayed would outsell others by ten to one. This girl is double cursed. Once by a Greek myth, and secondly, at our Roman stretch the mongrel party.'

'What exactly will happen if I got frisky? I have to admit getting a hard on thinking about waking up the Roman twins in the back...' he asked.

'You're on the right track,' she answered. 'Let's just say that one day, when I go to meet Pluto in the underworld, he won't have written on his list of wrong doings: 'Didn't warn Roberto'.'

'Only tricked him, maybe?' suggested Rob.

Venus gave a laugh and leaned over to kiss him on the cheek. 'The lips will tell...'

* * *

Rob looked at the three latest women in his life, standing in one corner of the lounge. Med in the centre looked the tallest by a few inches, although part of the reason seemed to be her thick mass of hair. Luna flanked her on the left, about five foot two, and the strongly build Bellona stood to her right.

'How about I give one of them a snog and pop her up in my bed while she's still stiff? We could have our evening meal and she'll be waiting for me when I go to bed,' suggested Rob.

'It's your choice,' replied Venus. 'I'm sure you'll have fun either way.'

He decided to toss a coin in order to choose. 'Heads, that'll be Luna then,' he said, after missing the flicked coin and chasing it across the floor. The shop manager ran over to the dummy and lifted off the T-shirt before turning to look at Venus.

'It may be weird but I feel shy...' he said.

Venus laughed. 'I won't watch. Is there some more of that modern wine in your cooling device? I think I saw some bottles yesterday. I'll go and have a look, Rob.'

He waited until she had left the room and looked at Luna. 'I'll tit you up first and then kiss your fanny,' he explained and received a non-committal response as expected.

'I'll take that as a yes,' he said and carried on with his plan, before placing her over his shoulder and carrying her upstairs.

He came back downstairs to find Venus in the kitchen drinking wine straight from the bottle and sawing large chunks from a loaf.

'I'll make the food, any cheese and olives?' she asked.

Rob directed her to a few cupboards and watched as the domestic goddess skilfully knocked up a Mediterranean style feast. He'd tried this idea before and had the ingredients, but her presentation, combined with the chopped salad and homemade *taramasalata*, using the tin of fish roe that he'd won in a summer fare raffle, definitely tasted made in the heavens.

At the end of the meal, he collected the plates and started the washing up. Venus had finished the white wine on her own and rose unsteadily to her feet.

'The love-goddess Venus needs to use your bathroom. I will check on the moon-goddess while I'm upstairs,' she said. He nodded and smirked as she wobbled upstairs.

'A drunken goddess, whatever next,' he said quietly and continued with the cleaning. A few minutes later, he heard Venus flop into the sofa in the lounge. He put the tea cloth back on its hook and went to hear the news.

'She's ok; survived the years fine. Very tired though and I've realised it's a full moon tonight. She can get a little crazy so I suggest cuddles tonight and action in the morning, stud,' she said. 'That means you can fuck this drunken goddess on the sofa.'

* * *

The next morning, a tired naked Rob sat at the table with two Roman deities.

'So in the *Indigitamenta*, my name should be used for prayers to ask for an improvement over last month's weather rather than the rain goddess, because of the lunar cycle?' asked the moon boss.

'It's all a bit woolly,' replied Venus, eating an apple. 'Your twenty eight day cycle only really works for ladies' internals. The latest yearly calendar has only one month with that number. They've cocked up a load of others as well. September which means seven, is their ninth month, October, the Roman eighth month is their tenth, it's just a mess.'

'What are you talking about?' asked Rob.

'Prayers,' answered Venus. 'The Roman state kept a list of goddesses and their specialities, suitable for praying to.'

'And gods,' added Luna. 'I fucked a couple of those. You never knew what offspring you'd get if you became pregnant. Could be a babe, horse, warrior, seductress, monster...'

'Or a half man/half beast, bear, bull or dog at the gates of hell. Here's a funny thought... Did anyone ever have a cat?' asked Venus.

Luna shook her head, 'Don't think so unless Roberto shagging my pussy counts. Nice cock by the way.'

'He really knows how to wake a girl up from a long sleep, doesn't he?' laughed Venus.

Luna looked at him and nodded. 'It's Bellona's turn tonight. Better have some more oats before you go into battle...'

* * *

Rob had taken a few days leave to help Venus, after initially believing her story. The promise of three nubile women, after a long break in his love life, seemed just what the doctor had ordered and he had looked forward to some soft female flesh and quiet conversation.

After his porridge yesterday, he drove his two Roman lady friends around the area, to see some of the sights and explain a little about modern technological advances. Luna turned out to be hyper. She seemed a non-stop chatterbox and kept groping him. She only stopped in the afternoon after he'd promised to service her before taking Bellona to bed. He couldn't believe that he'd actually given her some basic instruction in how to drive and let her sit at the wheel of his vehicle, in a pub car park. The two traffic policeman, who stopped them wheel-spinning amongst the other vehicles didn't book him, purely because Venus used her womanly wiles and gave them both a goddess style blowjob.

'That sounded embarrassing enough but did you really have to swallow?' moaned Rob, as he carefully drove away.

'At least I didn't cum swop with Luna,' she answered, 'All the rage at Roman orgies.'

'My turn to make dinner tonight to thank you for de-mannequining me,' said Luna, leaning through the gap between the seats. 'Fancy something with cream, Rob?'

When they finally arrived home, Rob tried to relax in an armchair, not sure whether to dread or look forward to the next few hours. Venus had slumped in the seat next to him, after necking a bottle of Sauvignon Blanc on the way home, and Luna chopped madly away with a large knife, as a lunatic would. He stood up after a few minutes and walked over to the amazon standing next to Med.

'Your turn, Bell,' and softly kissed her hard lips before reaching around and squeezing her ample buttocks through her

French knickers. He unhooked her frilly black brassiere and placed a palm on each breast. Rob noticed that his hands seemed to cover only a fraction of the boobs.

'Time to wake up,' he said, hoisted Bellona over his shoulder and took her upstairs to his double bed. As he looked at her lying there, he wondered how the models were so light to carry, but put on weight when they morphed into goddesses. This strapping girl's going to weigh more than him, he thought. Rob caressed her right thigh before he left and felt surprised to find it warm and muscular already.

The supper passed without incident and Luna's variation on *moussaka* with a Greek salad tasted delicious, apart from him constantly burping spring onions as he bonked her doggy fashion across the table afterwards, as she insisted.

* * *

The next day, a rather bruised looking Rob creaked into the kitchen to be greeted by three smiling goddesses.

'Saved the best until last,' shouted Bellona, punching the air.

'You probably need to work out a bit more,' said Luna.

'A little harder than you thought being super stud to the Roman myths, Roberto?' asked Venus.

'Let's just say I'm happy for you lot to go and carry on your search for the others,' he answered, and gingerly lowered his battered body onto a chair. 'When you said, 'be an animal', Bellona, I didn't realise that you planned to capture it, beat the beast into submission and finally suffocate it with your thighs...'

'I think you blacked out at that point, so sorry but your final spray of seed into my face looked magnificent, a true warrior,' said Bellona.

'He felt too scared not to please you three times,' laughed Venus.

'Anyway,' she continued, 'after breakfast, we will be on our way. I have found some women's clothes in a closet that nearly fit Bellona. We need no money because we can easily use our powers and goddess-ness to survive during our search.'

'Yes, we would like to thank you for our resurrection by phallus, Rob,' said Bellona.

'If you weren't so human, I could marry a crazy hero like you,' added Luna, with a tear in her eye.

Half an hour later, Rob stood at the front door and waved, as the trio stepped out of his life. The combination of his ex-girlfriend's too tight clothes on Bellona, Luna's crazy make up that she'd found in a drawer and Venus clutching his last two bottles of wine in each hand, made them look like a bunch of drunken tarts returning home, after an all-nighter.

He went back to his bed with its sheets smelling of sweat and wonderful goddesses. After only a few minutes thinking about the last few unbelievable days, Rob drifted into a dream of mythical creatures, heroic adventures and beautiful women.

The next day, Rob started back at Alldroits bright and early. He felt a bit battered, as he carried in the new model to replace Venus from his estate car. Rose, he thought, still didn't really believe his cover up story that on the Monday, when Venus wasn't on display, he'd received an offer for the fully clothed dummy, as soon as he arrived to open up.

He introduced Rose to Med, as soon as she clocked in. The deputy manageress seemed most impressed and soon carried her to the front display and began hunting for suitable clothes. He quickly settled back into the old routine and his bruises healed over the next few days; his only reminder of his week with the goddesses being the new model in the window.

* * *

A month later, as Rob looked around the store a final time, about to turn off the lights and lock up, he smiled to himself. It had been another long hard week. Venus had been completely correct, in that Med would increase sales of her clothes and any other associated goods. Her unusual appearance made women shoppers stop in their tracks; they just wanted to buy the clothes that she wore and be just like her. Alldroit's tills hadn't stopped beeping all month. The word had started going around the local hairdressers and 'ladies who lunch' cafés that this is the place to shop. He looked back into the sales area and caught a glimpse of the model at the far side of the room. Something stopped him from pressing the switch and he felt that he must have one more look at the beauty.

He walked over and stood in front of the mannequin. The fiery orange and red colour combination that adorned Med looked the epitome of autumn, which lay just around the seasonal corner.

'Let's get in early with the look, before the other department stores in the area,' Rose had encouraged, as they had scanned the various samples and online catalogues from their suppliers. Yet again, Med's dark olive complexion and complicated hairstyle formed a perfect marriage with the seasonal fabrics.

Rob stared at her beautiful face. He hadn't had sex since waking up the Roman lady trio. Maybe, he mused, Med could be secretly negotiated with? If Venus is right, this model next to him should be able to hear and understand even when cursed into solid form.

'I'm guessing that you're a bit jealous of your mates being able to run around again. That means another chance for you, Med. I know the girls advised not to touch you but I don't like rules set in stone. I'd like to know your real name. How about you show me just how hard a Greek girl can make me in bed, you sexy bitch?' he asked her.

'I wonder if Greek birds wake up differently to Roman,' he said quietly to himself and with Venus' warning voice ringing in his head, he leaned over and kissed the dummy full on the lips.

'Shit,' he said, as she blinked her eyes.

'Now listen honey, we have a bargain. I reckon that although you've just reacted quickly, that's all you can do. The other ladies needed more of my special wake up touch and a night in my bed before full recovery. No tricks now because we have a deal...' he explained, before placing one hand under her skirt and stroking her hair with the other.

Rob felt the hard plastic surface inside her knickers soften and he began to feel soft moist folds of womanly skin. Her coarse nylon hair began to soften and become alive under his touch...

'Fuck,' he shouted, as he jumped back clasping his hands. The crotch fingers seemed to be burning with her womanly juices and his other hand bled from several puncture marks.

He watched disbelievingly, as the model transformed into the most beautiful olive skinned woman that he could imagine. Her radiant smile and so kissable Greek facial features were perfectly complemented by her incredible black and blonde hairdo in a mythical style.

'Pleased to meet you Rob, I'm sorry my pets didn't agree to the contract. Oh, nearly forgot, I'm Medusa,' said the smiling model and the twisting entwined snakes on her head waved in agreement.

Rob had no answer to this, as the venom combined with the vision of the woman in the ancient tales to solidify him into just another male dummy for Rose to dress the next day...

Fairytail

Reed Hood hoisted up the handlebars of his stunt bike and performed a pirouette on the rear wheel, before fast pedalling along a makeshift ramp of bricks and ply. The combination of teenage boy and metal leapt over the row of parked up shopping trolleys, which were his appointed challenge. The landing however, looked less than successful, because the front wheel came into contact with terra concrete first and partly distorted. As the tyre rim jammed against the front fork, the resultant sudden deceleration sent him spinning off the machine, into a large St John's Wort shrub.

'Awesome, Red,' shouted one of his watching mates, saluting him.

'You're the man, dude,' joined in another, fatter boy, who stood by his own bike. 'Lemme have a go now.'

'There's no way, Piggy 3. You've eaten too many pies,' laughed a taller, thin kid.

'Bollocks to you, Sprat. I bet three quid that I make it, if I leave out the wheelie,' challenged the fat lad.

'You're on,' replied the thin one. 'I'll put up six skins against your money,' he offered, waving a packet of cigarette wrappers at him.

'He still owes me a fiver for a snog, last week,' warned a pretty long haired blonde girl, sitting on a shiny chrome plated cycle.

'Did P3's breath taste of swill, Goldie?' laughed the first boy, picking up his camouflaged hoody from the top of a traffic bollard. He unwrapped an egg shaped chocolate from his pocket and bit into it.

'Don't be rude, Kingsman. He said at first he had some fags but being as he lied, he owes me money,' replied the girl, cycling closer to thin kid. 'Any chance of a bite of your humpty egg choc?

I'll kiss you for it.'

The item disappeared into his mouth leaving only a trail of cream on his cheek. 'Too late, Goldie but I've got something else.' He reached into his pocket, as the disappointed blonde watched and pulled out a choc bar.

'A fanny kiss, maybe...' Kingsman suggested.

Goldie grabbed the sweet before he could react and sped off on her bike. 'Gotta catch me first and you left your bike at home...'

'Oi, you lot. I'm incredibly mortally wounded here and you're acting like tarts. I've wrecked my wheel, Jack. Can your old man fix it?' asked the forgotten Reed, as he came back from the crash site.

'I guess so,' replied Sprat. 'He can do anything like that. One of my wheels looked like a fifty pence piece after that bus knocked me over. Man; that's cool. They gave me morphine at the casualty place for my arm. Are you ok? You squashed that bush.'

'It's the only nice bush a ginger kid will ever see,' taunted another fat boy.

'Go toss with your twin, P2,' replied Reed, pulling up his hoody. 'Is Piggy 3 going to blast off because I reckon the manager will be out soon?'

'I know. I saw Mr and Mrs Jenkins watching us earlier. They've gone into the supermarket. I bet they're complaining now,' answered Sprat. 'I scratched their car last week zooming through a tight gap. Jenks probably guessed it might be the Grimms. Old gits; have you noticed that cute dark haired woman's been watching us again? She's standing over by her car, loading in the shopping,'

'You mean the one with the grey streak at the front? She's hot,' replied Reed, looking around the car park for her.

'That's called a mandarin mallard streak or something like that,' said Reed. 'Where is she?'

'Over there, you twat, she's in the black Mini with the white stripe,' pointed out Piggy Two.

'I'd give her one, boys. Milf points, eight out of ten, I reckon,' said Reed.

'Seven point five, dude. Anyway, the nearest you'd get with your knob is her car's exhaust pipe,' replied Sprat.

'You trying to say that I couldn't pull her, man?' asked Reed.

'Ginger boy shags orange duck Milf, no way. I reckon all the Grimm gang will bet against you. Wanna take the dare, Redman?' replied Spratt.

'He'd never prove it. Just his word and he's a piss-taker,' said Piggy 2.

'I've told you already P2, go ride in front of a road roller or help get the ramp into position for Piggy 3. Looks like he's gonna jump,' said Reed. 'Where's P1 twin, anyway, haven't seen him today?'

'Mam grounded him, for an E in tech homework and bunking off last Thursday. Bitch chained his ride to the shed,' explained Piggy 2.

'He's a twat. Anyway, I reckon a burger all round says I can nail the Milf. I'll bring her knickers back for you to sniff. Any takers?' asked Reed 'Look, she's struggling to close her boot. I'll go over to help and start talking to her.'

'I bet you the fixing of your bike and ten cigars, on behalf of the gang. Agreed P2?' inquired Sprat, looking at the fat kid.

'My bruvvers can carry the cost. Do it, he don't stand a chance,' encouraged Piggy 2.

'Just watch the Hood in action,' answered Reed, running over to fetch his bike from the Wort and seeing P3 flip headfirst into the trollies of doom.

'I'm calling the police,' shouted the manager, now standing at the front entrance, fifty yards away.

'Give Jack his six skins, you wanker and don't run off. Better start saving for my cigars as well,' Reed shouted to Piggy 3, as he picked up his battered machine, hoping that the sexy brunette remained in trouble.

Twenty seconds later, he whistled nonchalantly as he passed her vehicle, carrying his bike. She had leaned in through the open hatch, fiddling with something. Her shopping had been put back in the trolley. A slightly curvy but fit looking ass, wrapped in tight black corduroy, beckoned for his attention.

'Are you ok, Mrs? I saw you put the food in and then take it back out again,' he lied.

'Oh hello, thanks for asking, something's jamming on this lid thingy and stopping the boot closing. I don't suppose that you could have a look, young man?' she asked him and smiled.

'Sure and less of the young. You're not much older than me,' he teased.

'A charmer as well, I have struck gold.' she answered.

He looked at her face in close up, for the first time. The attention seeking trousers hadn't lied. This is one attractive middle aged woman that would make any self-respecting, porn watching teen happily whack one off, he thought.

A combed back, magnificent head of slightly greying raven hair crowned her pretty visage, topped off with a grey wave across the front. Reed almost fell in love with her at that point, but reminded himself that this is a bet. With any luck, he'd lose his virginity, feel some large tits and get a pack of Cuban cigars into the bargain. He knew the latter existed, because Sprat's dad had a stash hidden in the garage roof, well away from his wife.

Reed looked into the rear of the vehicle. He wasn't particularly mechanically minded, preferring his computer games machines to his father's offers to help fix his parents' old cars. He poked his head inside and had a look around, remembering the lady's broken lid comments.

The split back seat didn't seem to align properly and, when he pushed the right side, it moved forward.

'That's not right. It would do that in an accident,' pointed out the woman. 'I'm Mrs Wolff by the way, call me Fiona.'

'Cool, I'm Reed Hood,' he replied, freezing slightly at the name Wolff. He remembered his woodwork teacher's banter, about him needing to marry a wolf. Even the way that she pronounced Fiona ended in a little howl. He happened to be scared of dogs and the thought of getting spliced to an old one...

'I'm sure the seat should click into place, Reed,' she said, pulling him out of his thoughts, 'Is it jammed?'

Her perfume became stronger as she came closer and it slunk up his nostrils to kiss his olfactory nerves. Reed thought only he had sniffed, until her head came close to his shoulder and she said, 'Last Saturday at the cinema, third row from the back. You sat there because I recognise the deodorant and aftershave combination. I love your cropped red hair and you look too young to shave...' She stroked his cheek and laughed.

'Well yeah, I went there with Goldie, one of my gang, to watch that new sci-fi film in the morning. Did you see us? I've noticed you here at the shop before. It's one of our meeting points but I didn't see you at the Palace,' he replied, noticing that her unblinking, grey eyes were almost challenging him.

'I have an amazing sense of smell,' Fiona replied. 'It's almost animal like. I can smell fear as well...'

Reed shuddered at the last comment.

'I can see that the belt has become jammed in the catch, as the seat has been forced back. I'll put it completely forward and yank it out,' he said, trying to change the subject. Reed began to feel a little uncomfortable with the woman.

After a few small pulls, followed by a final desperate tug, the harness came free and soon the seat made the correct metallic sound as the lock engaged. He then attempted to replace the hatch luggage cover and discovered another problem.

'This has been on backwards, before. I bet you it never sat level. It should rise up on these black cords,' he said, feeling pleased with his diagnosis as he clipped the mechanism together.

'Wow, that's amazing. Well done Reed, I could do with a man

about the house like you,' she answered, lifting the rear hatch up and down and watching the parcel cover move in unison.

Reed wasn't really listening; he seemed too busy watching her impressive cleavage move in unison, too.

'Tell you what, if you help me put the luggage back in the car, we could put your broken bike in over the top of the back seat and I could give you a lift home, as a thank you,' she suggested. 'I saw you crash it and I think your mates would like to see you leave with me...'

Reed looked over to the sea of nosy faces, watching their every move.

'Would you mind, Fiona? It's a bit of a bet,' he asked, cautiously.

'Get in, young man. We'll show them that you can pull an old Milf like me. It works both ways Reed. I'm always happy to get my teeth into young fresh meat,' she laughed and made a growling sound.

Reed waved to his mates and climbed into the passenger seat.

'What about the pound coin in the trolley?' he asked, as she switched on the car ignition, about to pull away.

'Here you are, about to escape with the woman of your dreams, to shag her stupid and you worry about a quid. Let your mates buy some sweeties with it...' Fiona answered, tossed her hair back and accelerated out of the car park.

* * *

Two months ago, Reed Hood had been standing with his mate in their local park, planning what to do over the summer evenings. He had left school at sixteen, having achieved two crap GCSEs in Art and Drama, put one teacher in a mental hospital, had the school evacuated twice, once for a smashed alarm glass, and another time for mixing a large quantity of illicit chemicals that became misquoted in the local paper as, 'smelling worse than a thousand aliens farting at once', according to his mother.

'What shall we call the gang, Red?' asked Jack, his friend of many years, who had stayed on in school after Reed left and now, two years later, awaited his A level results.

'Well, kids have called me Red Riding Hood for years...' he started to answer.

'And Red and Redman, because of your hair and Reed Ridiculous Hood when your mother knitted you a winter balaclava, years ago,' added Jack.

'Ha-ha, anyway, you can't talk, Master Sprat. You only hear it at nursery school but there's the old rhyme about Jack Sprat who could eat no fat. You're just like him, tall and thin,' said Reed.

'So you're thinking something to do with old rhymes? There used to be somebody called Grime?' suggested Jack. 'No, I'm getting mixed up, it had two M's; I mean the Grimm Brothers or maybe Brothers Grimm?'

'I like it... Grimm Death or the Grimm Gang, maybe, we should all have fairy-tale names,' agreed Reed.

'Yeah, I'm Jack Sprat, you're Red or The Hood, Gemima can be Goldilocks because of her hair...' said Jack. 'Have you snogged her yet, by the way, because she kissed my cheek last week?'

'Nah, she's frigid. I wouldn't mind being that saddle on her bike though,' laughed the new Red.

'Yeah and her brother said she's got a size thirty two inch bra,' added Mr Sprat, holding a pair of imaginary boobs.

'Wicked, and what about the other names? The twins used to be called Tweedledum and Tweedledee years ago, but now they're just as fat as Billy,' asked Reed.

'How about calling all of them the Three Piglets? We could call them Piggy 1, 2 and 3. They could choose,' answered Jack.

'Cool, and Jeff?' asked Reed.

'Obvious,' replied Jack. 'Something to do with Humpty Dumpty, he eats those chocolate eggs all the time. How about those soldiers, the king's men who put the egg back together? He wants to join the army when he leaves school,'

'Kingsman, then,' said Reed. 'Hey, we have a gang; the Grimm Gang. Look, here come the others on their rides. Wait till they see my new stunt bike.'

'My nan says I'm too old to be doing cycle tricks at eighteen, Red,' said Jack, looking jealously at the shiny new red machine, with its small wheels and extra foot rests.

'Maybe Goldie will give me a snog for a test ride?' asked Reed.

'Or maybe more, she's sixteen now, last month,' replied Jack. 'You still a virgin, Mr Hood?'

'Nah,' Reed lied. 'Have you done it, yet?'

'Yeah loads,' Jack lied back.

* * *

The next day, Reed went back to work. After he'd left school, he eventually found himself a part time job with a local gardener and, when that business took on more serious tree work, he took a few courses at the local technical college to gain some certificates in chainsaw use and health and safety. He felt so proud of them that his mother had them framed and put up on the living room wall, the first thing since his childhood paintings. The only other thing in the intervening years on the walls from him, according to his parents, had been handprints.

He'd learned how to climb small trees and secure himself without falling and similarly trim off and safely lower branches, avoiding danger to himself and onlookers. His greatest moment turned out to be when he arrived for a job driving the business van and it turned out to be his woodwork teacher's house. Mr Chorley seemed amazed at Reed's new range of skills and made great play of how Reed Riding Hood had become the Woodchopper from the nursery rhyme. He said again that Reed needed to marry a wolf, to complete the job.

The first proper meeting of the Grimm Gang occurred a week later.

'And old Chorleychops said that you'd done well, Red? He used to hate you, man,' said Piggy 1.

'That's because you nicked a chisel from the woodwork room and carved a picture of Kylie Minogue on the gym floor,' laughed Piggy 2. 'He got the flak for not locking up properly.'

'They never actually found out who did it,' laughed Reed.

'Everyone knew only you would have the balls to do it,' said Kingsman. 'The carving looked crap though. Her tits were far too big. The only way to tell it's really Kylie, is to read the name.'

'You spelt her last name MINOG, you dick,' added Gemima.

'Boobs as big as Goldie's,' taunted Piggy 1.

Gemima delivered a well-timed apple core that bounced off P1's forehead, as he tried to run away.

'You should be in the army cadets with an aim like that, Goldie. Fancy coming along next week, there's loads of other girls, it's quite fun?' asked Kingsman.

'Well, maybe,' answered Gemima. 'Becky goes and she says there are some hunky soldier boys doing the teaching, sometimes.'

'That's why Kingsman goes,' laughed Reed.

'No way, I'm no bender. I mean I've got nothing against them... It's just you could get to learn a trade and earn some money. You're lucky just finding a job, like you did, Red,' he explained.

'Guess you're right, Kingsman. Only thing I want now is a steady girlfriend, really,' said Reed.

'Yeah, too many one night stands mess with your head,' agreed Jack.

'Well, I'm still a virgin so that means you guys are out. I'd only do it with another virgin,' said Gemima, before riding away on her bike, in a standing up position.

Reed and Jack stared at the bike's warm leather seat, as her long legs propelled it away.

'Fuck, Sprat. We just cocked up then,' said Reed.

* * *

The hatchback roared onto the main road after waiting at the traffic lights. Reed watched the Milf's legs as she changed gear, the clingy soft black trousers outlining her curvy thighs. She seemed at one with the controls as it shot along the road.

'Which way to your mum's house?' she asked.

'Maybe I live with mates, you know?' he answered, cockily.

'You're a mummy's boy. Your T-shirt's ironed,' she laughed.

'Have you got a boyfriend at all? I know you joked about needing a man. Maybe we can go back to your place?' he asked, getting bolder.

'My, you've grown up all of a sudden. Maybe my shag suggestion impressed you and your mates?' she asked.

'I'm ready, if you want to do it. You're quite sexy for an older lady,' he replied and then wished he phrased it better.

'Ha-ha, lucky I'm thick skinned. I'm glad you fixed the car so I'll make you an offer...' she said.

'I'm not desperate, you know,' Reed lied.

'Fancy a blow job, as a reward? It's safer than sex with me. You don't know where I've been,' she asked and laughed.

'If you're trying to say that I can't handle you, think again. I've had loads of experience,' he lied again.

'Well you've got to do it properly, like a gentleman. I just hate selfishness...' she said. 'When I start to take off my clothes, you have to kiss me all over and then follow me to the bedroom. I like to make love in comfort, with the curtains open, in full view of the romantic night sky. Do you chavs do emotion or thoughtfulness?'

'When my cock's all the way inside, you'll be satisfied,' he boasted, wondering what she meant.

'I'll take that as wanting to shag me then. Seems like a rather splendid reward for fixing a seat. Do you have any other skills?' she asked, as her car carefully merged from a slip road onto a dual carriageway and accelerated into the outer lane, to overtake a line of lorries.

'You're a really good driver, Fiona. So focussed and totally in charge... Are you always like this or just showing off? Most girls drive like...well, girls,' he asked.

'I'm a sheep in wolf's clothing, Reed, or maybe the other way around,' she answered and moved her hand over to squeeze his right thigh. 'And your job is...'

'Oh sorry, I do gardening, look after lawns, climb trees, trim bushes etc. I could probably check yours out,' he offered.

'Can't wait,' she grinned at him before looking back at the road. 'Especially the last bit...'

'Ha-ha, I didn't mean...' he stopped in mid-sentence.

'Getting cold feet? My sense of smell detects a little lack of confidence, mixed with a hint of inexperience...' she suggested and laughed.

'Maybe I trod in something?' he replied, warming to her and joined in the laughter.

'What is your job then, Fiona? You haven't given me one clue,' asked Reed.

'You never asked. Solicitor, and I teach music part time,' she replied. 'I'm quite good on the organ, I'll show you later...'

'Ha-ha, I guess there's lots of music jokes,' he said.

'I could blow your reed, Reed,' she laughed, 'But I've already offered.'

Ten minutes later, they were pulling into the drive of a nineteen forties detached house, set in a leafy residential area.

'Wow,' said Reed, as he climbed out of the vehicle. 'Looks like suing people, really pays dividends, Fiona. I'd love to spend the rest of my days here, especially in the garden.'

'Are you proposing to me, Reed? It could be arranged,' she

answered with a straight face.

He looked at her. 'You're joking, right? Or do you mean spare room and all that stuff?'

'See what you think after a look around. Like I said before, I could do with a man about the house, especially a fit muscular one...' Reed jumped as he felt his ass being squeezed.

'Isn't it somewhere near here that someone found a dead body buried in their back garden?' asked Reed, looking at some bushes.

'Yes, that's right, a couple of streets away,' replied Fiona, walking towards the front door.

'Jack's older brother knew him. He can't have been much older than me. The police said he had his heart ripped out by a vampire or something,' said Reed, following her.

Fiona stopped and turned around to face him.

'Believe me, I know a few vamps and that's not their style,' she said with a curious smile. 'There are lots of strange creatures lurking about in the middle of the night...'

'Ha-ha, you're trying to scare me, aren't you?' he said but the little wobble in his voice, gave his feelings away.

'Still happy to stick your cock in a Wolff called Fiona?' she asked and laughed. 'Grrr,' and the Milf chased him back down the garden path, with her pretend claws outstretched.

She caught him at the car and wrapped her arms around his neck and locked lips. After a smouldering kiss which left him wiping his wet face, she pulled away and said, 'You've never kissed a girl before; I can tell. Reed is actually a complete virgin, how sweet is that? I'm going to pluck your cherry, little man.'

'Well, of course, I've...ok, ok, it's true. I've just never had the chance, it's not like I haven't tried, you know...' he answered, looking down at the gravel by the side of the path.

The grey pieces of stone stared back at him, quietly shouting, 'Go for it.'

'Reedy, Reedy, I love fresh meat. Do as you're told and I'll be gentle,' she said, and stroked his hair.

* * *

Half an hour later, after arriving back at Fiona's house, he sat at her kitchen table. They had earlier spent a few minutes in the garden looking at the trees and plants. Reed had offered several suggestions on how the layout might be improved. She had asked about the type of work carried out by his employers and how much they'd charge, before finally asking him if he'd like a hot drink.

Fiona approached him with two mugs of steaming coffee, placed one in front of him and the other at the empty seat opposite. She went back to one of the kitchen cupboards, opened the door and reached up to the top shelf.

Reed caught a view of her white soft tummy as she did so. He noticed how a small flabby excess hung over her belt. Her womanly curves seemed so much more enticing than Goldie's slimness or the bodies of other young girls of his age.

She sat down opposite with a packet of chocolate biscuits, skilfully sliced the end of the packet open with a long red painted fingernail and clattered some onto a small plate in the centre of the table. He watched Fiona take her seat and run both sets of fingers through her greying hair, before resting her chin in her hands, elbows on the table, and staring at him, square in the eye.

He felt mesmerised by her presence and a few seconds of silence passed by before either one spoke.

'You're falling for me, aren't you, Reed?' she asked.

'You're a nice chick,' he replied, watching her lick her red lips after a sip of coffee.

'I'm not really a spring chicken, you know. Young boy's hormones see things differently. An older lady's bits start to pad out or droop, just when she wants to impress. We have to use all sorts of support girdles and potions to keep up with the teenagers,' she explained, gently tapping her cheekbone with her fingers, as she spoke.

'I think you're beautiful,' he blurted out.

'Good answer, don't stop...' she giggled.

'I mean it's just so nice sitting here with the coffees, looking across at one another talking. It's like being, erm...' he paused, trying to think of a word to describe the unusual feelings in his body.

'Married?' she suggested, 'Or at least girlfriend and boyfriend. Do you like the feeling?'

'It's kinda really cool sitting here with you. I wouldn't mind doing it again,' he said.

'Wow, I've still got it then, fatal attraction. Would you like to be my toy-boy?' she asked and leaned back to adjust her top, to show a little more cleavage. 'You sort the garden in your spare time; I pay the big bills and get satisfaction in the bedroom.'

'You mean move in?' he asked, wide eyed.

'As long as you obey the rules, my needs come first and never forget that. I'm the leader of the pack and if I'm not satisfied, look out,' she explained.

Reed nodded.

'Now then, this bet about me, earlier. How much am I worth?' she asked.

'Oh, loads,' he fibbed.

'Tell the truth...' she probed.

'Ok, a burger for all the gang, against some cigars and fixing my wheel,' he admitted.

Fiona laughed. 'That's all? You'd swop a fuck with me for a few smokes? And how were you going to prove that you'd done the dirty deed?'

'Borrow something suitable,' he said vaguely, 'I would have returned it, of course.'

'Maybe I should just give you an opened letter now or you

could take a mobile pic of my bedroom? I may drop you straight home, then…' she suggested.

'But what about the toy-boy deal. I would like to be one,' he pleaded.

'Reed Riding Hood belongs to Mrs Wolff? Ok, and the only chopper I get is in your pants?' replied Fiona, raising an eyebrow.

'Deal,' agreed Reed, hoping that she didn't notice he had his fingers crossed…

* * *

After watching an hour or so of TV and sitting on the sofa at Fiona's behest, it had started to get dark. She had insisted that Reed's deflowering, as she called it, would happen by moonlight because only then did she feel at her best during sex. He'd phoned his parents, to say that he'd left his bike in the business lock up and would be staying over at a friend's house. They'd been used to some odd hours kept by the teenager over the past few years, so weren't the slightest bit interested.

To match the story, Fiona had taken him around to the gardening firm compound, where the spare equipment, not carried in the van, had been stored. He had a key and the bent bicycle ended up left there. Jack's family lived a couple of streets away so his mate could easily pick it up for his dad to fix. He made Fiona park around the corner and carried the bike himself. Reed deliberately spoke to the old guy next door who knew him, and said he will be off drinking with a mate on the other side of town.

When the news on the television finished, Fiona stood up and said, 'I'm going to have a shower.'

Reed carried on looking at the screen and simply said, 'Ok.'

He received an unexpected whack on the arm. 'That means you as well, stupid…' she shouted.

'Oh sorry Fiona, you mean both of us at once? Sure thing,' he answered quickly, and nearly jumped off the sofa in anticipation. She led him upstairs to the bathroom and ordered him to take off his clothes. As he started to do so, somewhat embarrassed, he asked, 'You are joining me?'

'Of course sweetie, but for the moment, you are my private stripper-gram. Get 'em off,' she encouraged.

Reed never liked being told what to do. It felt like being at school. He pushed the thoughts to the back of his mind to focus on the joy of new sex to come and ways of proving it to the Grimm Gang. There might even be the possibility of winning the bet and still seeing the Milf for a bit of loving on a few more occasions, he thought.

'Swing it baby,' enthused Fiona, as Reed wiggled his ass in his boxers, before lowering them and tossing them at her head.

She stood there laughing for a second with her new underwear hat. 'Sex with a toy-boy makes you go blind,' she said, before shaking them off and grabbing his willy.

Fiona pulled him towards the shower and turned it on saying, 'Get in there, you dirty beast.'

A stinging smack on his ass encouraged him into the cool water, which happily soon warmed up. She squeezed some shower gel into her hand and passed him the bottle.

'Hold this, Reed. I'll soap you up.' she said.

He didn't realise at first what she meant until he felt her hand pushing him backwards towards the rear of the cubicle and Fiona climbed in, fully clothed. She started soaping his chest and slowly worked his way down to the start of his pubic hair just below his belly button.

The water quickly soaked through the material of her top and he could easily make out her dark bra showing through the now transparent fabric.

'Please take it off, Fiona,' he asked quietly, his voice almost lost in the hissing of the hot shower.

'This?' she inquired, pulling out the front of her sopping top to expose even more cleavage. Reed just wanted to dive head first into the promised wetlands as he gazed downwards.

She quickly undid the small black buttons on the front, removed it and tossed the garment over the shower doorframe onto the bathroom floor. She reached behind herself to unhook the bra, which immediately followed suit.

Before his eyes could fully focus on her exposed chest in the shower spray and steam that had built up, she took the shower gel from him and squeezed blobs onto both of his open palms. The noise of the plastic container clattering around on the curved floor of the shower enclosure, after she dropped it, joined with the echo of her loud sigh, as she clasped both his hands to her bosom and rubbed her soft skin.

He couldn't help nipping the hard bullets that flicked between the gaps in his fingers, as she guided his palms from side to side, massaging her wicked thoughts.

Fiona then bent down again to retrieve the bottle. He watched the water from the shower bouncing off her naked back and forming small rivulets, which ran off in all directions. For a split second, he realised that a major part of his dare had come true; he stood alone with a half-naked woman, she had taken off her top as he'd asked and now he had just groped her bare breasts...

He jumped as she got up and realised that she was soaping his knob. The wonderful feeling of another human touching your privates increased rapidly, as her hand moved to his bollocks. Fiona pulled him way from the shower wall, towards the centre of the cubicle, and she poured more gel into either hand.

'Close your eyes and I'll do your back,' she instructed.

Reed followed her exact words and awaited her soft hands on his torso.

Instead he jumped again, as a lathery hand grabbed his balls and another slid down along his back side and between his legs.

'I lied,' Fiona said, as she soaped all around underneath from stem to stern, finishing with a finger in no-woman's land.

The ball hand started tugging his cock, whilst the nether digit performed a little to and fro dance, 'This may be a little advanced for you but it cleans and satisfies…' she explained.

'Shit, Fiona that feels weird,' he said trying to wiggle away.

She opened the cubicle door and at first he thought that the bathing had finished but she started to kick off her shoes and drop her jeans. He moved back to let her in again and felt surprised how much shorter she stood, without her footwear. It seemed as though she had to stand on tiptoe to put her arms around his neck in order to snog him.

The sensation of her warm wet breasts pressing against him felt heavenly and he soon became aware of another new feeling, a prickling sensation on his cock. As she pulled away he looked down to see what on earth had happened and then realised that he had discovered a fully grown lady garden at work.

The only fanny that he'd seen before had always been trimmed or completely shaven, in porn magazines. This woman's bush looked a delight to behold and he reached down to push his fingers through the mass of dark curls.

'You're catching on, Reed,' she said and bent down to retrieve the shower gel again.

He held out his hands in anticipation and received his allotted double ration.

'Now do my bits. Don't forget the spyhole, sailor,' she ordered.

'Aye, aye, captain,' he replied, before it dawned on him just what she meant. 'You mean like erm…mine?' he asked. 'Advanced stuff?'

She nodded and seconds later he had produced a frothy bush with one hand and skirted around her unmentionable with the other. A little help from her knowing hands guided the lost finger into place and the other hand to her fun button switch. He had no idea just exactly what to do, but loved watching Fiona squirm, as his hands fondled the sexy older lady.

A few minutes later they were towelling one another down and laughing their heads off as they explored each other's bodies and compared drying off techniques.

Reed finally decided that Fiona's fanny looked a little too bushy to be called pretty and could actually do with a trim but no worries, he thought; all he had to do later should be poke, shoot, grab her knickers and go.

She pulled him upstairs to the bedroom and pushed him onto the bed before jumping on top and pointing her finger directly between his eyes.

'Just remember the deal. Considerate sex equals happy Mrs Wolff,' she commanded.

'Sure thing, Milf,' he lied and rolled into a ball to protect himself from her slapping.

'Time to be a man, little boy,' she said, when she seemed to realise his defences were Wolff-proof.

Fiona knelt down on the bed in an all fours position and said, 'Take me like this; I'm sure you'll enjoy losing your virginity this way.'

Reed positioned himself behind her, rubbing himself hard.

'Do I just jam it in? I guess there's a technique?' he asked, somewhat shyly.

'Just get closer and I'll pop it inside to get you started. Don't worry and if you feel like things are going too fast, just pull out and calm down, ok?' she instructed.

Reed obeyed and a few seconds later the bet had been won. He watched his cock getting moist as it slid back and forth. 'This feels better than I imagined. I could do this all day...' he enthused, several minutes later.

'You'll be lucky. Now just vary your depth and speed, see how the sensations change,' she suggested, before kneeling up a little straighter.

Reed obeyed like a robot, biding his time and enjoying the moment.

'Good boy,' she added two minutes later. 'Now lean over me. You can feel my boobs and kiss my back, if you're still ok.'

He obeyed and after squeezing her nipples, decided that his time had arrived. The feeling in his loins became too powerful to resist but he knew there might just be enough time to pull out and calm down as Mrs Milf-Wolff had insisted...

Reed viciously bit her soft neck and gave one more final thrust, as the moon came out from behind the clouds and flooded the bedroom with light.

He shuddered as his penis pulsed and sent his hot semen racing towards Milf-haven.

'You fucking lowlife,' Fiona exclaimed, as she realised what he'd done.

'Like I care, grandma,' he replied...

'Don't you little brats have any sexual manners, nowadays? The lady should cum first, you just committed a capital offence...' she shouted.

'Sue me then... Just wait till I tell the guys about this. You look pretty hot, for an old lady, in the moonlight, Fiona. I don't suppose you want a threesome with the little piglets?' he asked cruelly.

Reed reached down to force her butt away from him, but something brushed his hand so he tried to move it, first. 'Shit,' he shouted, as he grabbed and traced the object, back to its origin.

'Surprise,' said Fiona, as she grasped his still hard but sensitive cock with her muscular vagina.

'You've got a tail, for fuck's sake,' he cried out.

'And you still have a task to complete,' she replied and started forcefully moving on his phallus.

'Jeez, please let go,' he pleaded as the tailed lady wriggled back and forth mercilessly on his entrapped member. The room went dark as the cloud covered the impossible scene, with a fairy-tale duvet of madness...

He pressed his hands against her back, in a vain attempt to

push the nightmare away. 'I'll do anything, I'm sorry. I'll cut your trees, dig the garden and trim your bush,'

The coarse grey hair emerging on her shoulders suddenly stroked the fear receptors on his feeble palms.

'Arghhh...' he shouted, still trying to pull his meat-key out of her lady-lock.

Reed's screams merged with the blood curdling, orgasmic howl of Mrs Wolff, as she thanked the lunar orb for being a Milf before finally, with one swift movement, she rolled over and her jaws crunched through Reed's ribcage, emerging with its dripping, still beating prize.

She gulped it down whole and said, 'Milfs always swallow.'

Reed's dying brain realised the missed opportunity.

'Kids today, just so heartless...' said the Were-Wolff.

Epilogue

'So you've finished *The Twelve Stories*, Mr Baker; what did you think of them? The book's been very popular since it arrived at the library,' asked April, as she checked the return date.

'Very good and there's a great twist at the end of each story. You should read it, if you can find the time,' replied Alan. 'It's a shame that the men always lose, though. There should be another story, in which the lady gets her comeuppance.'

'Maybe you should write story thirteen and slip it in the back of the book? Call it *A Baker's Dozen* and surprise the readers.' she suggested.

'Great idea, how about we collaborate on it? I'm new to this town and don't know many people yet. Fancy a date? I can't see any rings on your fingers so I'm guessing you're unattached...' He looked closer at her name badge, 'April Spring?'

'My father's sense of humour, I'm afraid,' she answered, 'Although better than my schoolgirl alternatives of Rusty, Coil and Slinky.'

'A slinky spring, I remember them. They used to walk down the stairs. Slinky can be sexy as well nowadays, April. I don't suppose that you have a cat-suit?' he asked.

'If you're working up to a pussy joke, stop right now,' she laughed. 'I'm free Friday evening. I quite like the sound of writing the final secret chapter. I'll have a think about it. It seems appropriate to meet at *The Writer's Rendezvous*, in the old print works near the square. The new owner did a nice refurbishment there last year. It's where the creative clique hangs out.'

'Cool,' replied Alan. 'No tricks mind, like the women in the book...' he warned.

'It would never cross my shy, unassuming librarian's mind,' she answered.

April watched him through the dirty old sash window

overlooking the car park, as he left in his black BMW. The voice of her best friend Sasha, who he had shagged and dumped in one day, two weeks ago, spoke in her twisted mind. She had sat with her in the ladies room, looking at the blue colour on the end of a pee testing stick. 'I would kill the flash git, if I had half a chance...' her friend had shouted, with tears in her eyes.

* * *

April looked across the table at the handsome devil in front of her. His hair looked impossibly dark for a man supposedly in his mid-thirties. Her jury had gone walkabout on his exact age; she suspected some wash-in hair dye to match the washed-out jeans.

In her younger days, she'd have fallen head over heels in love with a chap like him, but the events and disappointments of recent years had left a bitter taste in her mouth, just like the jizz that several dolts with bad timing had deposited there and then laughed at her discomfort.

She no longer felt in a mood to receive red eye from premature shots or have an expensive perm ruined by flying toss. Ideally her soul mate would enjoy her company for who she is, cuddle her at night and flush the condom away himself...

The guy in front of her looked like he needed a French maid to do everything for him.

'How's the drink?' he asked. 'If you need another, I'll get a waitress,' and he clicked his fingers at a girl clearing some tables nearby.

'It's usual to go to the bar,' April pointed out.

'She won't mind, I'll tip her. Watch this,' he said.

'Hello, thanks for coming over. I've pulled a disc in my back and can't walk too well. Be a dear and fetch us two more glasses of white wine. My lady doesn't like to leave me on my own, in case I have a spasm. Please keep the change,' Alan said to girl, after she walked over to their table with an armful of dirty plates.

She looked at the twenty pound note proffered and then at the size of the glasses on the table. A bite of her lip followed, as she did some mental arithmetic before answering, 'Just this once.' She bent swiftly down and took the note away in her teeth.

A few minutes later, she returned with the ordered items and carefully placed them in front of the customers next to their unfinished drinks.

'Thanks for the tip mate. Give us a shout if you want the same deal again. I like a man who flashes his stash,' she said, fluttering her eyelashes at him.

Alan playfully tapped her behind with his hand as she walked away.

'You see, some girls are easy...' he said to April.

'And some girls are much harder to crack, like me,' she replied, finishing his sentence.

'Is this part of the new chapter thirteen, *Challenge of the Librarian*?' he suggested.

'Better write down your old successes then. Maybe they're about to end?' she teased.

'My charms don't always work. Women seem to see through them for some reason,' Alan commented.

'No kidding?' replied April, trying not to smile.

He leaned over closer. 'I prefer casual sex, if you know what I mean. No strings etc. Of course if I fathered a child, I'd be prepared to pay the price,' he replied.

'I'm glad you said that. Makes my job somewhat easier,' answered April, wondering if the staff would notice if she just stuck a steak knife into his back at this very moment. She looked around to see if anyone had a T bone on their plate.

'If you're hungry, I could get that girl back to bring us a menu. I can see you're staring at the cakes,' suggested Alan.

'That might be a good idea. How about something like a toasted ham sandwich? Make sure the knives are sharp though; I hate struggling to chop stuff...' she answered.

After another conversation and passing of ten pound notes to Madeline, whom he had befriended by now, Alan started scribbling a few notes in a little black spiral bound pad.

'Are you seriously going to try writing an addendum to *The Dozen*?' April asked.

'Why not, how hard can it be? I know a few rude words like fanny and clit. All the stories seem to revolve around those two anatomical areas,' answered Alan. 'I'm thinking about calling the main character after you: *The Spring*.'

'Does she have a bladder problem?' April asked cheekily.

'No, she's a he and uses a spring loaded machine to kill people with,' he replied, adding, 'In April each year...'

She could hardly contain her laughter and held her hand over her face, to hide her sniggers.

'Make the heroine an alien transvestite baker, with an interest in taxidermy. She could use her dildo to stuff the dead bodies,' suggested April.

Alan wrote it down and finished reading it back, just as the food arrived.

'You're not taking this seriously, are you, April?' he finally said. 'She could use a baker's rolling pin, I suppose.'

'True,' grinned April, 'it's hard to see how they can say it takes years to write a whole story. I hope the sandwich knife is sharp.'

She wasn't sure how she managed to get through the rest of the evening without slitting his stupid throat. Only the presence of witnesses saved his bacon. Not only that, if a crime had to be committed, who knows, she might be tempted to carry out more, to avenge the dreadful acts that men do to the fairer sex.

The plan crystallised in her head, as the minutes passed away. He obviously sought a woman for the night; she'd seen him flirting with the helper for several hours so she told him that if he played his cards right, he could come back to her house in another hour.

April stated that she had an image to keep and didn't want to be seen leaving with a man by the staff. She would simply shake hands and say goodnight to him in front of Madeline and leave the pub, alone. He should stay chatting to whoever he fancied at the bar and drinking only orange juice because he would need his manly charms for later. Before he left, Alan should announce to as many people as possible that he needed to get a taxi to the next town, for some late night casino action but in reality walk the back lanes to her house. She made him memorise the address and not write it down, because that's what the bad lady always did in thriller books. Alan liked that part of her scheme.

'You're going to enjoy tonight, darling. I've watched lots of films and I'm good,' he promised, making a wanking gesture under the table.

'I could see that talent straight away,' she replied with a wry smile. 'Well, if you've taken all that in, I'll be off to prepare your surprise.'

'Black stockings please,' he suggested.

'If I have to...' April reluctantly agreed. 'See you later, stud,' she whispered.

'Should we have a password at your front door, such as, *Spring is in the air*?' he asked.

'No, there's a doorbell,' she replied, straight faced. 'Madeline's walking this way, let's shake hands.'

* * *

As Alan undressed her later at the flat, she felt mildly amused at how gentle he seemed and also the fact that he neatly folded every item of clothing and placed them on the arm of the sofa. He obviously had undergone a proper shower and used deodorant, which had been another pleasant surprise. As she knelt down to loosen his boxers, April became very impressed by the size of his slumbering manhood. The temptation to touch became too great, so she mentally re-planned his quick execution from the easily cleaned shower, to one in the bedroom, after enjoying some man meat inside her. A bit twisted, she thought, shagging the target, but every budding murderess must have a calling card...

'I'm glad you decided to wear the stockings, April,' he said, reaching down to cup both of her breasts as she took the tip of his penis into her mouth.

He surprised her with his skilful stroking of her nipples. They hardened quickly under his touch, their sensitivity increasing by the second. A gorgeous tingling sparked around, just under the flesh, almost making her rip his hands away as it tickled, almost as much as it pleased.

April soon became aware of his expanding rod. She had felt the short soft foreskin quickly retract, when she had earlier teased the frenum. His glans rapidly expanded in her mouth and knowing how much she hated to deep throat even a small man, her excitement got the better of sense and she managed to get her lips around his rim.

His shifting of weight from one foot to another, as he enjoyed her sucking, could be felt in her fingertips, which rested just above his hip bones. She had no wish to be choked and they were placed there out of experience, as a sharp nailed, safety buffer.

Her focus drifted away into a higher place as his musky pheromones warmed up and overcame the perfumed body deodorant. The man smelt so sexy and his hot body felt under total control, as her hands moved through the fine hairs on his muscular thighs and his rough fingers gently crushed and reformed her nipples. She continued to gently mouth her intended prey and at one point gently pressed her teeth into the hard but delicate flesh of the glans, just to let him know she had taken charge of the proceedings. Alan's body became one with hers, during this sensitive, petting dance.

'Fuck,' she cried out seconds later, after he'd given two sharp thrusts, past her tonsils. April coughed and tears started to run down her cheeks, before hearing him laugh above her spluttering face.

She felt like she'd swallowed a large light bulb and glugged back some bile before wiping her face with her arm.

'You bastard, you know that you're a big man. Does my gob look like a welly-boot? It must be two sizes bigger, you shit-head,' she cursed.

'I didn't mean it. I thought maybe you were more experienced, April,' he said. 'Hey, I've just had a thought for the last chapter. If April got covered in sperm, would it be April showered?'

'You'll be April hammered, if you try that move again,' she shouted.

He playfully tapped her on the head a few times with his erect penis. 'What next boss? Wanna feel the force inside you?'

'And knock off a space alien? No thanks but I'll settle for a good orgasm from a well-controlled sensitive man' she replied, standing up.

Alan came closer and wrapped his arms tenderly around her. She could feel his phallus pulsing as it became trapped against her tummy. She slipped her arms around his waist and ran her fingers up the bones of his back. He leant down and their lips locked for a few seconds in a passionate kiss.

'I'll try…' he promised.

'Follow me to the bedroom, then. I'll have a surprise for you if you behave…' she replied.

A few minutes later they were play wrestling on her double bed. She made the moves but his superior strength always enabled him to break free. Every now and then, her lustful body felt about to give in to his charms and fall for the rogue but the sensible mind inside her head kept treading water and saying kill him.

Alan constantly kept stroking her hold up stockings and she really hadn't realised the power that black nylon could have on a man. She soon found out that he turned most submissive, whenever she managed to sit on his face.

Finally they both knew that playtime had ended. She wasn't sure how it came about but suddenly the contact between their hands and one another's body became more forceful, more urgent, and their breathing deepened.

In a similar vein, she instinctively knew when to become passive, something in her genes, passed on from one generation of females to the next, when to roll over, time to be fucked...

April watched open mouthed as Alan had sensed her move and instantly positioned himself between her outstretched legs; his mouth opened and as he breathed, his tongue thrust like a micro-penis and his eyes were two bulging reservoirs of male seed, scanning the open furrow between her legs. She could swear that he looked like a godly farmer about to plough deep into her, for she had become mother earth...

In his rush to get inside her, his penis trapped one of her soft skin, sweet wrappers. April pushed her hand between their eager bodies; to allow it some escape room and re-guided his lance inside her hungry lips.

She shuddered as the rim of his soldier's helmet passed over her engorged clitoris, sending a tsunami wave of desire, crashing over the shores of her evil plan. As she gasped for air, she desperately tried to distance her rapidly growing passion for the cad from his imminent demise.

Alan reached under April's bum cheeks, to grab at her derriere and stop her being squashed into the soft creaking mattress. As he thrust deeper, his breath felt hot on her face and his stubble threatened to plough furrows of desire, across her soft cheek.

She grabbed his muscular back and dug her fingernails deep into the flesh, to control the animal between her legs, but it seemed to no avail, as the beast simply moaned with lust at the pain from her claws and continued to pound her innermost parts.

'Please don't stop, Alan,' she pleaded and moved her hands

onto his hips.

A tortured bedspring creaked a rusty melody to the mattress bashing.

'You tarts can never get enough, once you start,' the man said, as he pulled out and started to sit up.

'No please, I only jok...' Her words faded away as a new galaxy of stars appeared in her head. She closed her eyes as he rubbed the tip of his member, up and down her slit, paying particular attention to her fun button.

'Oh, God,' April cried, 'wait a second,' and she reached down between her hot thighs to part her annoying lips, which were interfering with the ultimate contact.

'Again, now,' she ordered.

'Hungry bitch,' he cursed and pushed her hand out of the way to take over the job.

She flinched as he roughly grasped her delicate flaps of skin between his left hand fingers and stretched the womanly folds outwards. For a split second, April felt as though he had pulled them completely over her head. The sudden pain almost made her scream, but the reappearing of the stellar scene of multi-coloured moons and shooting stars in her psyche felt so sweet and sour that her protest disappeared into the bed sheets.

Alan redoubled his rough efforts to massage her sensitive spot, using his phallus in his right hand, and she couldn't help wriggling with sheer pleasure at his touch. She tried once again to focus on her original aim but his overwhelming sexual presence stood firmly in front of her vagina. A voice inside her shouted to roll over and be forced into missionary submission.

'Shit, do you treat all your girlfriends like this?' April gasped, as he thrust partly into her depths, again.

The bed frame squeaked in annoyance again, at the overuse of its mattress companion.

As his helmet hit the G spot and as she felt her eyes roll, he answered, 'Only the dangerous ones.'

His second thrust went further than any other man had done and felt as though it had stretched the neck of her womb into an impossible shape. As it sprang back, she screamed and realised that her body could not take much more of his erotically vicious technique. If her insides carried on with this sexual barrage, her reproductive parts would surely split in two but she sorely wanted to climax with her male nemesis and decided that the moment had arrived.

'I want you to come inside me now, Alan,' she panted out, between shudders of pleasure. 'I have to pretend to be chained to the headboard.' Her hand reached under the pillow and surreptitiously grabbed the handle of her killing knife.

She watched as Alan's gaze filled with an intense male longing to beat the lady to the end game. But, as his breathing deepened and movements became more stabbing, she knew he would lose, she had almost peaked and become unstoppable and armed...

The bed stopped its noisy protest against the copulation combat and watched with baited breath and sweat sodden sheets, as she climaxed and raised the knife high above his back.

'Remember the faces and cries of your past conquests, for we have together written the last chapter,' she gasped, as his penis throbbed deep inside her, sending sharp, curly tailed daggers towards the heart of her womb.

His final thrust also sent the sharp, recently fractured bedspring, through the protective mattress cover and deep into her heart...

Blurb

Twelve men, twelve stories of heroes chasing the beaver.

But watch out guys, the ladies are sassy, armed and very dangerous...

The girly menu has Cleavers and Cleavage, Bondage and Boobs, Greed and Goddesses as the main course with Voodoo and Vaginas for dessert.

Hold onto your credit card and man-meat, if you dare to pay their unusually hot price of erotic pleasure...

BEDROOM BOOKS

Romance, erotica, sensual or downright ballsy. When you want to escape: whether seeking a passionate fulfilment, a moment behind the bike sheds, a laugh with a chick-lit or a how-to - come into the Bedroom and take your pick. Bedroom readers are open-minded explorers knowing exactly what they like in their quest for pleasure, delight, thrills or knowledge.